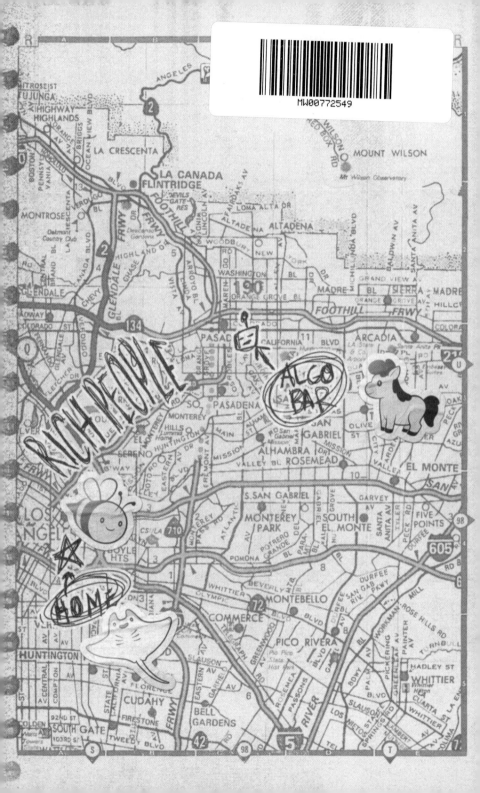

RICH PEOPLE

ALGO BAR

HOME

TWO
TRUTHS
AND A
LIE

TWO
TRUTHS
AND A
LIE

Cory O'Brien

PANTHEON BOOKS

New York

FIRST HARDCOVER EDITION PUBLISHED BY PANTHEON BOOKS 2025

Published by Pantheon Books, a division of
Penguin Random House LLC,
1745 Broadway, New York, NY 10019.

Pantheon Books and the colophon are registered
trademarks of Penguin Random House LLC.

Library of Congress Cataloging-in-Publication Data
Names: O'Brien, Cory, author.
Title: Two truths and a lie / Cory O'Brien.
Description: First edition. | New York: Pantheon Books,
a division of Penguin Random House LLC, 2025.
Identifiers: LCCN 2024021052 (print) | LCCN 2024021053 (ebook) |
ISBN 9780593687284 (hardcover) | ISBN 9780593687291 (ebook)
Subjects: LCGFT: Science fiction. | Detective and mystery fiction. | Novels.
Classification: LCC PS3615.B7433 T86 2025 (print) |
LCC PS3615.B7433 (ebook) | DDC 813/.6—dc23/eng/20240509
LC record available at https://lccn.loc.gov/2024021052
LC ebook record available at https://lccn.loc.gov/2024021053

penguinrandomhouse.com | pantheonbooks.com

Endpaper map from the 1989 California Thomas Guide used
with permission Publishing Holdco, Inc. d/b/a Rand McNally
Publishing. Updated and illustrations by Elizabeth Perez.

Printed in Canada
2 4 6 8 9 7 5 3 1

The authorized representative in the EU for product safety and compliance
is Penguin Random House Ireland, Morrison Chambers, 32 Nassau Street,
Dublin D02 YH68, Ireland, https://eu-contact.penguin.ie.

For George O'Brien and Cayce Weintraub.
I think you'd get a kick out of this.

TWO
TRUTHS
AND A
LIE

SUBMISSION

1

The L.A. sun squeezed in through my building's cracked roof and poured itself onto the sheet-metal ceiling of my compartment, cooking me awake almost an hour before my kortiko would've zapped me conscious otherwise. Mornings are worthless. Nobody wants to buy a memory of bloodshot eyeballs and nostalgia for last night's liquor, so my archives are loaded with identical copies of the same seven minutes of suffering, stretching all the way back to when I took the fact-checking gig at Info-Drip a decade and a half ago. Still better than your job, though.

I have some sympathy for you, since we're in the same business. Difference for me was, I corrected a higher class of information than you kids on the municipal blockchain. More work to verify, but worth more. I'm sure most of the stuff you get on commission is nothing but conspiracy theories—"No, the mole men are *not* invading your teeth," "Yes, gravity *is* a universal force, unaffected by how much raw beef you eat." This, I assure you, is not that. Listen till the end, and I promise to make this submission worth your while. And, just for you, I've included plenty of irrelevant detail to line your pockets with. So where was I?

Right. A perfectly awful Wednesday morning in July. I peeled off sheets that would've been drier if I'd pissed in them and began the forty-five-minute process of convincing my atrophied muscles to crawl out of bed and carry me to work. My commute was five steps long, bed to table. At my age, that's five steps too long, but I find that if I stay in bed to work my spine's a solid rod by the end of the day, and not the kind of solid rod I like. At the table, I poured myself a bowl of Grape-Nuts drowning in caffeinated milk and slapped a handful of knockoff Think tablets into my mouth. Gotta keep the brain slippery, as the kids say. I stuck a lunch pack to my arm, strapped the Frosty to my face, and—with nothing else to do—made the fateful decision to clock in forty-five minutes early.

The InfoDrip buffer slid over my brain from back to front, giving my eyeballs the feeling of being goosed from behind. It's the worst feeling in the world. Well, okay, no, not technically the *worst* (I'm not giving you such an easy excuse to invalidate and collect this submission, checker), but I'm sure you'll agree it's a bad one. You sit there all day, in the back of your mind, fully aware that your brain is doing *something,* but unable to observe the smallest sliver of it. Can't have us actually *knowing* any of the data we interact with, can they? That'd be financial suicide. Anyway, if you know how the buffer works—and I know you do—you'll understand why I didn't hear the cops come in. What you might not understand is why I screamed at them anyway.

See, back in the drone corps, we didn't have the bandwidth to monitor our meat and our metal at the same time, so we had to get creative. You could tab back and forth, but mess up the timing and your gently twitching body could be target practice for a Union scout, Russian "aid worker," rogue AI dogbot, actual wild dog . . . The list goes on. We needed a fail-safe, Commonwealth funds were tight, and that's when some sadist invented the Frosty.

A Frosty—named for the type of blowjob you do with ice cubes in your mouth—is just a can of compressed air inside a welding mask, with a little fishing line around the trigger. You wear the mask, point the air can at the roof of your mouth, and tie the fishing line to whatever door you're trying to monitor. Door opens, air can goes off, and 150 psi of brain freeze wakes you up out of whatever immersive routine you're running. What worked in the war works just as well in peacetime. Over the years, I've caught one or two of my neighbors trying to sneak in and tap my trode while I worked—though they mostly stopped trying to hack my kortiko after I bit one of them and gave him a staph infection. Still, I rigged the thing faithfully every morning before work, because if I stopped doing it and got killed for my carelessness I'd feel like a real asshole. Anyway, I don't know what the two cops expected to find when they cut the lock and walked into my crate, but I'll wager a scandal it wasn't a sixty-eight-year-old ghoul shrieking his guts out as he somersaulted backward over his threadbare office chair, clawing an air can away from his face, and inventing a new language just to curse in.

I heard my spine pop and felt my hip crunch before finally completing my somersault and colliding with the mess of domestic machinery along the back wall of my crate. I tried to land in a battle crouch, but the best I managed was a menacing sprawl.

"Monastery graymatter hotswap!" I said, before I could get my language centers fully under my control. Then I collected myself and said something very cool and intelligent. It came out as a bundle of exotic vowels. The cops waited to see if I was going to try any other linguistic experiments. Then the shorter of the two spoke.

"LAPD," she said, unnecessarily. Who else in this city wore black riot gear in July?

"So?" I managed.

"We traced a drone to this address," said the taller one. He held out an early-model Dragonfly painted baby blue with a matte finish. One of mine, all right. But, of course, I couldn't remember what I'd just been doing with it.

"I have a license for that one. Fact-check only, through my employer," I slurred, my tongue still numb from the compressed air. I had managed to get the welding mask off my face.

"Maybe you do," said the shorter one. The two of them seemed to have a deal about alternating who was talking.

"Am I under arrest?" I asked.

"Not necessarily," said the tall one, sticking to the deal. Now that my eyes were starting to focus, I noticed how thoroughly he failed to fill his uniform. The way it bunched and wrinkled around his torso made it look like there might just be a spine and a rib cage under that shirt. The short one filled hers too well. Between the two of them, they had exactly the right amount of fabric, just poorly distributed. They each wore sleek black police-issue kortikos—carbon-fiber commas over their left eyes. Removable, unlike my ancient model. A green LED blinked on the short one's kortiko as she spoke. Recording.

"We just want to ask you a couple questions down at the station, Mr. Vue."

"How much data are we talking?" I asked, knowing I'd hate the answer.

"Not much," said the tall one.

"Following up on a couple Rumors that'll maybe roll up into a minor Scandal," said the short one.

I did the math. Two Rumors and a Scandal was a month and a half's rent in this place. And that's only if the Scandal really was minor. A major Scandal could easily get me through October. I couldn't afford to be questioned right now, not this close to the end of the month.

"Suppose I don't feel up to answering questions right now?" I asked hopefully.

"We're authorized to compel your obedience," said the tall one, his unofficial smirk belying his official-sounding words. The two cops took a step forward. I would have scooted back, only there was nowhere to go. My back was already pressed against an ugly chunk of metal and plastic tubing, which was itself pressed against the rear door of the shipping crate I live in, which was suspended by steel cables thirty feet above the warehouse floor. Even though that floor was covered with a thick cushion of sea-water and salty garbage, going out the back way didn't seem like a very clever option.

While I was considering whether I had any clever options, I noticed that the two cops had stopped advancing after that first step. I followed their uneasy gaze over my right shoulder to the peeling plastic label that identified the machine I was leaning against: "HOY FONG FOODS AT-HOME DIALYSIS SYSTEM" and, below it, beneath a wonderfully intimidating yellow-and-black icon, "CAUTION: CONTAINS ORGANIC BLOOD." The idea that occurred to me then wasn't clever, but it had a certain appeal.

"Okay, so I get that you're authorized to compel my obedience," I said, "but you're not . . . *compelled* to compel me, right? You could choose not to?" As I spoke, I felt around on top of the machine for one of the plastic pouches of used blood I'd been too lazy or sentimental to send out for recycling.

"Mr. Vue," said the short one; then, her eyes twitching up and to the left as she checked some unseen kortiko overlay, "Orr, don't make this difficult." She tried to take another step forward, but I coughed theatrically, and she froze. Belatedly, the two cops twitched their eyebrows, raising breathing masks from their collars.

"You know what's difficult?" I said, emphasizing the rich undertone of phlegm in my voice. "Hepatitis. Your piss turns the color of maple syrup, you're tired all the time, nobody wants to share needles with you anymore . . ." As I spoke, I brought the corner of the plastic blood pouch to my mouth, and ripped the corner with my teeth. "But that's just the sort of bug that breeds in organic blood. Wish I could switch to synthetic like you two, but, well . . ." I spat on the ground between my legs, and the two cops took an involuntary step back. "My kortiko's the invasive type, it only runs on organic blood, and it's drilled too far into my brain to remove now."

The cops' eyes flicked to the dull silver contact plate cooking the flesh above my left eye, then to each other, then reluctantly back to me. "Though I hear synthetic blood's not all it's cracked up to be, in terms of immunity," I said, idly gesturing with the blood bag. Their eyes couldn't help following it. I squeezed a little too hard, and a few drops trickled out of the torn corner. "The nanobots in the synthetic blood fight infection, but a life without disease means no antibodies. In the time before the 'bots get there, an organic virus can do some real damage, no?" I raised the plastic bag above my head, and the cops' hands went for their guns. Always going for their guns, cop hands are.

"Put down the—"

"Drop the bag, Orr," interrupted the short one, forgetting their deal about taking turns. "Assaulting an officer is—"

"Relax," I said, not moving, "I'm not gonna throw it at you." Instead, I clenched my fist around the bag, squirting its contents onto my bald head. The blood oozed down my scalp, onto my shoulders, and down my bare arms. The tall cop looked like he was considering hiding all that blood under a thick layer of whatever he'd had for lunch. I took the opportunity to get my feet under me and push ever so painfully upright, the dialysis machine carving its name into my spine as I did. I tried (and failed) to keep the pain out of my voice, but, honestly, it only added to the effect.

"You two are free to do what you like," I said. "You can take me in, by reaching out and touching my body with your hands, or you can let me walk out of here. The choice is yours."

And with that I walked between them, out the door. Their hands came up to stop me, but their brains seemed to veto the idea. I had already lurched the remaining five steps to the door before the tall one thought to say, "Hey . . . stop."

But, rebel that I was, I kept going. Leaning heavily on any

surface within arm's reach, I shuffled out of my crate and onto the chain-and-polymer rope bridge that connected the rooms on my level. All around me, the other shipping crates that contained those rooms swayed gently, suspended in a web of ropes, wires, and steel cable that would have been illegal if all the saner real estate in the neighborhood wasn't underwater. Hell, even the bottom floor of my building was underwater, with the crates of the lucky bottom-dwellers floating on the oily seawater. You'd think I'd be used to the swaying after twenty-plus years in the building, but I stumbled and lurched my way along the walkways as if I'd moved in yesterday. Nice thing about getting older: it keeps you young.

The blood gag wouldn't hold the cops long—I could already hear them digging in their belts for latex gloves to apprehend me with—and I wasn't getting any quicker, so I entered phase two of what I was now calling my "plan." With the remnants of what was once a pretty impressive lung capacity, I yelled: "Hey, everybody, Orr Vue is covered in blood, and the cops are here!"

The response was about as relaxed as the one you get when you kick an anthill. My voice echoed through the jungle gym of chains, epoxy, crates, and girders, summoning scarred and wrinkled faces from every cranny and crevice. The lucky ones had crates of their own, and they scurried out onto the walkways laden with telephoto lenses and boom mics. The unlucky ones lived in webs of nylon rope that would have made a shibari master blush, strung between the crates of their richer neighbors, and they crawled along the girders and scaled the scaffolding to get a better view. Their cameras were cheaper, but their angles were better. Behind me, my fellow tenants were already crowding the walkway, dragging nano-nets through the air to capture my stray pheromones, and scraping skin samples off the cops as they struggled to push through. It was near the end of the month, and nothing interesting had happened in the building since at least May. For a lot of these folks, a juicy Rumor here was the difference between paying rent and finding another home. I was doing a little better, but only if I managed to avoid any tricky questions from the police.

While the cops attempted to fight through the sudden crowd, I limped ahead and ducked into the communal toilet. Inside, I threw the bolt behind me and squeezed past the toilet. The bathroom's got doors on both sides, so it can service more tenants. JB Splunge, my beneficent landlord, sifts through all the waste and sells whatever data he can scrape from it as demographics. You can pull a good five or six hundred demos from a full septic tank—enough to buy a handjob and a hot meal if you're not picky about the meal or the hands.

What Splunge did to the tanks, I now needed to do for my mind. I didn't need to stay ahead of the cops forever. (Which was good, because I wasn't going to—the tall one was already doubling back to find another way over to me, while the short one put her shoulder into the door I'd bolted.) All I needed was to buy enough time to figure out what they wanted to learn from me, then sell off the memories for demographics before they could ask me about them. Demos spend easier than fat facts— they're the closest to the old fiat currency we've got left—and on top of that a head full of Bangladeshi soft-drink preferences isn't so incriminating during a police interrogation. The only problem was, I had no idea why the cops wanted to talk to me. In the old days, it wouldn't have been a question, but I'd been disappointingly well behaved for the last couple of decades. Whatever they were curious about, it was probably something I'd learned under the buffer, a fact I'd corrected and therefore been allowed to keep on commission. Hence the sifting I was gonna have to do.

"Get back here!" the tall cop called out. The last word was garbled by the sound of one of my neighbors sticking a cotton swab into his mouth. I ignored him, and faced my greatest nemesis: the stairs.

My average daily step count, according to my medical monitor, is twenty-seven. Six days out of the week, I only get about ten. The average is only so high because once a week, on Sunday, I walk the sixty-two steps down to street level, buy some street produce, breathe some air with a little extra oxygen in it, and hobble back up. Today was not Sunday, but the cops after me didn't seem to care. I gripped the railing and started down the first flight.

I stumbled on a slippery metal step, narrowly ducking under a kid who was hanging from a girder, trying to snip a lock of hair off my rat-tail. The crowd was thinner around me—even the old and the poor can afford synthetic blood these days—but a few brave souls still shot their shots. On the second-floor landing, I accessed my memories. My left eye—the worse one—went blind, and then hallucinated a messy desk with a pile of old memory cartridges on it, content summaries scrawled on their surfaces in black marker. I know I could just see a list as an overlay, but I got my niece to show me how to implement the custom interface. I find it comforting.

"Local," I muttered, too focused on getting down a creaking ladder to make it subvocal. The cartridges sorted themselves into two piles on the table. Only three files in the local pile. Still probably too many to read while one of my neighbors swabbed bloody sweat off my scalp with a mechanical appendage. "Value greater than ten k demos," I muttered. The three local facts split into two high-value facts and one low-value. I grabbed the first juicy one and mimed stuffing it into my mouth. The headline exploded across the backs of my eyes.

POP IDOL SHIVA STALLION DENIES EATING
OWN CLONES

I spat out the cartridge. That wasn't it. Just a continuation of a battle I'd been having with an entertainment reporter for the past three days. "Shiva" (formerly Mars Trampoline, formerly Alabaster Wankhome, formerly DROP TABLE Starlets) had been changing her name on an almost hourly basis in an attempt to evade the rumors going around about her. The reporter who submitted the story had called her Mars this time, and in a few minutes "Shiva" probably wouldn't be right, either. If I'd had the time, I would have cashed the fact in for demos before another name change made it worthless, but I could hear the cops starting to throw their weight around on the walkway above me. I stuffed the other fat fact in my mouth.

TEXAN AMBASSADOR PLEADS GUILTY TO ARMS SMUGGLING CHARGES

The writer of this one had misidentified the make and model of the assault weapons the diplomat had been importing. I got a lot of corrections like these—civilians are clueless about guns, and nearly everyone's a civilian these days. But I wouldn't have needed a drone to check that fact, and the cops don't tend to meddle in international business anyway. Another dud. I spat out the cartridge. A stick-thin woman hanging spiderlike from a web of rope above me caught the spittle in a plastic grocery bag. My lungs ached, and my throat was dry. The blood on my arms and head was starting to turn crunchy and brown. I dragged myself onto the final staircase, leading with my "good" leg. The cops were only a floor behind. I needed more time. I brought up my chat interface and flashed Ty. After a couple pings, his avatar bloomed inside my head, more smell than visual, a stink like coffee grounds and fish.

> **TydeeTy:** What you want? Doing my route.
> **me:** Good. I need a pickup. Cops after me.
> **TydeeTy:** Wow, blast from the past.
> **me:** Is that a yes?

TydeeTy: 50k demos.
me: I could always let them catch me.
me: Tell them who dumped that load of rotten
pumpkins in front of City Hall during the
sanitation strike.
TydeeTy: Ok how about you owe me a drink.
me: Deal, trashman.

I was down at sea level now, on the rotting wooden pier that rings the outer edge of the bottom level. I could practically hear my kneecaps grinding against bone as I forced myself to keep walking. The curious crowd thinned out down here—tenants who can afford a bottom crate aren't nearly so hungry for data—which meant the cops would be catching up any second. I could hear their boots clanging on the staircase. I barely made it to the back door before the short one hit the bottom of the stairs and put a boot through the rotten wood. I shut the door on her curses.

The midday sun insisted on sautéing my eyeballs the moment I was outside. Didn't matter where I looked—up at the gray-blue sky, across at the bleached concrete buildings of the warehouse district, down at the gently stinking seawater in the canal—the sun used every available surface to make sure my corneas stayed molested. My medical monitor congratulated me rather sarcastically on venturing outside twice in one week.

"Shut up," I muttered, and it did.

The off-white plastic sidewalk bobbed beneath my exhausted feet, just out of sync with the building's dumpster on its heavy steel chain. One last feat of acrobatics. I hauled over the dumpster by its handle, shoved the lid open, braced one foot against the disintegrating concrete wall, and (against the muffled complaints of my medical monitor) half jumped, half fell in. More than half fell, actually. I hit a disappointingly thin layer of moist garbage near the bottom of the bin. Damn dust eaters get nearly everything these days. Even I have one. You can't beat the convenience, until one day you're trying to hide in a dumpster and there's nothing soft to break your fall.

I heard the door bang open next to me, and two pairs of boots stomped out onto the sidewalk. They'd check the dumpster eventually, but not before they'd exhausted every less disgusting option. That gave me, unfortunately, a little more time to think. Neither of the high-value facts I'd corrected that day seemed to be the reason they were after me, and anything nonlocal I'd checked would be out of their jurisdiction. That left the one I'd skipped for being low-interest. My hopes weren't high, but I was out of options. I shoved the cartridge into my mind's mouth.

YOU WON'T BELIEVE HOW THESE SIX RICH ASSHOLES SPEND THEIR DATA

A gossip column. Pure clickbait. I stifled a groan. InfoDrip doesn't usually vet low-rent gossip. That's more of a job for someone like you, no offense. ID does make an exception, though, for gossip about its top execs. Keeping corrections of that stuff in house means the execs aren't getting snooped by municipal checkers, which helps keep their data private. And, sure enough, one of the Six Rich Assholes on the list was InfoDrip's toppest exec of all, Thomas Quentin Mahoney, CEO. My corrections were all in his section, and they all seemed to be fairly minor line edits. I skimmed them:

> *The CEO of InfoDrip, Thomas Mahoney, spends 14 trillion demos every . . . => . . . Mahoney,* **spent** *14 trillion demos every . . .*

> *Mahoney eats genuine beef, drinks unlimited water . . . => Mahoney* **ate** *genuine beef,* **drank** *unlimited water . . .*

Mahoney lives in a repurposed missile silo . . . =>
*Mahoney **lived** in a repurposed missile silo . . .*

And so on, changing every present tense to the past tense. What, had Mahoney lost his fortune overnight? A quick scan of the public feeds didn't turn up anything with his name. And a rich guy getting poor all of a sudden probably wouldn't have the cops poking around my building. I had a feeling that Mahoney's past tense was a lot more permanent. I checked the supporting files I'd attached to verify my corrections, hoping for more context. There was only one file attached: "Live drone footage captured 8:47:22." I tried to open the file, but got the missing-tooth feeling of a file-not-found error instead. Red text blinked before my eyes, filling my HUD:

DATA MISSING
    REMOVED FOR REASONS OF ORGANIZA-
TIONAL SECURITY
    AUTHORIZED BY A.M.

I had no idea what that meant, which I guess was the point. That was fine, though. I knew enough: Thomas Mahoney, CEO of InfoDrip, was dead. Recently dead, probably, and—judging by the cops—murdered, to boot. Given all of that, the fact that I knew so little was actually a blessing. I just needed to find a broker willing to buy the Rumor of Mahoney's death off me, and I could pay my rent with the proceeds. If that sounds ghoulish to you, spend a couple decades sharing a communal toilet with a diaper fetishist, and then we'll talk.

I heard the dogged burbling of Ty's trash barge coming down the canal. There was a mechanical grinding and a sharp jerk, and then I was tumbling out of the underfilled dumpster and into a proper heap of everybody's leftovers. My face landed in something wet that smelled like sharp cheddar and urinal cakes, my chest landed in a forest of springs that used to be a mattress, and my legs landed in what felt like a nest of cockroaches. I had a couple guesses what my feet had landed in, but then it started slithering and I stopped trying to guess. From up in the cab, Ty's sweet stink messaged me.

> **TydeeTy:** Where to, geezer?
> **me:** Just finish your route while I handle this, then
>   Villains for that drink.

Ty responded to that with something I'm sure was incisive and clever, but another chat request grabbed my attention before I could read it. The name on the chat request made me forget the pain in my knees and back and hips, the layer of slime and seawater coating my skin, even the unidentified trash creature now shyly slithering up my pants leg. It was a name from the old days, the Braining Wheels days, when this sort of thing was a daily affair and I was busy racking up the maladies I was now paying off. It was the name of a man whose kortikode I'd tried to block, more than once, but never quite managed to. The name, for all I wished it wasn't, was Auggie Wolf.

I accepted the request. Auggie's avatar bloomed in my brain, sharpened teeth and flayed ears unchanged after twenty-five long years. But there was something in the simulated eyes I'd never seen before: he was nervous.

> **Auggie:** Hey, Orr.
> **Auggie:** Long time no see.
> **me:** Not long. Only two and a half decades.
> **Auggie:** Listen . . .
> **Auggie:** You know I'd never . . . kill anyone, right?
> **me:** . . .
> **me:** Where are you?

Auggie: The police station, dummy. How about
bailing me out? I've only got the one call.

I told Ty to stop the barge. I pushed myself upright in my nest of
wet trash, and waved to the furious cops on the sidewalk below.

"Hey," I said as the barge drifted to a reluctant stop, "I've
decided I'd like to go with you after all. No hard feelings?"

SUBMISSION
2

Welcome back. Forgive the multiple chapters, but I just don't have the stamina to give you the whole story in one take. I know it's you, though. Fact checking's so dull, any one of you would jump at the chance to flag a story like mine. At least, I like to think so. Either way, I'm gonna act like you're the same person. So.

It was a tense ride from the trash truck to police headquarters, where they were keeping Auggie. The cops didn't bother putting me in the cage at the back of their boat, but the short one did take it upon herself to repeatedly hold my head underwater as we sped along the canals—"to sanitize you," she said. The way the water tasted, I'm not sure it was any cleaner than the garbage, but the high-pressure wash did get the rest of the blood off.

We motored through J-Town, passing the half-sunken Little Tokyo Market Place, with its red-plastic plaza floating amid what were once the second floors of all its shops and restaurants. The bottom floors were still there, I knew, their doors sealed with boat glue and their windows looking out at a curated selection of tropical fish. The boat didn't slow down, and I watched our wake swamp more than a few pedestrians navigating the bobbing plastic sidewalks behind us. Between the Commonwealth, C-SEC, and the Strategic Core, cops have to get by with whatever petty authority they can cling to.

LAPD HQ looked like an enormous steel housefly on dozens of plastic stilts. The place was built before the levees broke, and the plastic legs were added to keep the exciting concrete architecture from crumbling into the sea. The bulk of the building was a cube of windows that someone once told me was meant to symbolize transparency in policing, but if those windows had ever been transparent, they had been obscured by half a century of acid rain and salt accumulation on top of their mirrored glass. The building bristled with antennae, scrutinizing the sunken neighborhood around it from every angle. My captors docked among the building's many legs and lugged me inside.

They left me in what was either a waiting room or a holding room, depending on which side of the badge you were on. I felt something I hadn't felt in at least fifteen years, though I thought about it daily: air conditioning. The air was cool, the furniture was modern, and as I stepped through the door, my kortiko autoconnected to the building's guest AR layer, which attempted to soothe my unsoothable nerves with pleasant lobby music. Commonwealth or no, Investigation pays well in a city like Los Angeles.

A shortish, stocky Black cop with a cheap suit and a sharp fade seemed to be waiting for me when I came in. They reminded me of an artist's rendering I'd seen once of a spacecraft designed for stealth. It'd been blocky and angular, not the kind of aerodynamic you'd expect, but, then, in space it didn't need to be. The cop had the same silent blockiness, the same unexpected efficiency of build. The guest layer gave me the cop's name and pronouns on an overlay: Detective Mar Coldwin, they/them.

"You the one he messaged?" they said without preamble. They had eyes that sucked in light and gave back nothing, and their mouth was a jail of teeth that only let out questions. They were not the sort of cop I'd been hoping to deal with.

"Orr Vue," I said, extending a hand, "Fact Checker for Info-Drip. Pleased to meet you, Mx."

Instead of taking my hand, they summoned an LAPD breathing mask from the collar of their dress shirt, further inhibiting my ability to read them.

"Why did he message you?" they asked, as if they were continuing a conversation we'd been having for hours.

"I . . . I don't know," I said. "All he told me was that you all had him here, and it had something to do with a murder he didn't commit." I'd expected questions, but not two steps inside the front door. They hadn't even invited me to sit, and I could already feel the cramps creeping up the sides of my legs. I was uncomfortable, and they could tell.

"What murder?" they asked. "If you had to guess?"

"If I had to guess?" I stalled. I knew they weren't just looking at me with their eyes. A cop HUD is one of the most powerful lie-detecting interfaces data can buy. From Detective Coldwin's perspective, my face probably looked less like a face and more like a weather map—microexpressions, temperature fluctuations, subvocalizations, all lit up with shiny green labels. I got to look through one once, back when I used to fuck a cop, and it felt like seeing people naked. Once a cop knows you're lying, they can apply for a warrant, and once they have a warrant, there are much more effective methods of data extraction than asking questions. That's leaving aside the minimum ten-year sentence for counterfeiting info. Basically, lying to a cop at my age is suicidal, and I promised I'd only off myself by autoerotic asphyxiation, so I gave my best guess: "The murder of Thomas Mahoney."

"How do you know about the Mahoney murder?" I could see what was happening now. They were rushing me, hoping I'd give something away. But you don't survive on a fact checker's commission by just giving data away.

"I'm a fact checker." I shrugged. "We end up with all kinds of info and no clue why."

"I didn't ask why," they said. "I asked how you knew, and that sounded suspiciously like an evasion."

"All right, all right, I checked a fact about him during my shift today," I said. "Something written before he died, so the whole article was in the wrong tense. That's how I know, okay?" I wasn't trying to evade the question, but acting like I might be had broken their rhythm and given me a chance to stabilize. For the first time, I glanced down at their stub-fingered hands, and noticed that the right one—the one that had very deliberately not shaken mine—was deftly spinning an expensive-looking pen. It seemed more like a nervous tic than a conscious affectation. If I couldn't get any information out of their mouth, maybe I could get some from their hands.

"When did you learn that information?" they pressed on. As much as I would have liked to give a vague answer for frugality's sake, the memory was timestamped.

"Eight thirty-one a.m.," I said. My forthrightness was rewarded by a little twitch in Coldwin's right hand. The pen faltered mid-spin before resuming its hypnotic motion. The time was important. They looked down, caught me staring at their hand, and stuffed it into their pocket. Along one wall, a tasteful gray couch beckoned, begging me to rest my weary joints on its soft cushions, if only I were invited to do so.

"Who is Auggie Wolf to you?" they asked. A rapid change of direction, designed to retake the initiative. It worked.

"No one anymore," I said, dropping my eyes. "I haven't heard from him in twenty-five years." When I looked up, Coldwin was staring at me, prompting me not so subtly to continue.

"He was a friend," I said, unsure whether I used the past tense because he wasn't a friend anymore, or because in my mind he had already died.

"Where did you and Auggie meet?" Coldwin's words cut a gash through my reminiscence. I grimaced, which is the closest I come to a smile when I'm sober.

"Braining Wheels. Old mindracing club in WeHo. Still open, last I checked, but I haven't checked in a long time."

"Before I take you in to see him," they said, "I'd appreciate it if you shared any potentially relevant information about your relationship with Auggie—the last time you saw him, any aspirations he shared with you, people he fought with, that sort of thing."

Would you believe I almost answered? I was that out of practice, and they were that smooth. But instead I shook my head, made my grimace as grinlike as it would go, and said, "Sorry, Officer, but by my count that was a *who*, a *what*, a *where*, a *when*, a *why*, a *how*, and a *yes-no*. By law, you've run through all the questions you're allowed to ask a civilian in a routine conversation. Now, can I see my friend?"

Detective Coldwin narrowed their eyes, but didn't press. I shudder to think how much data the cops would've pumped out of me over the years without the Seven Questions Legislation.

They weren't done yet, though. Without breaking eye contact, they gestured over my shoulder at the short cop who'd powerwashed me on the way in. Officer Menendez, the overlay told me, she/her. Menendez pressed the powder-blue Dragonfly drone into Coldwin's palm. Coldwin didn't even bother looking at it.

"You don't have a permit for this," they said. They were out of questions, but this I had to answer.

"Not personally," I replied. "It's licensed through InfoDrip, my employer. Strictly for use under the buffer."

"Mahoney's company," Coldwin said. Not a question, a threat. "Okay, come with me."

Coldwin made no allowance for my decrepit shamble, so I was breathing heavy before we were halfway down the corridor. I knew, though, that aching limbs and shortness of breath were the least of my problems. I hadn't given away much in their little question game, but only because I didn't have much to give. The fact that the cops were so interested in what I knew made me mighty nervous about how much I didn't. What had my drone seen that tipped me off about the murder? Why did

Coldwin seem surprised at the timing? And what did Auggie Wolf, the mindracing wizard who walked out of my life twenty-five years ago, have to do with any of it? I was rich with questions, but you know what they say: If questions were answers, then children would be richer than popes, and who wants that? Children are assholes.

I finally caught up with Coldwin at the door of the interview room, and they opened it for me—more, I suspect, to keep my dirty hands off the handle than out of any kind of courtesy. They closed it behind me, too, but didn't lock it. The inside was like any other interrogation box in the city: gray-blue acoustic pads bolted onto lead-shielded walls, a scar of fluorescent lighting blaring from the equally shielded ceiling. Gummy gray floor that'd probably eaten more than its fair share of blood. The only unusual thing in the room, just like in any room he inhabited, was Auggie.

Auggie Fucking Wolf. Literally, had his middle name changed so he could introduce himself that way without irony. Five foot five, a hundred pounds soaking wet, a build that might have looked frail if it wasn't constantly animated with such frenetic energy. His vicious leanness made the tendons stand out on the backs of his hands, the sinews dance in his ever-active forearms; made his neck look like the roots of a tree digging curiously into his lithe body. His eyes were green, his chin was knife-sharp, and his ears were cut into a wicked fringe that ran from lobe to helix. At least, that's what he'd looked like when I'd last seen him, twenty-five years ago.

Now, in the interview room, most of the parts were still in the same places, but they seemed to fit together differently. His elbows, which rested on the dull gray interview table, had become as sharp as his chin, and the olive skin that once clung so tightly to his muscles had grown looser and taken on an ashy tinge. His always-too-long nails had yellowed and thickened, his green eyes had sunk, and he'd lost one of his front teeth. All the hair on the front left quadrant of his skull had been burned away by the heat of his invasive kortiko, same model as mine, its position marked by a four-centimeter aluminum square ringed with puckered flesh five centimeters above his left eye. Even now, fifty years old, he looked too young to be wearing one of those.

Then there was the invasive itself. I stared at the dull metal plate a little too long—maybe because I never keep mirrors around, so I forget what mine looks like. There was a millimeter-long spur of bone poking out from the ridge of flesh around the edge of the contact plate. Our heads don't want these things inside them. The machine's incompatible with synthetic blood, the weight gives you neck pain, and the outdated hardware saves all your memories in a format that looks like plain text to anyone with newer-model headgear. If we'd waited just a few years, we could have gotten all the same benefits without drilling a hole in our own brains, but the military wasn't willing to wait that long. Neither was Auggie, though no one forced *him* to get the operation. Seeing that little spur of bone trying desperately to push away that invading hunk of metal made me especially sorry for him. Imagine the things he could have done if he hadn't been limited by our crummy hardware.

He caught me staring and smiled at me, and I noticed one of his canines was missing, too. Somehow, all his flaws only added to the appearance of dangerous solidity he'd always had, like the years of grease accumulated on an ancient monkey wrench.

"Orr," he said. "Good to see you."

"Better than good," I said, pulling out a chair for myself and gratefully slumping into it. "Assumed you'd died."

"Working on it," he said.

"You always were," I replied.

He chuckled and leaned back in his chair. That's when I noticed the thing that was most different about him: the still-ness. His fingers rested flat against the tabletop. His eyes held mine steadily. His jaw was relaxed, no sign of the grinding that we always joked would turn his teeth to powder. His constant activity had always made him fascinating to watch, but this inaction was somehow even more fascinating, if only because it was new. Also, he was wearing a dark-gray monastic robe. That was new, too.

"I'm glad you're here," he said. "These guys think I killed Thomas Mahoney." He nodded at the two-way glass behind me, beyond which Detective Coldwin surely loomed.

"Why do they think that?" I asked. He blew a breath through pursed lips and put a bare foot against the edge of the table, tipping his chair back.

"Probably because I was in the area when he died, and I don't have an alibi, and I was the only one around who knew him personally."

He said it in the same tone he used to use when describing the latest challenge the admins at Braining Wheels had cooked up for him. Like, "Oh, they just want me to sword-fight five guys while riding a unicycle, and also solve a Rubik's Cube with my tongue." He'd had reason to be cocky then. I couldn't see the reason now.

"Why are you so calm about this?" I asked him.

"Side effect of the monastic life, I guess," he said, gesturing at his robe.

"The monastic life?" I said. Then, finally putting it together, "Auggie, don't tell me you joined . . ."

"Yup." He smiled. "I'm a blockhead now. I live in the Barnsdall Monastery. So did Mahoney, until, uh, I guess this morning. They're not done wiping my memories yet, but I'm already seeing the benefits." He paused, chewed his lip, and gestured at the interrogation room. "And, I guess, the drawbacks."

The blockheads. Formally known as the Brotherhood of the Uncarved Block. If you're fortunate enough to be unaware of these crackpots, I'm sorry to burden you with the info. You know how some monks in olden times used to take a vow of poverty?

Well, with information being currency nowadays and all, ten or so years ago some wackos got the bright idea to invent a Vow of Ignorance. An anonymous code monkey going by the moniker "Brother Null" wrote some kortiko firmware that pulls out all your memories and wipes your short-term cache every so often to keep you ignorant. They set up a couple locations around L.A. where you can live and work for free, as long as you agree to strap on one of those special kortikos. What they do with all the data they suck out of their members' heads, no one's quite sure, but let's just say there's a reason they never need to pass a collection plate. People call them "blockheads" because of the blocky kortikos they wear to wipe their memories, and because it's a play on their name, and because they're idiots. I'd never thought I'd hear Auggie describe himself that way.

"How . . . how long do you have?" I asked.

"Until my memories are all gone?" he said. "A few days, likely. Assuming they give me back the kortiko. Which they should!" He addressed the last bit to the two-way glass. "They took it off so they could question me without me forgetting what they'd asked. Lot of good it did them." He chuckled.

"Still doesn't explain why you're so calm," I said. "You're a murder suspect, with no memory of the murder in question and no way to prove you didn't do it. If it was me, I'd be pissing myself."

"Really?" he said. "Has old age made you incontinent? I'm jealous, I've always wanted the excuse. Anyway, silly, I'm calm because you're here."

"Me? Why?"

"If anyone can clear my name," he said, "it's you. There's a reason you became a fact checker and I became, like, a drug addict and then, you know, this. You are still a fact checker, right?"

"Yeah, for InfoDrip. But come on, Auggie, you've always been smarter, you—"

"That's great!" he said. "InfoDrip was Mahoney's company, right? Hey, maybe you even already know who killed him, huh?"

I clenched my teeth to keep from telling him the whole story in front of the cops. "If I ever knew, I don't know now," I said, trying to make it sound like a joke.

He didn't take it like one, though. His green eyes, which, even sunken in his skull, had watched the whole conversation with a twinkling vigor, abruptly lost their twinkle. He laughed to cover it, but he seemed truly disappointed that I hadn't just swung in on a golden rope to rescue him outright. The Auggie I knew would never hang his hopes on something so foolish. Then again, maybe this wasn't the Auggie I knew.

"Hah, that's fine," he said. "You'll figure it out. You're tenacious. And you, uh . . ."

"What?" I said.

"Well . . . I'm fifty. I last saw you twenty-five years ago, and met you five years before that. The Brotherhood's memory wipe goes from the front and the back and meets in the middle, so . . ."

"So I'm one of the last people you still remember," I finished for him. If he was as far gone as he said, he wouldn't remember his parents anymore. No recent friendships, either. Just me, and a few of the guys we used to run with at Braining Wheels back in the day. It was piss-poor company, but I was glad he still knew us at least. Still knew me.

"Yeah," he sighed. "So . . . you're gonna help me, right?"

I looked at the walls and ceiling, suffocated with acoustic padding. I looked over my shoulder at the two-way glass, felt cold cop eyes peering in from the other side. I looked at the door I'd entered through, heavy with shielding, and so far away. Then I looked back at him, at those familiar flayed ears, the dexterous hands, the green eyes watching me from within the sharpened skull with their look of worried intelligence. I couldn't remember Auggie ever asking for my help before. He was always too clever, too quick. By the time I got there to help, he would've moved on to an entirely different predicament. It brought me a sick kind of pride, there in the interrogation room, to know that now, in this brainwashed and weakened state, twenty-five years past his prime and uncountable decades past mine, he finally needed me for something. That was the reason I gave myself, when I chucked my better judgment in the trash and said, "I'll try."

"You'll do better than try." He smiled, exposing one of his three remaining canines. "I don't know much, but somehow I know that."

"We'll see," I said. Then we just sat there, studying each other across the table. I felt the tickling in my stomach I used to get before a match, or a fistfight, or a viciously good lay. It felt like he was waiting for me to say something, or maybe I was waiting for him to say something, or maybe we were both being very quiet so we could hear the thing that neither of us was saying. It felt too nice, so I pushed myself to my feet.

"I guess I better get to work, then," I said.

"What are you gonna do?"

I supported myself against the back of my chair as I shuffled around it toward the door. "The most dangerous thing a guy can do these days: ask questions."

Auggie chuckled. I put my hand on the door handle. A thought stopped me.

"Speaking of questions," I said, "you mentioned you knew Mahoney personally. How did you know him?"

Auggie raised his eyebrows at me, his forehead deforming as it scrunched against the contact plate of his kortiko. "You don't remember? You've been keeping too much of yourself in that storage unit of yours. I don't know what we were to each other when he died, but, back when you and I met, I was his 'live-in personal assistant.'" He winked at me. "There are worse arrangements."

"Huh," I said, suddenly angry for no clear reason. "Good to know." I knocked on the door a little harder than I needed to, but the feeling passed as suddenly as it had arrived.

"Take it easy, Orr," he said, as the cop outside opened the door for me. "And thanks."

"Sure," I said, and walked out the door directly into Detective Coldwin's implacable stare.

"Well, that was a waste of time," they said flatly.

"What," I said, "you expected him to tell me something he hadn't told you, in front of you? How dumb do you think he is?"

"You don't get to ask me questions," said Coldwin. "Officer Menendez will show you out."

"Hang on," I said, as Menendez moved in to "escort" me. "You can't keep Auggie in here like this."

"Sure, we can," said Coldwin. "He told you himself what a prime suspect he is."

"You've got nothing on him," I said, "no hard evidence. So he was in the monastery when the murder happened, and he happened to know the victim. That's a paper-thin case. Toilet-paper thin."

"You're talking like you've got something to poke holes in it with." Coldwin raised an eyebrow. "Some 'hard evidence' of your own. If that were the case . . ."

"No," I admitted, "I don't . . ."

Coldwin nodded, and Menendez resumed her approach. I held up a hand.

"But . . . I know you don't think he did it, either. You're only holding him as an investment. Maybe he gives you some useful data you can roll into a deduction. Unlikely, given his memory loss, but worth it just in case. But if someone made you a better offer in exchange for his freedom . . ."

"An offer like . . ." Coldwin prompted.

"I'll register an investigation on this subject. You can invest for . . . ten percent of what I learn. Hell of a lot more than the zero you're getting out of him." I jerked a thumb toward the interview room.

"You'd have to quit InfoDrip," they pointed out. "Conflict of interest, C-SEC regulation. That'll cancel your drone permit, too."

"Yeah." I winced. "But I figure the solution to this case is a little more valuable. Consider this my retirement plan."

"Thirty percent," said Coldwin without hesitation.

"Fifteen," I said. "And I get to see the body."

"Eighteen," said Coldwin, "and ten minutes with the body. Final offer."

"Fine," I said, wondering why. Did I really believe investigating Mahoney's murder would make me rich? Or was I doing this for Auggie, whose glittering green eyes still hung in the darkness between my temples? I couldn't tell you, even now. Intention's not a thing that encodes well in memory.

Coldwin put on a latex glove so we could shake on the deal, and the two of us went to fill out the paperwork. When it was done, and I'd filed my severance papers with InfoDrip, they gave me a curt nod and turned to leave. The formidable Officer Menendez was still near at hand, already guiding me toward the exit.

"Wait," I said. "What about Auggie? You agreed to let him go."

"Oh, he's already gone," said Coldwin. "We got a call from the Brotherhood's lawyers while you were in the room with him."

"The blockheads have lawyers?" I raised an eyebrow.

Coldwin shrugged. "The Barnsdall Monastery does, apparently. With the amount of data they take in there, I guess they can afford a retainer. The lawyers challenged his detention on religious grounds and got him released back into the Brotherhood's custody. He's probably halfway to the monastery by now."

They turned to look at me, clearly expecting some kind of

30

half-cocked response, but I had nothing. I'd been too thoroughly played.

"Pleasure doing business with you," they said.

A sharp pain in my right thumb cut through my annoyance. I looked down to see that I'd been picking at the cuticle again. The skin at the corner of the nail was a gnarled mass, scabbed over from previous attacks. I used to have nice hands, once, but that was before my years as a fact checker. You pick up all kinds of habits under the buffer, without knowing why. I wonder what habits you've picked up.

Bright blood welled up within the gash I'd picked. I stuck the thumb into my mouth and sucked at the wound.

"Pleasure doing business with you," I muttered back. "Now let's go see a dead body."

SUBMISSION
3

Mahoney was pale, big-boned, strong-jawed, and very dead. A thick purple line across his throat marked where his rope belt had been used to strangle him and crush his windpipe. Aside from that, though, he looked all right. His skin had that plumpness that comes from always having enough water, and his white beard was so well trimmed it looked like a prosthetic. I made a note to join the monastery next time I wanted my own patchy beard groomed. He had a tattoo on his shoulder of a winged brain impaled vertically by a sword, and two snakes coiled around the whole mess—service tat, brain corps. We used to call them shrinks—the guys they sent from Palo Alto to make sure our kortikos didn't burn holes in our skulls. (Although most of them seemed more concerned with protecting our headgear than protecting us. The magnesium charge in our heads in case of capture wasn't for our benefit, I'll tell you that.)

Mahoney was bald, too, though some white stubble down the back of his skull showed that it was by choice. The invasive kortiko above his left eye would have burned away all the hair near the front, so he must have decided to roll with it. I had to admit, it was more elegant than the rat-tail I'd cultivated on the back of my own skull. But dead's a lot more elegant than alive, too, once they clean the shit off you, and I didn't fancy trading places with him.

The lab brain gave me a tour of the body, its simulated monotone making its boredom childishly obvious. In its defense, there wasn't much to get excited about. Signs of a struggle, but, judging by the fibers under his nails, he'd only struggled with the rope and his robe, not with the strangler. Nothing but blood in his bloodstream, nothing but rice and beans in his stomach, and nothing at all in his kortiko. It was an invasive, so the killer couldn't have taken it out easily, but the Brotherhood mindwipe had done the next best thing. It'd completed, according to the logs on the invasive, at 5:46 a.m.

If he'd had synthetic blood, the embedded nanomachines could have told his time of death down to the second. Just another advantage of organic blood; after all, they say it's sexy to cultivate a certain air of mystery. In the absence of nanomachines, the coroner was forced to go old-school. The ninety-seven-degree day made body-temp analysis worthless, but, based on the state of the beans in his stomach, it hadn't been long after breakfast. Maybe seven, eight, or nine in the morning. Just a couple hours after his mindwipe finished. That was handy. The monastery had called the cops around ten, and the cops had intercepted my drone sometime after that. No wonder Coldwin had seemed interested when I shared the timestamp on my correction. I'd apparently been snooping with my drone right inside the time-of-death window. Add it to the pile of facts I didn't love about this whole situation. I said goodbye to the lab brain and walked out feeling dumber than I had when I got there.

Coldwin was in the hall when I came out, leaning against the wall and cleaning their nails with a pocketknife. They looked up, but didn't say anything.

"No wonder you let me see the body," I said. "It's a piñata without any candy."

"Do most bodies have candy where you come from?" They raised an eyebrow half a millimeter. It was the Coldwin equivalent of a fit of breathless laughter.

"You're still out of questions," I reminded them. "Which makes me wonder what you're doing here."

"Nails needed cleaning," they said, returning to the task.

"If it's a manicure you're after, I used to frequent this place in the Garment District. Only nail salon in the city that'll file off your fingerprints while they're at it."

"We shut that place down three years ago," said Coldwin.

"Wouldn't have told you about it if you hadn't," I said. "So— what do you want from me?"

"Only what your contract says. Regular reports amounting to eighteen percent of your collected data by file size."

"Right," I said. "I'll send a packet to the precinct before bedtime."

"You'll send a packet to me," they said, still studying their nails. A numerical kortikode appeared in my HUD. A private chat address.

"Rats in the walls?" I asked.

"Something like that," said Coldwin.

"But not exactly?" I pressed.

They flicked the pocketknife closed. It was the Coldwin equivalent of putting a fist through a wall.

"Look," said Coldwin, "the death of somebody like Mahoney ought to have attracted some pretty high-profile investigators, yes?"

"You're still out of questions—"

"You're the most experienced investigator who's registered. Mahoney's death has been on the feeds for hours. The department's not moving on it, either. They didn't even canvass the area around the monastery for witnesses." Coldwin opened and closed the pocketknife with a thumbnail. "Either everybody already knows what's going on . . ."

". . . or they don't wanna know," I finished. "Family's paying them to keep quiet, I guess."

"For that he'd have to have a family," said Coldwin. "Twelve years divorced, records show two kids. The elder, Aiden, has no records for the past thirty-four years, and the other's got no public records at all. Not even a name. Just a birth date and a gender assignment."

"So that's the one covering it up, then," I said. "The invisible man."

"Woman," said Coldwin. "According to the records, anyway. Could be her doing the cover-up. Either that or his 'live-in personal assistant.'"

"Leave Auggie out of it," I snarled.

Coldwin looked at me with all the tenderness of a staple remover. "Don't let your history with Auggie Wolf fool you, Orr. He's in this, whether you want him to be or not."

I wanted to tell them that I had no history with Auggie Wolf, not anymore. But that's not how history works. You spend enough time with anyone, and they leave a trace in you. Mannerisms, ways of looking at things. Sometimes, you do a thing not knowing if it's you doing it, or the *them* inside you. I spent five years with Auggie Wolf, and another twenty-five thinking about those five. Even if he wasn't in *this,* he was in *me.* I picked at my thumb and pivoted to business.

"So the big brains aren't on call, you've got no departmental support . . . Sounds like I'm doing you a favor. I have yet to hear what's in it for me."

"The courtesy of this conversation," said Coldwin. "And Auggie's continued freedom."

"This conversation isn't exactly overflowing with courtesy, and you couldn't bring Auggie back in if you wanted to."

"Don't haggle with me, geezer," Coldwin said lightly. "I know you intended to register an investigation before you even walked into that interview room. I just gave you a reason. Go do your job."

I snorted. A high-profile murder that all the high-profile investigators were mysteriously avoiding, a religious organization with limitless legal reach and a penchant for secrecy—only an idiot would take on that kind of risk without a guaranteed reward. It's always painful, so late in life, to realize you're an idiot. I consoled myself by asking Coldwin a question that was bugging me.

"Why do you care, if nobody else does?"

They skewered me with their black-eyed stare.

"I may be out of questions," they said, "but you never had any to begin with. I'll expect a packet by ten p.m." Then they went back to cleaning their nails. I shuffled down the hall and didn't look back.

SUBMISSION

4

I spent almost two hundred demos on a water taxi across town to the Barnsdall Monastery of the Uncarved Block, formerly the Barnsdall Art Park and now one of the few parts of East Hollywood not underwater. We came in from the south, past the tarnished gray cubes that made up the old Kaiser Medical Center, and the converted parking garages that house the old and infirm who need it most. They send me pamphlets. The pamphlets edit out the greenish rust stains weeping from the plexiglass windows and the pale-yellow scabs of corrosion climbing up the walls from sea level.

The driver helped me onto the bobbing sidewalk in front of one of these prime real-estate opportunities, averting his face to keep from breathing my air, and I tipped him the memory of a good breakfast for his trouble. Across the waterway, beyond a row of wilted palm trees, atop a chunky concrete wall with pretensions of architecture, the green hills of the monastery grounds presided over the decaying medical district. I stared. There was a time when that color hadn't been so rare around this city. When this alley had been dry, the sidewalk made of concrete. I superimposed the past over the present, and decided I didn't much care for the change.

Those lush hills weren't for me, though. The whole compound was surrounded by a wall, and a couple blocks down I could see that the wrought-iron gate was shut tight and flanked by cameras on prehensile stalks. For an organization that was supposed to be guileless and voluntary, it was an unusual amount of security.

I pulled my gaze away from the compound and turned back toward the hospice facilities on my side of the street. Each floor was just slightly slanted, betraying their origins as parking garages, and the openings on each level had been bolted over with tinted glass to make huge dark windows that peered toward the monastery. The pamphlets did say the apartments offered unbeatable views. Across the street, a Google Puppet lurched along the sidewalk, wearing his trademark red-blue-and-yellow striped shirt, that customary expression of sincere bafflement plastered across his face. I wondered who was piloting the kid today, who he'd been before he rented his body to Google, but mostly what he was doing ogling the homes of the elderly in the middle of the afternoon. Our eyes met for a moment, but it was like looking at a dog, or a particularly intelligent dust eater. He lurched on, and I turned my attention back to the buildings. One of them had a sign out front, on a buoy in the canal: "SUNSET VILLAGE." I went inside.

The lobby was a little cozier than a glacier, but only because it was two or three degrees warmer. The building had to be pulling in good data to afford that kind of A/C. The girl inside the attendant's booth glanced up at me as I came in, then defocused her eyes and went back to whatever mind game she was playing.

"Who do I talk to about renting a room here?" I asked her. She reluctantly refocused her eyes.

"You can fill out a form," she said, sending one to my kortiko with a gesture. "Waiting list's about three years."

"I'd prefer to speak to somebody in person," I said. "Old-fashioned, you know."

She shrugged and pointed to a cinder-block enclosure with tinted windows—what must have once been the parking attendants' office. A plaque on the door read "Y. GLOB, OWNER/

MANAGER." I hobbled past the raised parking barriers (left in for effect, or because it would have cost data to take them out), and rapped on the door. A voice grunted at me to come in.

With careful interior design they say you can make a small space seem larger. The office of Y. GLOB pulled off the opposite and much easier trick of making an office meant for four adults feel just large enough for two parakeets. A brief scan of the room revealed a microwave, a dozen dead-eyed baby dolls, the skeleton of a six-foot saguaro cactus, two refrigerators, a stationary bike, a cardboard cutout of Cecil the Sensible Centipede, and enough shoeboxes, postcards, and commemorative vapes to start a shoebox, postcard, and commemorative-vape store. The only clear space was a single window, the one that looked out at the street.

In the middle of this altar of junk, behind a mahogany dining table halfheartedly repurposed as a desk, sat Ms. Glob herself, a meager collection of bones in a Hawaiian shirt half an acre too big. She sat in an ornately carved dining chair with her fists balled tightly on the tabletop, unwilling to allow even the dead skin cells from her palms to escape her grasp. The placard on her desk said her first name was Yelena, and she looked just young enough to outlive me.

"You're not here to apply," she said. "Real applicants either come in with their kids or on a gurney. Whaddaya want?"

"Efficient," I said. "I like that, in a lover *and* a business partner. Time is money, as they say. Mind if I sit?"

She shrugged. I pulled over the closest thing to a chair and straddled it. It was a plastic brontosaurus.

"You know what else is money, though?" I said. "Information."

Yelena smirked. "The Mahoney thing. I figured you dicks would start poking your heads around here sooner or later."

"And I figured an enterprising manager such as yourself might have demanded an early rent payment this morning in anticipation of just such a scenario. Those top-floor apartments have a good view of the monastery. Get any interesting memories from those tenants?"

"Sorry," said the enterprising manager, "but you're not the most reputable-looking dick I've ever seen. You look like you should be solving mysteries for smut clips up in Ten-Town, not badgering the proprietor of a high-class establishment like this."

"I wish I was, Ms. Glob," I said sincerely. "But, believe it or not, nobody more reputable would take the Mahoney case. It's just me."

"Fib," said Yelena, crossing her arms. "The Pinkertons'll be here any minute, and you'll be shit on their shoes."

"Really," I said, "you think I beat them here? On these legs?"

"Other amateurs, then," she said. "I'll have a bidding war on my hands." She flexed those hands to show how capable they were of facilitating a bidding war. Her blue acrylic nails clacked against each other.

"Yeah, you're probably right," I admitted. "Bunch of young kids in here, clamoring for that data. You'll net a scandal, easy. I'll leave you to it, then. Just let me sit here for a minute, yeah? My legs are exhausted from outrunning the Pinkertons."

She shrugged, and I sat. The dinosaur wasn't the most comfortable thing to sit on, but, then, my poor tortured pelvis isn't the most comfortable thing to sit *in*. I saw her eyes drift past me to the one uncluttered spot in the room: that street-facing window.

"You know, I remember when all this was above water," I said. Her eyes snapped back to mine, and she narrowly stopped herself from gasping. I continued as if I hadn't noticed. "Yeah, I was nineteen when the levees broke. Army put this in about six months before." I tapped the contact plate of my invasive, the home of every memory I'd made since it was installed. At least the ones I haven't sold, or traded, or lost. Her eyes flicked up to the plate, like a lizard's tongue tasting the air.

"You ever go inside the park?" she said, feigning a lack of interest. "Back when it was a park?"

I glanced over my shoulder, ignoring the shooting pain in my neck as I twisted. There was a sliver of green visible out there, atop the concrete wall.

"Oh yeah," I said. "Got the whole tour. There's an original Frank Lloyd Wright up there, or there was. And trees."

She gave a slight shiver, as if I'd said something naughty. Then she shook her head.

"Your memories are in the old format," she said. "Hard to read on a new-model kortiko. They wouldn't be immersive."

It was my turn to shrug. "Immersive for who? I'm just reminiscing. Besides, you try finding someone who was wearing *any* kind of kortiko before the levees broke, let alone a noninvasive."

Her eyes flitted from my contact plate, to my face, to the window, and back to the plate.

"You remember that section of street?" she said, pointing out the window. "That one, right there?"

"They put the trode in me at Kaiser," I said. "That street was the first thing I saw when I came out. The sun was shining, the palm trees were alive, and I was still a little high from the surgery." It'd been a good day. I smiled a little, reliving it.

"You paint a nice picture," said the woman behind the desk. She laced her fingers together and squeezed, then abruptly released them in a gesture of surrender. "Couple of my tenants got a look at somebody entering and leaving the monastery, over the wall. Face doesn't come up in any public databases, probably temporary. Still, it's data, and it's for sale."

"Sure you don't wanna wait for that bidding war?" I said.

"Consider it a charitable act. I've got a soft spot for the elderly. Why I run this dump." She grinned at me. Even her teeth were skinny, with wide gaps between them. One of them had been swapped out for something silver-black that glinted in the fluorescent light—a dental kortiko, pried from the mouth of a deceased tenant, if I had to guess.

I looked out the window as we made the exchange. I felt the exact moment when the memory left my head and entered hers. The view didn't change, but something vanished from it anyway—something I'd been projecting on it without knowing. I recalled smiling a minute before, and found that I couldn't remember why. I shook my head and turned away from the window. There was nothing there for me now. I shifted my attention to the data Ms. Glob had so charitably given me.

The fact was timestamped 8:47 a.m., and the midmorning light didn't do its subject any favors. Compared with a memory of an idyllic landscape on morphine, the face of the guy the tenants had seen was a definite downgrade. You can do a lot with vat-grown flesh, but you can't make a person smaller, and this was a guy I definitely wished was smaller. He had the kind of shoulders that each need their own zip code, and he didn't so much climb the walls as step nimbly over them. He wore a black bodysuit that barely contained his various muscles, and where his skin was exposed it was a pale, inhuman gray. Sharkskin, lab-grown, used almost exclusively by contract killers who wanted to make a statement.

His face was an obvious fake—cheekbones out past his ears, eye slits that stretched around to his temples, and a scalp full of thick purplish stubble that was about as organic as the food at Renaldo's Meat Factory. He was in the monastery for about ninety seconds, then back out again, sprinting down the grassy hillside, over the fence, and away. I had a feeling that, if I asked around long enough, in enough dangerous places, I could find the guy. But the genius of a guy like that isn't so much that he can't be found—it's that you don't want to find him.

In the foreground, there was something else, something I wouldn't have noticed unless I was expecting it. To the untrained eyes of the tenant whose memory I'd purchased, it was just a blue-gray smudge against the green of the monastery's unnaturally grassy hills, about the size of a pencil. Blue-gray, the same color as the unchanging L.A. sky, perfect for a gizmo meant to be invisible from the ground. It was the drone the cops had snagged, the one that led them to me. It hovered silently in the memory, a version of me inside it who I no longer remembered. What had led me to send a drone to the monastery? Why had I spent so much effort to check a gossip column? That, like every other thought I had under the buffer, was in InfoDrip's servers now. I thanked Yelena for the memories and dragged myself up the nearest refrigerator to a standing position.

Someone knocked at the door right as I grabbed hold of the doorknob. I opened it to see a clean-cut kid with slicked-back black everything: hair, sunglasses, suit, shoes. He took an involuntary step back when he saw what I was. I shook my head sympathetically.

"Sorry, kid," I said. "She doesn't know anything. Next time, be quicker."

He scrambled out of the way as I limped out of the office. Outside I saw a crowd of other amateurs stampeding in, the whole wave of them crashing against the black-suited kid, who sadly explained that they were all too late. I saw him pointing at me, gesturing frustratedly, saying my name, though I hadn't told it to him. I turned away from them and headed back outside, out of the cold of the A/C and into the merciless warmth of the canal. It felt dingier than it had when I went in—the colors less bright, the palm trees more dead. I fixed my gaze on the toes of my shoes and trudged down the gently bobbing sidewalk to find a cab. I hoped Ms. Glob enjoyed her new memories. I doubted I'd end up enjoying mine.

SUBMISSION
5

I pinged the local cabbie network to let it be known that I was looking for a ride, and shambled toward the Sunset Canal, where I'd be easier to find. I knew the plastic sidewalk beneath my ratty shoes should offend me—an attack by the present against a kinder past—but without my memories it was just a sidewalk. I knew it had been dry once, but only in the way I knew about September 11 or Custer's Last Stand. It was a story told by the dead, attempting to infect the living with their nostalgia. Even so, I was one of those dead at heart, and a flicker of the memory still burned deep in my neurons. They say you never totally forget anything, even when you trade it off your kortiko and wipe the synapses behind it. A certain chemical tendency remains, a clot of abandoned neurotransmitters. The body remembers. As if to prove the point, the sidewalk bucked beneath my feet, and my feet—expecting dry land—stumbled.

It wasn't a bad fall. I landed on my hands and knees, saving my hip to die another day. A husky voice from the intersection up ahead cut through my pain.

"Orr Vue!" it yelled. "Over here!"

I looked up from the highly absorbing task of feeling like shit to see a bruiser of a woman in a white button-down and wrap-around shades waving energetically at me as she climbed out of her water taxi. Two other water taxis were anchored beside hers, and as I watched, three more pulled over to join them, blocking traffic on the westbound side of the canal.

"I'm at the front of the line, Mavis," barked a guy in a yellow three-piece suit, climbing out of the front-most cab.

"Orr!" said a smiling young pixie of a woman in a rhinestone cowboy hat and white leather bodysuit, gesturing from the driver's seat of her cab. "How are you?"

"Don't you dare ask him questions, Shirley, he's not in your cab yet," spat Mavis, the bruiser. The other cabs were nosing their way in between the first three, causing them all to rock in the shallow water. A guy in a tuxedo and top hat scrambled onto his prow, waving and smiling like he was shipwrecked and needed saving.

"Heard you got picked up by the cops this morning," he called, "around the time of the Mahoney murder! People are saying the two events might be related!"

"Dwight, you moron, don't tell him why we're interested. That's perfectly good data you're giving away," the pixie in the bodysuit shrieked. Up above all of them, in a color only I was trained to spot, a handful of Dragonflies hovered, their compound eyes feeding my face back into InfoDrip's servers, where fact checkers would be busy checking the data against all the gossip that was surely being spread about me by now. It was unsettling being on the other side of the buffer. This is what you get for going outside.

I looked the cabbies up and down, with their slick new haircuts, and their trendy formal wear, and their fashionable greed, and spat in the water.

"All right," I said, loud enough for all of them to hear. "My fare goes to whoever's willing to carry me to their cab."

When that many people go silent at once, you get a special kind of quiet. I could hear the hollow knocking of one plastic hull against another, the squawk of a nearby seagull, the bashful throat-clearing of six cabdrivers trying to calculate the probability of catching SARS from a temporary celebrity at close range.

"I'll do it," said an impossibly refined voice from just down the sidewalk. We all turned to look. Silhouetted against the afternoon sun, he looked like a prim cutout in the fabric of space, walking steadily toward us. His shoes knocked against the plastic in a way that told me they were very fancy indeed. He passed the row of silent cabdrivers and stopped about six feet from me. Without the sun behind him, I could see that he was, in fact, entirely navy-blue. His shoes, his suit, his shirt, his tie, his skin, his hair, even the flesh under his fingernails, all the exact same shade. He looked like a model—not the kind you photograph, but the kind you paint. He half turned his head to address the group behind him.

"Leave now. You will all be compensated. Half now, half upon trading in all memory of ever having seen us. Goodbye."

The drivers scrambled to obey, muttering hurried thank-yous to him as they went. When they were gone, I said,

"Who are you?"

"Not important," he said. "My employer wishes to speak with you."

"Why?" I asked. "Who's your employer?"

"You test my generosity with all these questions," he replied. "Come with me and you can meet her."

"I guess I don't have much choice. You're gonna have to carry me kind of a long way, though. I don't see your boat."

He didn't answer. He just looked up. I followed his gaze to a dark rectangle set against the hazy blue L.A. sky. It got bigger.

"Fuck me," I said. "It's been a long time since anybody felt like wasting a flying car on me."

"Yes, well," said the blue man, as the car settled into the canal behind him and he rolled up his sleeves to make good on his promise, "it wasn't my decision."

After five or so minutes of wrestling me into the back seat, and another ten minutes of sitting in the driver's seat and wiping every inch of himself with disinfectant, the blue man finally started the car, and we took off. I watched the monastery recede beneath us and thought about the man who'd died there . . . and the man who still lived there.

There was a question I hadn't asked so far, because I didn't know who to ask: Why? Why would Thomas Mahoney, a man with more data than he could spend in a lifetime, choose to forget it all and join the blockheads? He'd been in the war . . . Maybe those memories were painful enough to warrant forgetting. But if so, why now? I was worried that the only person who could answer that for me was already dead.

The monastery became a toy castle on a green backdrop, then vanished as we turned northeast. I was left with a bird's-eye view of the city I'd lived in since the war, but very rarely saw. From the ocean in the west, to the mountains in the north, the sea-soaked city sprawled, a bowl of piss overlooked by the fine people who'd pissed in it. Down below, the flat gray roofs of buildings struggled to stay above the choppy gray water—except in the hills, where the water can't reach, and on the elevated byways of Ten-Town, which has neither water nor flat roofs.

Sea traffic was bumper to bumper along the deeper water of the L.A. River Basin—lines of barges waiting their turn to cross corroded intersections. Land traffic was a high-speed demolition derby up and down both sides of Ten-Town, and along its railings insect-sized people leaned and fought and used jury-rigged poles to hook jugs of water off the Sparkletts barges below. They seemed like models in a diorama, and even the barges in the canals were toy-sized. I could imagine how a person who spent most of their time in a vehicle like this might develop a certain perspective.

We passed over the Silver Lake Reservoir, its concrete walls built up three stories above sea level, the ramparts patrolled by guards with machine guns and drone swarms in Commonwealth blue. The Commonwealth's supposed to be "a loose affiliation of city-states," but that laid-back attitude ends where the water supply begins. The big boys in Silicon Valley are rolling in data, and the cops have piles of it, too, but you can't drink data. As long as the Commonwealth controls the reservoirs, the C-SEC can impose any limitations it wants: ban drones that aren't ours, only ask seven questions, etc. The cops put up with it, because who are they going to complain to? I looked down at the clear water in the reservoir, suddenly aware of how dry my mouth felt. You'd think they'd hook me up with an extra ration, given my years of loyal service. Then again, if we wanted gratitude, maybe we should have won the war.

Past the reservoir, the landscape started to dry out a bit. First it was isolated homes built up on stilts, then whole neighborhoods connected by bamboo bridges. Finally, we crossed over into the only place we could have been headed—the hills. Mount Washington, the area's called, out of some misplaced loyalty to the founders of the former Republic. I glimpsed crumbs of ancient asphalt scattered through the undergrowth. Nowadays, the only way up these hills was in a car like the one I was riding—a hefty price tag that kept the riffraff at a safe distance. Hidden among the trees I could see what looked like rock formations of many different colors—the ostentatiously "disguised" houses of the wealthy few who could afford to live on dry land. One of those houses was our destination.

We touched down on a concrete landing pad amid a grove of eucalyptus trees that leaned in as we landed, to better shade us from view. There was plenty on that landing pad worth hiding. Two other aircars, for a start: a Maybach in cerulean chrome and a Daimler-Tesla that looked like it was made of waterfalls. An actual waterfall pounded away at the hillside behind it, fed by a crystal-clear stream that flowed in a perfect cascading zigzag from a peak a few hundred feet up, where I spotted a structure that looked like a giant sapphire someone hadn't quite finished mining out of the hillside. The distribution of walls and angles made it look like the building, instead of being designed and built, had developed over a billion years of geological accidents. Only the size and the color gave it away as something man-made. Three stories tall, and dark blue all over. I wondered what the owner's favorite color was.

The dark-blue driver opened the door for me, but didn't help me out. I hauled myself to my feet, and was immediately nauseous. You spend enough time on the city's shifting sidewalks, dry land under your feet will do that to you. On top of that, there was the smell: the medicinal sting of eucalyptus, the savory sweetness of sage, the ripe acidic stink of mulch, and the disturbing absence of carbon monoxide. Birdsong rang from the tops of the tall trees—tunes that a quick search told me hadn't been native to these hills since before I was born. It was nice, once I got over the nausea, the disorientation, and the fundamental iniquity of massive wealth.

"If this meeting goes well," I said to the blue man, "you think your boss will put me in touch with your landscaper?"

"My employer does not use a landscaper," said the employee, starting toward the waterfall. "She retains an ecologist."

"Ah," I said, "Mahoney's daughter, is it? What's her name?"

The blue man stopped walking and gave me a look with almost no murder in it.

"What?" I said. "Lots of money, a hard-on for secrecy, she/her pronouns . . . Call it a lucky guess."

"Come along," he said, and turned. It could've been my imagination, but it seemed like he walked faster, just to spite me. Luckily, our charming banter had given me enough time to get my nausea under control, and I was more or less able to follow him. The waterfall parted for him, and stayed open just long enough to wet my ass and the back of my head as I lurched through. Inside, glowing lichen in exciting patterns lit the way to a staircase elegantly embedded in the cave wall. The staircase was made of blue crystal and, regrettably, stairs. The blue man stood at the bottom, giving a passable imitation of patience. I took my time joining him, fearing the climb almost as much as I feared what he'd do to me if I refused to make it. When we stood on the first wide step, though, it carried us upward like a river flowing in reverse. The spiraling journey up the inside of the mountain brought my nausea back with a vengeance, and in a few moments we were back in daylight, my watery breakfast was decorating the hillside, and the house of blue gemstone loomed before us like an engagement ring for a small planet. The front door, a smooth slab of blue beneath a delicately carved archway, separated into vertical slivers, each the width of a pack of cigarettes, and drew itself open like curtains parting. The interior was entirely pitch-black. The driver entered, but I stopped at the door. He looked back at me and did not sigh in exasperation.

"Network: 'Sapphire_Eye,'" he said. "Password: 'a sphere made of wind.'"

I manually requested the network and got a password prompt. I couldn't picture a sphere of wind, because wind is invisible, so instead I imagined a bunch of sand and leaves blown into the shape of a sphere. The system didn't accept that, so I imagined the same thing but without the leaves and sand. A door opened in my head, and then there was light.

Every wall that was opaque from the outside suddenly became transparent on the inside. Even the internal walls were made of pale-blue crystal, and I stood in a prism over paradise. Through labyrinths of lighter and darker blue, I could see the outer walls—if "walls" was even the right word. Through some kind of camera magic, the house's boundaries made themselves invisible, revealing the landscape outside as if there were no walls at all. The desert scrub on the foothills outside seemed more green, and the distant mountains more purple. The normally hazy sky was a paralyzing blue, except where it was full of ivory clouds. Up here you could pretend you were living in the Los Angeles of a hundred years ago, back when the world was just as ruined, but at least we didn't know it yet. The only difference was that there were fewer houses than there used to be, and the houses that remained were bigger.

The man in blue led me along the entryway to a sunken living room that took up the majority of the floor. Three royal-blue couches nestled in a hexagonal depression, around a fire pit that leapt with blue flame. He motioned for me to sit, which I did, and then he went upstairs, glad to be rid of me. I was so busy watching him navigate the transparent stairways that at first I didn't notice my host come in. I don't imagine it happens to her often.

There's a week in boot camp when they just torture you. For seven days, it's nothing but tear gas, Tasers, panic attacks, water-boarding, mental scarabs . . . They're not even trying to get any information out of you, but after a couple days of that kind of treatment, you want to start telling secrets, any secrets, just to satisfy them.

The woman who came gliding into that living room had a body that hit my eyes harder than tear gas, lit up my nervous system like a dozen Tasers, made my heart pound harder than a panic attack, and took my breath away like a week of water-boarding. The only thing it didn't give me was the scarabs, because it was hard to believe insects would even exist in the same hemisphere as the woman I was looking at. In short, her body was a weapon, an instrument of torture beyond the reach of any nation's military. I wanted to tell her secrets until I ran out of them, and then make some up just to keep on talking.

Her face wasn't something that grows over a lifetime—it was designed, like a cruise missile. Her skin was white without being pale (and here I struggled to suppress the memory of the dead

Mahoney on the coroner's slab), and her blue-eyed gaze was cool without being cold. Her hair was black and fell in thick waves—a portable cloaking device.

She wore a blue dress that was almost black, with a floor-length skirt that made her look like she was floating on a column of genie smoke, and she had a sapphire pendant on a silver chain around her neck. The sapphire was modest—only about as big as a hand grenade. My medical monitor warned me that my brain wasn't getting enough oxygen.

"Shut up," I said through gritted teeth. If the woman in front of me heard, she didn't show it. Instead, she smiled with a mouthful of teeth that must have cost more than certain military satellites.

"Orr Vue!" she said. "I'm Marianna Mahoney—no, don't get up—and I'm just *delighted* you decided to join me."

" 'Decided' is a strong word, Mrs. Mahoney—"

"Miss," she corrected. "Thomas is my father."

"Was your father." It was my turn to correct her.

The smile stayed on her lips but fell out of her eyes for a moment. She got it back quick enough. "Force of habit, I guess. Though to be fair, one's father is one's father, alive or dead, wouldn't you say?"

I thought of my corrections from that morning, the ones that'd gotten me involved in this mess. "That's a question for a philosopher, I think. Me, I'm just a fact checker. Former fact checker, I guess I should say."

"I know," said Miss Mahoney, lowering herself into a plush blue love seat across the fire pit from me. "That's part of why I've been so anxious to meet you. But before we get to that, will you have a drink?" She crossed her legs in a way that stole roughly three months off my remaining life span, and I didn't begrudge her the time.

"I'm hungry *and* thirsty," I leered.

"I'm afraid there's nothing I can do about the former," she said.

"I don't keep food in the house. I have the mod that lets me live on sunlight."

"I'll have a Bloody Mary, then," I said. "There's food in that. Salt the rim until it's too much salt, then double that."

"So much salt can't be good for a man your age," she said. My medical monitor snarkily agreed.

"You make me feel young, Miss Mahoney." I winked, ignoring the medbot. A hovering crystal tray brought our drinks so quickly they must have already been made—a Bloody Mary for me, and a martini for her, plus two glasses of water we hadn't even asked for. She plucked her martini delicately from the tray, sipped the water daintily before putting it back, and let the tray drift to me so I could grab my drinks.

"My sources tell me you've registered an investigation into my father's death," she said, gazing at the warped reflections of her crystal palace in the martini glass.

"What," I said, slurping a tiny pickle off the generous skewer that came with my drink, "no small talk?"

"Small talk is expensive," she said lightly.

I lifted the water glass in my other hand, and pointedly took a sip from each drink. "You care about expense?"

"How do you think the rich stay rich?" She gestured at the walls around us with her martini, so smoothly that the liquid hardly stirred.

"You don't want me to answer that," I said, working an olive off its skewer with nothing but my teeth. I thought it might impress her, but it didn't seem to.

"So you don't like answering questions, either," she said. "I respect that. Shall we talk business?"

"If you insist on skipping over pleasure," I said, licking salt off the rim of my glass.

"It's almost cute, how you talk," she said, briefly holding my gaze with those blue eyes of hers. "As if you think someone could possibly find you attractive." The fire danced between us, laughing at me. "Let me tell you why I called you here . . ."

"Let me guess," I said. "You want me to lay off my investigation."

"What makes you think that?" she said, doing all the gestures a surprised person would do.

"Well, you are the invisible sibling, aren't you? The Mahoney heir with no data on record? The one making sure nobody works this murder who has the skills to solve it?"

"So they taught deductive reasoning at the one-room schoolhouse you grew up in. That's terrific." She swirled her martini and broke off a portion of a smile to feed me. "Yes, I'm the 'invisible sibling,' as you put it. My business benefits from keeping a low profile. But no, I didn't bring you here to warn you off. In fact, I'd like to invest in your inquiry. I'm willing to provide an . . . in-depth interview as seed capital, plus expenses."

"And in exchange?" I finally took a sip of my Bloody Mary. The horseradish immediately made me sweat, just how I like it. "Let me guess, unfettered access to my nubile young body?"

"I'm simply a daughter who wishes to see her father's murderer brought to justice." She plucked the olive skewer from her martini and considered it. I wondered what food looked like to her, a woman who never ate.

"And if I happen to learn something unsavory about the guy?" I asked.

"Publish it, sell it, I don't care." She stirred her martini with the olive skewer. "Father's reputation is his own business. I just want to make sure you have the resources to follow the investigation wherever it leads."

Again, I noticed the present tense. Was it habit, like she said, or did she genuinely not believe her dad was dead? If it was the latter, there was a hell of a wake-up call waiting for her in the morgue.

"His will hasn't executed yet, you know," she said, as if sensing my thoughts. "A standard automated will would have resolved the moment his pulse stopped. But the lawyers say the document is just sitting on the blockchain, still waiting for some unknown condition to fulfill. Don't you find that strange?"

I was beginning to get an idea of what Marianna was really hoping for from my investigation. I leaned back on the couch. "So you don't care so much what happened to your father. You want to know what's become of all his data."

"I know what's become of his data," she scoffed. "It's all locked up in the servers of that ridiculous cult he joined."

"The Brotherhood? You're mad he shared his memories with them instead of you, is that it?"

She laughed, but there wasn't any humor in it. "The Thomas Mahoney I knew wouldn't have shared his memories with *anyone,* least of all a crackpot religion worshipping at the altar of ignorance. Do you know, when my brother and I were growing up, he never told us stories, not even at bedtime. Aiden would beg to hear about the war, but Father would always say, 'Never ask a soldier what he did back there. It's enough that I'm here, now, with you.'" When she imitated Mahoney, her voice dropped half an octave, her shoulders drew back, and an ironic smile curled her lips. She gestured expansively with her martini. It wasn't an impression she had practiced—he was just in her head that way.

"Maybe he sold his war memories to the service," I said. "It's common enough."

She gave a single, scornful laugh. "If there's one thing I learned from Father—and that's debatable—it's that the data you keep is infinitely safer than what you give away."

"You saying he was embarrassed about his work in the brain corps? Those guys . . . I'd call them butchers, but at least a butcher uses the whole animal."

"No, no." Marianna shook her head. "I believe Father was quite proud of that assignment, from what little he shared. It's what he did before he volunteered for the front lines . . ."

"He was on the kortiko research team?" I shook my head in disbelief. I'd heard rumors about that crew of psychopaths. To make something like a kortiko, you've got to burn through a lot of brain tissue before you land on the right design. Best to make sure it's brain tissue you don't mind losing. Prisoners were their test subjects. Of course, most of their dirty work was done by the time I enlisted, but we still heard about captured ruralists with experimental models jammed into their skulls, forced to stare at test patterns projected on the walls of underground bunkers until their eyeballs dried out. On the rare occasions when we managed to take an enemy combatant alive, we'd sometimes joke that we were "sending him to the doctor's office."

"If he was one of those bastards," I said, "he could have spent the war safe behind the lines, carving up the meat and making a killing in data for his trouble. Why'd he volunteer for brain corps?"

"He said he was eager to serve"—Marianna rolled her eyes— "but I suspect he was eager to get away from Mother's family. He never spoke well of Palo Alto, and he never went with us when we'd visit." Her eyes got distant for a moment, examining the simulated skyline projected through her walls. Then she shook herself and continued.

"So, you see," she said, "Father didn't sell his war memories. He used them as seed capital." She took a long sip of her vodka and exhaled the vapor through bared teeth. "Besides, as far as he was concerned, he *was* his memories. Giving them up would mean giving *himself* up. That blockhead nonsense—about the mind existing separately from the body—that's just what it was to him: nonsense. For Father, the body was meaningless, just a vessel. The mind was all there was. Besides, he was forgetful enough without joining the monastery."

"People like Thomas Mahoney don't generally get rich by being forgetful," I observed.

"*Selectively* forgetful," she clarified, making a witheringly careless gesture with her free hand. "If he forgot a birthday, or said something cruel, or drunkenly seduced your college boyfriend, for example, you could never bring it up with him again. It was as if such things simply vanished from his mind."

"What, you think he got rid of those memories somehow? But you said he thought he *was* his memories."

"Yes, and he had a very clear idea of who 'he' was," said Marianna. "So, like I said, he had little reason to enter the monastery. Miles and Ernest I almost understood, but I really thought Thomas would be the last one to join those idiotic memory thieves."

"Miles and Ernest?" I asked.

She stiffened. A drop of vodka splashed over the side of her martini glass and dripped down her knuckles.

"My ex-husband," she said, "and my son. They joined as well, years ago." In the few moments before she collected herself, I saw a different version of Marianna Mahoney—without the self-conscious performance to hide it, she was a siren at the center of a glass labyrinth, awfully beautiful, but horribly lonely. It didn't occur to me until much later that this, too, might be a kind of performance. I should have pressed her then, asked her another question while she was still off balance. But I couldn't bring myself to do it. Instead, I watched her quietly collect herself as the Bloody Mary burned my lips.

"Got any other prying questions for me, Mr. Vue?"

"Don't rush me," I said. "I'm still deciding whether to take your deal."

"I was under the impression you already had." She smiled. "I'm counting this time against the in-depth interview you were promised."

"I could just walk out with the data you already gave me," I said, taking another sip of both drinks.

"I suppose you could, at least physically." She examined me appraisingly. "Actually, I'm not even sure about that. But I clearly informed you of the terms of the offer, and you went on blithely asking questions regardless. If you absconded with my data now, I'd likely be forced to take legal action—an unpleasant prospect for both of us."

. . . but mostly for you was how that sentence ended, but she tactfully left that part unsaid. I stayed sitting, partially because of her threat, and partially because she kind of had a point about me not being able to get up.

"Fifteen percent," I said. "Standard arrangement. Daily packet delivery amounting to fifteen percent of the data I've collected by file size. Investors may take an *advisory* role in the investigation, influence proportional with their stake. Deal?"

"Fifty percent," she said. "You could use quite a bit of advice."

"The cops are in for eighteen," I said, "as I'm sure you know. If I don't own a majority share in my own investigation, I might as well not investigate. I decide where this goes. You and the cops can sit on the sidelines and criticize. Or you can go down there in your fancy car and question suspects yourself."

She smiled at her martini. It was not an entirely pleasant smile, even on that violently pleasant face. "Very well," she said. "You keep fifty-one percent. Forty-nine minus eighteen is thirty-one. I'll settle for that."

"Twenty," I said. "I have to leave room for other investors."

"Promiscuous, aren't we?" She raised an eyebrow.

"If my promiscuity surprises you, you didn't do your research." I slurped another olive off the skewer, to prove my point.

"Oh, I did my research." She sighed. "And quite expensive it was. Someone's set an algorithm to bid automatically on any information even remotely related to you, you know. You're rather interesting at the moment."

Cops in my crate, cabdrivers hounding me, an algorithm set to surveil me . . . I sucked an ice cube from my drink, and chewed it. A drone operator never likes being the center of attention.

"There you go," I said, spitting crushed ice back into my

Bloody. "You might find another investigator interested in the case, but you're never gonna find another snooper with the case so personally interested in *them*. Twenty percent is a bargain."

"I said I did my research, Mr. Vue." She gently swirled her martini and watched the oily clear liquid spin, infinitely more interested in that subtle vortex than she ever could be in my health or comfort. "Twenty-seven years ago, you killed a man, a courier for a rival clan who tried to steal your cargo. Impressive, considering none of your drones had guns. Impressive you even had drones to kill him with, considering the C-SEC ban. Especially impressive you were never caught, considering he saw you orchestrating the attack from your rooftop perch, and saved the act to video. You're rather impressive, Mr. Vue, in a horrible sort of way."

The fire blossomed into a glowing blue rectangle between us. Some of the blue deepened, other parts lightened, until I was looking at a monochrome reproduction of the video in question. I saw tattered clouds against an azure sky, then a dot of navy against it, wheeling, growing larger, sprouting wings, diving. The eyes of the viewer followed it down, down, until it was level with the rooftops of the surrounding warehouses, where it cut a sharp arc and sped parallel to the ground toward the camera. Toward the eyes of the soon-to-be-dead man. And behind that speeding shape, that metallic parody of a falcon with the razor edges of its wings two flying knives microseconds from their target, behind that messenger of death, up on the roof of one of those gray-blue warehouses, stood a man who looked a lot like me. He was younger, and less haggard, but, perhaps most disturbingly, he was smiling. The blade made contact. The point of view swung wildly and landed sideways on the ground. A kortiko can keep recording memories as long as the brain's supplied with blood—up to ninety seconds after the head is severed. Marianna cut the video off after thirty.

The fire receded into its pit, and I receded into mine. She

had me, all right. But, worse than that, I had no memory of the killing. Not the dead man, not the moment of his death, not even what had happened to my Falcon or, come to think of it, the rest of my once-extensive menagerie. Maybe killing came so naturally to me I'd forgotten, but the raw-wound feeling I got when I probed for any recollection told me otherwise. I'd taken the memory out of my head and put it somewhere else. And if I'd done that, who knew what else I'd hidden away?

"Thirty-one percent," Marianna repeated calmly, "and this can remain our little secret. I'm *very* good at keeping secrets."

I took a gulp of water to calm my nerves. If she was gonna blackmail me, I'd at least make sure to cost her a scandal in drinks. "You negotiate like a real piece of shit," I said.

"Coming from you, I can only assume that's a compliment." She smiled. "Do we have a deal?"

"Deal." I spat into my left hand and extended it. "Shake on it?"

She actually leaned forward slightly to keep from recoiling. I took more pleasure than I should have in that momentary discomfort. Then she summoned a contract with a twitch of her forehead. I wiped the spit on my jeans and checked the language before signing.

"Now," I said, settling back to enjoy the rest of my Bloody, "I believe we still have an interview to conclude."

"I suppose we do. What else would you like to know? Enemies, I imagine, and people with a financial interest in his death?"

"No, I figure that won't be much help. I'm guessing he had thousands of enemies, and almost anyone could make a quick bombshell off a rich guy's death. I'm more curious about you. For example, how'd you pay for all this?" I gestured with my drink at literally everything around us. "Trust fund from Daddy, I'm guessing?"

She shook her head. "I told you, Father never *trusted* us with anything. Actually, the fact that you don't know how I make my living is marvelous news for the state of my business. I'm a privacy consultant, you see, for half the people living in these hills. It takes quite a lot of effort to remain unseen these days, and it isn't cheap, either. But, of course, it pays for itself many times over as the value of one's personal data appreciates."

A privacy consultant. Of course. Whatever happened to the days when we actually made things in this country, and the rich people owned people who actually made things? Well, if her personal data was so valuable, I was gonna make sure to get me some of it before I left. I'd ask her some questions about the case, sure, but there was nothing in the contract that said that was all I could ask about. Any details not relevant to the case were mine to keep, and I still needed to make rent. I switched to a topic that seemed lucrative.

"You mentioned an Aiden," I said. "That your brother?"

"Yes." She didn't elaborate, just watched me carefully. I pressed on.

"He died, didn't he? Cops only have records of him up to thirty-four years ago."

"Was there such a thing as tact," she said, "back in the bygone era you hail from? Or did they invent that around the time we harnessed fire?"

It was my turn not to respond. Less because I had a tactic in mind, and more because there was still liquid in both my glasses.

"Yes," she said finally, "he died. When he was sixteen, I think."

"You think?" The water did nothing to cut the spice of the Bloody, but I drank it anyway, because how often do you get free water?

"I was young when it happened," she said, her eyes far away. "Around eight years old. My memories of him are pre-kortiko. Fuzzy. I'm sure you understand."

"Only too well." I nodded. "How'd he die?"

"Is this really relevant, Mr. Vue?" Marianna sniffed.

"I don't know," I said, trading my two empty drinks for two fresh ones from the floating tray. "Probably not. But you owe me an in-depth interview, and I'm still mad about the blackmail. So how'd he die?"

"Pneumonia," she said, almost sulkily. "No one knew in those days how much risk a person with organic blood could pose to someone with synthetic." She looked meaningfully at the wrinkled skin on my forearms. Organic blood gives you a slightly redder skin tone than synthetic; I might as well have a biohazard symbol painted on my forehead.

"Your dad," I said. "It was his fault?"

"We never talked about it," said Marianna, "but I don't know of anyone else with organic blood who was allowed anywhere near our family. As a matter of fact, Mother hardly allowed Father near me when I was growing up."

"But she allowed him near Aiden? What, did she have something against boys, or—"

"Why don't you ask me about my father?" she suggested icily.

"Hey, I'm just interviewing you, like we agreed." I tried to make a placating gesture with my hands, but it didn't quite read the same with a drink in each of them.

"We agreed to an interview. I didn't agree to be tormented. Or to answer every one of your cruel little questions." She crossed her free arm over her chest and rested the other over it. All of a sudden, it felt as if the stretch of empty couch between us was a thousand miles long. It was my first indication that the house's overlay was doing anything other than faithfully representing its contents.

"Fine," I said. "When was the last time you saw your father?"

"When he told me he was joining the Brotherhood," she replied. The couch was just a couch again—bigger than the entire crate I lived in, but smaller than Los Angeles. "He didn't come in person, of course, but we spoke in full VR. He was drunk—the avatar hid most of the signs, but I could tell by how carefully he chose his words—and he told me he was sorry. I asked him why, and he said he couldn't tell me. Then he said he wasn't really apologizing to me, but the people he should've been apologizing to weren't around anymore. He said that was why he was going away.

"He explained about the Brotherhood, about how it would be so nice to forget. I did as I've always done—I cooed and soothed, comforted him without really saying anything. We hung up, and I didn't hear anything from him after that. I assumed he'd sobered up and forgotten all about it. Then, a few days later, Exley showed up."

"Exley?" I asked.

"My manservant, the one who brought you here. He showed up at my door and said Father no longer had need of his services."

"Exley was Mahoney's guy?"

"He was my mother's," she sighed, "before Father . . . bought her out."

I got the toothpick from my Bloody in my mouth and sucked the brine from it. "Either your kind does marriages differently than I'm used to, or . . ."

Marianna rolled her eyes and began to speak quickly, as if reciting a poem she'd memorized in grade school. "Father wasn't born rich, Mother was. But she was money-rich, and money went out of style when I was still a toddler. Father had the foresight to found InfoDrip with his war research as the initial reserve data, and so, almost overnight, he became the one who held the purse strings. She still owned land, of course, but . . ."

"But he owned lawyers," I finished for her.

"I never quite understood," said Marianna, staring into her martini. "If it were me, I would have put up more of a fight. But I'm sure there are details I was never privy to. One thing that runs in our family: secret keeping. She's dead now," she said, answering my next question, "something to do with pills, naturally. Everyone agreed she left a lovely corpse." She took a sip of vodka to mask the grimace on her lips.

"So Exley's your only reminder of your old lady," I said, not knowing how to say anything more tender.

"Don't be so morbid," she said, pulling a convincing smile across her face. "He's just a manservant. Though I suppose I *am* quite attached to him. I've known him since I was small."

"Wait," I said, belatedly doing the math. "How old is he? He looks . . ."

"About ninety, I think," said Marianna. "It's amazing what you can do with synthetic blood and a few organ transplants, isn't it? Sooner or later, something will give—probably his brain—but for the time being, he's quite the specimen."

Not for the first time, I wished my invasive could run on synthetic blood. "Was he always blue?" I asked.

"I had him dyed," she said airily.

Leave it to the rich to make sure their employees match the drapes. I returned to the subject at hand.

"Did anything strike you as odd about that last call? The one Thomas made?"

She looked thoughtful. A bit too thoughtful to really be thinking. "Well, yes, in retrospect. That's a large part of why I hired you. You see, Father and I rarely talked after I moved out. There were the obligatory calls on holidays and birthdays, of course, and twice I even managed to get him to Thanksgiving dinner, back when I was still married. But it seems a bit strange, doesn't it, that he would call me out of the blue to let me know he'd had enough and was joining a monastery?"

"Maybe. Maybe he wanted his daughter to know about his last big life decision."

"I think you would have to have been there, listening to him, to see it the way I do. Everything he said seemed to have some sort of . . . purpose. Like he was taking care to make sure I got it all on record."

"I thought you said he always spoke carefully when he was drunk."

"You're impossible." She rolled her eyes.

"What I am," I said, "is curious. You've gone pretty far out of your way to hire me, only to spend half this interview dancing around my questions. What are you hiding?"

"Have you ever been to Paris?" she asked.

". . . No," I said.

"The cathedral, *Notre Dame.*" She said it with the exaggerated French accent of someone who paid for good wine and people to explain it to her. "It burned down many years ago, and they restored it, exactly as it was before. The thing I remember most from when I visited was *Notre Dame's arches.* Have you seen pictures?"

"Maybe," I said. "All churches look the same to me."

"Ah, but there's something special about *Notre Dame's arches,*" she said, leaning forward slightly. She seemed excited, almost nervous—like she was about to kiss me or pull a gun on me. "Sometimes I feel like I'm *under Notre Dame's arches,* even now. Do you understand what I mean?"

I thought about Braining Wheels, the mindracing club where I met Auggie. The crowds, the ring, the twisted overlays casting simulated shadows on the distant warehouse ceiling . . . It had been a cathedral to us, in a way.

"I think everybody does, to some degree," I said. "Why?"

She sat back, and her shoulders slumped slightly. Disappointed, by what I had no idea. "No more questions," she said. "I'm tired." She briefly traced a circle in the fabric of her dress with a blue-nailed finger, then seemed to remember herself, and put on a smile. "Here, before you leave, I have some things for you." The tray that had brought our drinks reappeared and floated over to me. On it were a sealed envelope and an elegantly machined bronze disc about the size of a poker chip.

"I don't need this," I said, pointing at the disc.

"Isn't it better to have it and not need it?" she inquired innocently. "After all, mendacity credits aren't exactly easy to come by for someone of your means."

The disc gleamed saucily at me on the tray. One free lie, no legal repercussions. A chip loaded with enough real data to pay for a web of fake backstory even a cop couldn't cut through. That little piece of metal probably cost as much as the aircar that'd brought me there. It hummed as I picked it up—just to examine it, I told myself—and with a brief flash of heat, it molded itself into the wrinkled skin of my palm. When the heat faded, there was nothing to betray the complex circuitry embedded there—nothing but a new weight inside my right hand.

"What about the envelope?" I grunted. "That some other rich-folk witchcraft I'm unacquainted with?"

"It could be, I suppose," mused Marianna. "It's an invitation to a party. Tomorrow night, at this address. You'll have to come early to be sterilized and clothed, of course. Ernest, my son, will be there."

"Your son the blockhead?" I said.

"The former blockhead," she corrected. "He left the organization years ago, unlike his father. I thought you might find him interesting. I'll see you then?"

"If you're that hard up for a date, I suppose it's my duty as a gentleman," I said.

"Wonderful!" She beamed at me as if she hadn't more or less kidnapped me to talk about her dead dad. "Exley? Take Mr. Vue wherever he wants to go. I'm sure he has a lot to do before our engagement tomorrow evening."

The manservant was so well camouflaged against the décor that I hadn't noticed him come in. He motioned for me to follow him in a way that told me he wasn't above dragging me out by the braid if he had to. By the time I was done clawing my way up the arm of the couch and limping over to him, something else seemed to have occurred to Marianna.

"Mr. Vue? Why *are* you so interested in my father's death?"

"Like I said, almost anybody can make a quick bombshell off a rich guy's death." It sounded good, but Marianna didn't look convinced. I couldn't blame her. Auggie's haggard face still hovered at the back of my mind. The police had let him go, so why did I get the feeling he was still in danger?

"Admirably callous," she said, laughing. "But I can tell you're not as hard-boiled as you pretend. You care about this, just as much as I do."

"I'm flattered," I growled, "but I don't stand to get nearly as rich off this as you do. Have a day."

Without waiting for a reply, I followed Exley down the hall. At the door, I disconnected myself from the house AR. The walls turned opaque. No crystal windows or majestic vistas. No light at all. It was just me and Exley, in the dark. Exley opened the door without a word, and we walked out into the blinding light of another perfect Los Angeles day.

"Where to?" he asked me, as we rode the stairs back down to the car.

"The Self Storage on Seaboard Industrial," I said. "I need to remember some things." Marianna's advice, and that video of the murder I didn't remember, had convinced me of that.

Exley didn't answer, or seem to care. I looked over my shoulder at the house. It was just as opaque on the outside as it was on the inside, doing its very best to hide the woman it contained. A woman in a pitch-black house, pretending she could see it all.

SUBMISSION
6

Exley didn't seem inclined to talk to me on the drive over, which made me extremely inclined to talk to him.

"Marianna says you're older than me," I said when we were safely airborne. No answer.

"You must have known Thomas for a long time," I continued. "What did you think of him?"

Exley's eyes met mine in the rearview mirror.

"It was not my place to have an opinion, Mr. Vue."

"Come on," I prodded. "Did you like him? Did you think he was a first-class bastard?"

"My employers did not tolerate familiarity of any kind from the staff," he said. With a voice that cold, it was a wonder he'd bothered to turn on the A/C. Any other questions I might have asked froze in my throat. The guy was probably under half a dozen NDAs anyway, and hardcoded NDAs exert a powerful influence on a person's kortiko.

The car touched down gingerly in front of the Self Storage, like it was afraid of getting its chassis wet. The water in the warehouse district is relatively clean by city standards, but the scattering of plastic bottles, used needles, and doll heads that knocked against the glass bottom as we hit sea level was enough to make any self-respecting automobile feel skittish. Exley spoke to me without turning, his doll-like eyes watching mine in the rearview mirror.

"Mr. Vue, you should know that I don't share my employer's affection for you."

"That's what you call affection?" I snorted.

"You were allowed to remember her face," said Exley. "And her name. Don't make her regret it, or I'll pass the regret on to you. Understood?"

It occurred to me then that the car likely didn't need a driver. That there were hungry families all up and down Ten-Town who'd love to drag down a car like this and strip it. That what a car like this really needed was a man in the driver's seat willing to kill a hungry family.

"What she regrets isn't really up to me," I said.

The doors didn't unlock. We just sat there, bobbing in the surf, as Exley examined me in the rearview mirror. Finally, he reached across the passenger seat and got something out of the glove box. Against all odds, it wasn't a gun. It was a tattered paperback book.

"Take this," he said, thrusting it into the back seat. I read the title: *Amy Vanderbilt's Complete Book of Etiquette.* "Read it. Try not to make a fool of yourself at the party tomorrow night."

I took the book but didn't say anything. The doors unlocked themselves with a sound like a gun cocking. Exley's silence was worse than any further threat he might have made. I fought my way out of that silence, through the door and into the reassuring cacophony of an L.A. afternoon. Seagulls swore at each other, the sidewalk clunked against itself, and along some side street a disgruntled driver leaned on his foghorn. I didn't even mind the spray of oily saltwater Exley's car doused me with as it took off—it meant he was leaving.

On the outside, the Self Storage looked like it always had—a reassuringly ugly concrete brick with the name painted near the top in green letters. On the inside, like most things, it'd changed. You don't want the place where your surplus memories are stored to change, but, hey, you don't want to feel a burning sensation when you piss, either. There's a reason the universe doesn't have a complaints department.

The dingy fluorescents were gone, and the scuffed concrete walls. The newly renovated reception area gleamed yellow, black, and silver, with excitingly shaped plexiglass windows in internal walls that didn't need them, and polished metal benches that seemed like they would resent being sat on. The AR autoconnected when I entered and insisted on playing soft classical music. The kid behind the desk wore a vest and bow tie, and his skin was traced with subtle channels meant to make the planes of his face look segmented, like an android's. It wouldn't have surprised me to find out that those were his street clothes. What passes for streetwear these days would've been appropriate for a damn wedding in my day. So I guess I was underdressed. Underdressed for a Self Storage.

"So this is why the rental rate keeps going up," I said, looking around. The kid at the desk politely ignored the comment. I had a feeling the kid at the desk would take a shit politely, too.

"How can I help you, sir?" he crooned.

"You know how you can help me," I snarled. "Lemme in, so I can look at my stuff."

He wrinkled his nose ever so slightly, and—with the utmost civility—retrieved a breathing mask from beneath the counter. "Of course," he said.

With exaggerated courtesy, he stepped around the counter and led me into the facility. He remarked with pride on the improvements they'd made there: intelligent climate control, X-ray shielding, embassy-class ICE . . . until, finally, we arrived at the rusty steel closet where I kept my other selves.

"You know," he remarked, as if it had just occurred to him, "if you would authorize it, we could upgrade the door here to one much more penetration-resistant and . . . aesthetically pleasing."

"I'll bet you could. Now, can I get some privacy, or is having you staring over my shoulder another 'upgrade' I'm gonna have to deal with?"

My tone didn't even faze him. He must have had his kortiko locked into a powerful customer-service temperament. He clasped his hands in front of him, bowed slightly, and said, "At once, sir." I watched him go; then I leaned my head up against the door.

"It's me, bud. Sorry, but I didn't bring any biscuits."

I willed the lock open, then the door. Roy, my 250-pound mechanical Rottweiler, sat obediently in the open doorway, hydraulic-press mouth hanging open in a pretty convincing imitation of animal dumbness. They could add whatever shielding and countermeasures they wanted to the rest of their compound. I prefer security I can pet.

I walked past Roy, toward the storage brain at the back of the tiny closet, but stopped in front of the single shelf of dusty physical keepsakes I bother to hold on to. My combat fatigues, neatly folded; somebody's barbed nose ring; a bottle of wine too valuable to drink; a rusted coffee can full of state quarters, from back when we were a state and used quarters. I plunged my hand into the coins and drew out a handful, ignoring my medical HUD's warnings about tetanus. The coins might be useful, if I found myself needing the help of the Carnival.

With the quarters jangling in my pocket, I hobbled the last few steps to the back wall, where the black storage brain sat on its yellowed folding table, drinking contentedly from its outlet. I lowered myself gingerly into the creaking folding chair, eyes locked on the brain. They make them without senses or voices, but you need something a certain amount of brainlike to store a brain's memories. I don't trust anything with that much me inside it. Which meant I trusted myself even less, especially after Marianna's creative little blackmail session. I figured it was better to know what I didn't know, so I wrote down what I wanted to remember on a pad of Self Storage stationery and connected to the device.

A minute later, I looked over at the list on the paper, and kicked myself for my stupidity. Why had I written down a list of things I already remembered? Then I kicked myself for kicking myself. This is exactly why you write down what you want to remember before you remember it—it's impossible to remember not remembering, once you do. And once I remembered it, I also remembered why I'd chosen to forget.

See, the thing about war is that it trains you to do a very specific thing: kill people. It turns out that killing people, though incredibly valuable in a war, is sort of frowned upon in, for example, every other situation. The snipers in my unit had it worst when the treaty was signed—there's just not a lot of civilian jobs for a guy whose main skills are shooting people in the head from very far away and holding his pee. I had it a little better, because there are theoretically reasons to fly a drone that don't involve ending a life. After the war, I worked for years as a courier, and an investigator. You can learn a lot by hovering a drone outside the right window at the right time, and if you're even a little clever about it, no one will know you're doing it. Which is, of course, exactly why drones were banned for civilian use. They were free data, at the expense of privacy. They were, said the Commonwealth, a "destabilizing force on the economy."

It didn't feel right to me that the one thing the Commonwealth Army had taught me how to do well was now the thing they were telling me not to do. So, instead of turning my drones in for recycling, I hid them, and then I forgot where I hid them.

Now I remembered.

I flipped through the locations of all my old mechanical friends, saying hello. I said hello to the school of Stingrays buried in the silt of the L.A. River Basin, and to the Sparrowhawks living peacefully among the doves atop the Museum of Jurassic Technology. I checked the status of the Beehive hidden in the broken air-conditioning unit on top of the Bradbury Building, and the one nestled in an ornamental archway outside the Griffith Park

Observatory. I woke up the Solar Eagle pretending to be a solar panel on the roof of the Self Storage. The den of Taskrabbits under the mound in Triangle Park had been destroyed when the park was replaced with more condos, and the MotorBats hiding on the Commonwealth Canyon golf course had gotten confused and burned out their motors avoiding each other, but I still had thirty-six D-Rats in a subway alcove underneath Hollywood and Highland, and one RealHorse owned by the Santa Anita Race-track that would obey my commands in a pinch. And, of course, there was the Falcon.

The drones recognized the touch of my mind immediately, and stopped whatever random walk or crawl or flutter they'd been doing just to listen. I wanted to dive into each one of them, leap out of my tattered meat, and lose myself in fifty sleek metal beasts. Along with the locations, I remembered now what it was like to become a swarm, to use all the parts of your brain you never even knew you had because you've only ever had to control the one body, to fly and swim and scamper and gallop at the same time. I remembered the vicious joy of meeting an enemy one-on-one and *outnumbering him*. Before I really knew how much time had passed, I—we—I noticed the sun sinking below the horizon. I watched through the optical sensors of each drone I touched. The Sparrowhawks and the Eagle saw it like I would see it—an atomic sunset in pink and orange, painting the wispy clouds that seem to come out only at that time of day. The Stingrays saw it as spears of golden light piercing the water's sur-face. The RealHorse saw a spot of reddening light crawling down the stable wall. The Rats saw nothing, but the TwinBees . . . the TwinBees saw a sky that glowed deep purple, the color I always imagined a heart would turn if it was in love. I saw all of these, not one at a time, but all together, as a composite image my brain recognized simply as "sunset."

The Falcon didn't see the sun. It was hooded, masquerading as a statue on a column in the ruins of the Ace Hotel. I probed its vitals, searching for any evidence it knew about the murder it'd helped me commit. But it was only a tool, a mute idol, a blood-stained knife. The killing was in its memory when I checked, but there was no animal glee in the attack. It had sliced through that courier's neck with all the passion of a guillotine.

That memory linked to another in the brain's recesses, and that one linked to another, as memories tend to do. After a while, I retreated from the Falcon's blind eyes and into Roy's, as he sat guarding my door. I turned him around and looked at myself: a grizzled old fart in a crusty black T-shirt and jeans, hunched over a metal desk. No hair besides a short gray braid on the back of his head. He held that head in one liver-spotted hand while the other picked dumbly at its thumb, his skin so thin the bones seemed ready to cut right through it. His arms were covered in bad tattoos gone blue with age, memorializing events no one else remembered. When he smiled, which he was doing now, it was with small gray teeth peeking over shriveled lips. His was a small body, in a small room, the last fragile vessel of a bunch of memories better off forgotten. I rested my metal head on the old man's thigh and closed my telephoto eyes. I couldn't tell you if he cried. I was just a dog.

When I finally left dronespace, I held a single memory before my mind's eye, peering into it like a preserved insect. It was the end of the chain of memories triggered by the Falcon: waking up tangled in Auggie's bedsheets, smelling Nag Champa and banana pancakes, watching the sun find its way through the ivy on the windows. The night before, he'd poured me gin until I stopped talking, after he'd spirited me away from the murder scene on his junkyard Jet Ski, after he'd bought my victim's final memo-ries, after I'd called him, after I'd done the deed. As I held that memory, afraid of crushing it in a mental fist, it unfolded—not a chain, but a spiral staircase lining the inside of my spinal col-umn, tunneling down to the basement of my body, where our first kiss lived in chemical darkness.

SUBMISSION
7

I'd met Auggie thirty years ago, on the mindracing circuit. And let me tell you, mindracing then wasn't like mindracing now. Back when I used to play, it was a programmer's sport. The whole game was based on one simple principle: your brain is smarter than your kortiko, but your kortiko is faster. Winning at mindracing—that is, surviving whatever twisted challenges the emcees had devised for that evening's entertainment—was all about concocting a set of scripts that made optimal use of your trode, allowing you to think as little as possible while, ideally, forcing your opponent to think as *much* as possible. Walk randomizers, dodge calculators, twitch enhancers, aimbots . . . Everyone was competing to make the best use of their kortiko's limited RAM, to cram in as much thinking as the circuits could handle without overheating. (Or with overheating. Every arena came equipped with extinguishers in case of scalp fire.)

Today's trodes, on the other hand, are good enough that hardware limitations aren't an issue. Wetware's the limiting factor. Tune in to a stream nowadays and you'll see a bunch of genetically perfect sport gods proudly showing each other their muscle collections. Everybody's just running the same pack of standard scripts on the same bleeding-edge Mindracing-Grade™ kortikos, spending all their off-hours in the gym or the gene editor's, because the only competitive edge left in the sport is how hard you can beat your meat. You put that much data and time into a body, you're gonna be skittish about letting anything happen to it, so the challenges in "modern" mindracing aren't what they used to be, either. "Chess-boxing"? "Paintball-trivia"? In my day, we had tasks that couldn't be summarized in a cute compound word. Try "winning a philosophical debate while disarming the improvised explosive devices your opponent keeps flinging at you." Or how about "fencing on a tightrope over a bed of nails while frantically searching the internet for information that might allow you to blackmail your opponent into forfeiting the match." People say traditional mindracing was "too violent" *and* "posed unacceptable risks to the lives of the athletes and audience," but in all the time I was on the scene, hardly anybody died, and those who did probably liked it.

I joined the scene after the war, like a lot of the original players. Back then, we were pretty much the only people with kortikos, we were used to hacking our headgear just to stay alive in the field, and we had what you might call a distorted perspective on violence. I was never very good at the game. My gimmick was, at the start of every match, I'd kick my opponent in the crotch. Make them waste brain cycles protecting their sensitive parts from my boot. Then, after I was known for doing it, I started only doing it sometimes, and keeping my opponents guessing like that gave me a cognitive edge that almost made up for my piss-poor code. My win record wasn't great, but my strategy was novel enough that I became a meme. When new competitors joined the circuit, Lijah Lye and the other emcees would conspire to match them with me first thing, as a form of hazing. That's how I ended up as Auggie Wolf's first opponent.

First thing I noticed about him was that he was too young to be wearing an invasive. He had this look of danger about him, too. It was the way he showed his teeth when he smiled, I think. He hadn't flayed his ears yet, hadn't lost any teeth, but he already looked like the sort of person who *would* flay ears and lose teeth—his own and others'. He had olive skin, a tight black topknot, and muscles that slithered under his tank top like they wanted to get out and see the world.

"Where'd a boy like you get a trode like that?" I said, tapping my own contact plate.

"Beat me and I'll tell you," he said.

I don't remember what the challenge was for our match. Something with a halfway functional speedboat and the alligator pit Lijah found at a police auction. I don't remember the details, because our match only lasted twelve seconds. Soon as they yelled "Go," Auggie raised one booted foot, I went in for the crotch kick, and he brought his boot down on my extended knee.

He found me in the locker room after, where I was lying on a bench waiting for the meat sleeve to knit my knee joint back together. He brought two bottles of beer and sat down on the bench next to me so that the crotch I'd failed to kick was at eye level. He wore a pair of loose gray basketball shorts, which encouraged the imagination.

"Sorry about your knee," he said, handing me one of the beers.

"No, you're not," I said, smiling. When I nearly waterboarded myself trying to drink, he slid a folded towel under the back of my head to prop me up.

"True," he said, laughing. "You should've seen the look on your face."

"Oh, I have," I said. "Everybody's been sending me vids of it for the last two hours. How'd you know what I was gonna do, anyway? Lijah tell you?"

He shook his head. "Didn't know you were gonna do anything," he said. "I just figured, if I blew out somebody's knee in my first match, everyone who faced me after—"

"—would have to waste valuable brain cycles protecting their knees." I chuckled. That was how he was: he'd have the same idea as me, but he'd always take it further; execute it better. I was even more impressed when he explained the algorithm he'd

developed to calculate the most direct trajectory to his opponent's knee. Then he kept going. He told me about macros he'd
pieced together in assembly, the custom garbage-collector he'd
built to replace the kortiko's inefficient one, daemons he'd taught
to rewrite his own code for him on the fly during the match. I
was fascinated, but I have to admit I was only following about
half of it. I was distracted by the basketball shorts, and the way
he smelled—like he'd just sprinted through a motorcycle engine,
burning herbs to clear out the ghosts. He must have noticed I
wasn't fully focused, because he trailed off midway through a
tangent about hijacking the brain's natural trigonometric processes to augment the kortiko's onboard APU, and his expression
changed.

"You're not . . . mad about your knee, are you?" he said. It
was a different voice from the one he talked code with. It barely
crossed the distance between us, like it wanted to stay close to
his mouth in case it needed to hide.

I spat into a nearby bucket reserved for the purpose—or, actually, probably reserved for some other purpose—and grinned.
"Why would I be mad?" I said. "The meat sleeve will fix my knee
better than it was, my win record's garbo anyway, and apparently
your guilt got you to bring me a beer and sit with your junk near
my face. I'm a lucky man."

A deep blush darkened his face, but he didn't move his junk.
He rubbed his contact plate sheepishly.

"I guess I'm . . . unaccustomed to humility," he said.

I took a sip of my beer and ended up getting half of it up my
nose. I sputtered, and we both laughed. "I guess I'm accustomed
to being humiliated." I smiled. "I kind of like it, actually—and
not just in the way you think. Thing I learned a long time ago:
if you can let yourself be embarrassed without *feeling* embarrassed, it gives you power over the people who think you *should*
feel embarrassed."

"I like that," he said, managing to drink his beer without giving himself a sinus wash. "I don't think I'm there yet, though. I care too much about impressing people."

"Well, you're impressive! I mean, the code you were just telling me about? I've probably kicked every competitor on the circuit in the balls or ball-equivalent, and I never thought to write code about it."

He tapped his lips with the neck of his bottle in a way that made me think of other things. Eventually, he said, "I think I've got a different relationship to my kortiko than you've got to yours. Yours is a service weapon, a piece of equipment you were given. Mine is . . . Well, it's me."

"Mine's a part of me, too," I pointed out. "Pretty hard to remove at this point."

"Not a part of me," he said. "It's me. It's not a part, because there's no division. I don't pass thoughts back and forth between the trode and my wet brain. I live somewhere in between them. I'm not even *here,* exactly." He tapped his chest, which his green tank top did a good job of framing. "I'm not really sure where *I* am, to be honest."

"Because you got yours so young," I said.

"I guess so," he said, finally finishing his beer.

"And why'd you get the surgery so young? Your parents sadists or something?"

"Ah-ah-ah," he said. "I said I'd tell you if you beat me, and you didn't." He tapped the meat sleeve with the butt of his beer bottle, sending a dull, throbbing pain up and down my leg. We looked at each other in silence—the kind of drawn-out, horny silence that screams, *Kiss me, you idiot,* at a pitch only dirty dogs can hear. And, like always, Auggie got the idea before I did, and executed it better than I ever could have managed. He kissed thirstily, like he wanted to get drunk on me and find out what he'd do under the influence. I kissed him back hungrily. I wanted to swallow him and extract that energy that made him glow when I closed my eyes. That night, and for five years afterward, that was how it was between us: I was a drug to him, and he was my sustenance.

I was lying down when he left, too, five years later. We'd fought the night before—about what, I don't remember—but that wasn't why he left. We'd both been leaving for a long time, and that moment was only a formality. I woke up to find him in the open doorway of my crate, looking back at me, begging me silently not to follow him. Maybe wishing even more silently that I wouldn't listen. But I obeyed his eyes, and closed mine, and when I opened them again, he was gone. I've lived in that shithole of a crate ever since. Maybe I stayed there so that if he did decide to come back I'd be easy to find.

As for what happened between that first kiss and that last look, I don't remember much. I remember when he told me he was Thomas Mahoney's twink. I like to think I didn't begrudge him the arrangement—it wasn't as if I was exactly monogamous, either. But I do remember us fighting. I remember talking too loud. I remember him crying. I remember smashing a beautiful glass dildo and spending the rest of the night cleaning up the shards while Auggie consoled himself elsewhere. I remember those fights, but not what we were fighting about. It could've been Mahoney who came between us, but it could just as easily have been me. After all, Auggie'd walked out of my life of his own free will, and decades later he'd walked into the Monastery of the Uncarved Block with a guy I'd taken for just another sugar daddy.

No matter how I arranged the memories, they never formed a clear picture. It was all too muddy. Too many pieces missing. Maybe I spent the memories of the rest of it on the booze I drank to wash them down. Maybe I was too high most of the time to recall things clearly. Maybe there wasn't much to remember— just two lonely men faithfully following a romance algorithm older than men or faith. But now he was back, and our tidy little tragedy no longer had an ending. I had a chance to write a new one, and I wasn't sure I appreciated the opportunity.

SUBMISSION
8

I hadn't remembered loving Auggie, but I'd suspected. A love like the one in those memories leaves chemical traces in your brain, ghost-memories no kortiko can erase. Auggie's trace was a red-hot brand. Pretty much the whole sordid story was stored on the brain box: hooking up in the locker room at Braining Wheels, swapping knowledge at all-night diners, learning each other's spirituality, cooking each other breakfast. All the little details that build up over a years-long love affair. Must have been too painful to keep them in me once he disappeared.

The memory that had brought me there still nagged at me. Auggie'd saved me from the consequences of my drone murder all those years ago by buying the memory of my crime. I couldn't imagine why he'd sell that memory to someone like Marianna, but she'd gotten it somehow. Perhaps it'd gone to the blockheads along with the rest of his memories, and from there to Marianna's account. She hadn't seemed too thrilled with the Brotherhood when we spoke, but in my experience you don't exactly have to love someone to take their data. Still, it implied a closer association between her and the monastery than she let on. Just as it implied a closer association between me and Auggie than I'd assumed that morning.

Against my better judgment, I took the romance from the brain box and loaded it onto my kortiko. Then I closed the connection. I was just myself then. An old man in a metal coffin, thumb raw and bloody where I'd picked it. Auggie had always called me his wart, I remembered—tenacious, and impossible to get rid of. My own wart stung. I pressed it to my lips and sucked the blood away. I was already regretting my decision, which was reassuring—I'm not sure I'd know it was a decision if I didn't regret it.

As I sat there, working up the motivation to stand, that one decision unfolded into many more. I knew now why the case felt so personal to me, knew I wouldn't stop investigating until I was sure Auggie was safe. To make sure he was safe, I was going to have to investigate the Brotherhood. They were at the center of this—Auggie, Mahoney, even Marianna's husband and son—there were too many blockheads in this for it to be an accident.

Then there was the matter of Marianna's blackmail material. If I'd hidden that from myself, what else might I have hidden, and where might I have hidden it? I needed to talk to Auggie, while he still remembered something worth talking about. Another road that led back to the monastery.

Oh well, one step at a time. I used Roy's head to lever myself to my feet and made for the door. As I passed the shelves, my eyes caught again on the barbed nose ring. It'd been Auggie's, I now remembered. I left it where it was but picked up my old combat poncho with the jagged black-and-white dazzle camo. Doesn't do much against human eyes, but AI doesn't know what to do with it. That'd keep the InfoDrip drones from auto-recognizing me, at least. Then I was in the hall, the door obediently closing itself behind me, Roy taking up his position on the other side. Outside, I squeezed my meat-eyes shut, and put out a hand to steady myself against the wall. I was overwhelmed by the returning sense of omniscience my drones conferred. They were everywhere, looking at everything. Everything but me.

SUBMISSION
9

There was no mob of cabs outside the Self Storage. I guessed Exley was better at keeping his mouth shut about my whereabouts than the cabbie who'd dropped me by the monastery. I appreciated not being harassed, but it meant I had to hire a cab and wait for it, and by the time one got to me, the sun was down and the air had turned cold. The days have gotten hotter since I was young, but the nights have only gotten colder. I'd sprung for a higher-class cab—AI-driven, discreet. The boat was entirely black, with an enclosed cabin and tinted windows. I was so absorbed with getting my aching, shivering body inside that I was already sitting down by the time I noticed I wasn't the only passenger. There was an elegant white man in the seat across from me. I yelled, and threw the only thing I had on hand. He caught it.

"*Amy Vanderbilt's Complete Book of Etiquette*," he said, turning the book I'd thrown to read the title. "You've been talking to Exley, have you?" His voice was unbearably casual, as if he had just happened to find the words on the floor and was idly flicking them in my direction. I reached out to my nearest drone: the Solar Eagle atop the Self Storage. It wouldn't exit sleep mode for precious seconds, but if I was being assassinated, I could at least instruct it to avenge me. With a faint hum, the boat's motor came to life, and we drifted away down the canal.

"Orr Vue, isn't it?" The book sailed back across the cabin and landed in my lap, just barely tapping my balls. The whole cab smelled of him—of rose-water aftershave and clean linen. Somehow that was worse than the sudden pain in my balls. "You probably need this more than I do," he said, gesturing at the book. "I'm Ernest."

"Okay, but what's your name?" I growled.

He ignored the quip. "Forgive me, but I had my driver intercept your cab call. I thought we should get to know each other," he said. "After all, you've already met Mother, and she can be so . . . opinionated sometimes." He interlaced his long, pale fingers around his knee, and crossed that knee over the other. He wore a fat ruby on his right index finger and a diamond-encrusted gold chain around his left wrist. The wrist disappeared into the sleeve of a wine-red cashmere turtleneck sweater, and there was another gold chain draped around the neck. Ruby plugs stretched his earlobes, and a gold ring pierced his right nostril. The nose ring was connected by a gold chain to another ring, at the outer edge of his right eyebrow. To be honest, it was pretty much how I would have decked myself out if I was rich, though it looked a bit out of place on someone who I guessed was half my age. The gold-ringed eye winked at me.

"I can be opinionated, too," I said. "I've already got opinions about you, for example."

"I can't wait to hear some of them." He grinned. Lounging in the seat across from me, he looked like a young god—not one of the ones in charge, but one of the minor ones who go to all the parties and occasionally ruin lives.

"Well," I said, "you're the one who used to be in the Brotherhood of the Uncarved Block, aren't you?"

He nodded.

"Yeah," I said, "I don't have a lot of respect for anybody who chooses to forget their life instead of fixing it."

Ernest chuckled. "How does one fix something that has

already happened? The past is immutable. The only power we have over it is whether or not we choose to remember."

"So what did you *choose* to forget, then?" I pried. "What drove you to join the monastery in the first place?"

"If I knew what I chose to forget"—he smiled—"then I wouldn't have forgotten it, would I?"

"So you didn't get all your memories back when you left? They kept something? A little donation?"

His smile curdled into a grimace. "How would I know?" he said. "One thing I retained from my time in the monastery is a general distaste for questions."

"But you just asked me one," I pointed out. Outside, dark silhouettes of buildings drifted silently by. Ernest sighed.

"Look, you seem to have a chip on your shoulder about the Brotherhood. No doubt Mother biased you against it. She never understood its benefits, and she still holds it against Father and Grandfather. And me, of course. That's part of why I wanted to talk to you. The Brotherhood of the Uncarved Block is a voluntary organization, one that did Father and I a world of good—and Grandfather, too . . . until—"

"Until someone murdered him," I offered helpfully.

"Yes," Ernest replied. "And I'm worried you'll be tempted to connect that . . . murder to the organization. I'm sure Mother would just *love* that. She doesn't understand the value of forgetting, of being empty. She hoards her data like a dragon. Even worthless little trinkets like photographs and knickknacks. You know, there are rooms in that blue house of hers where you can hardly walk, for all the boxes full of useless things. Postcards, magazines, sweaters, snow globes. Combs with hair still in them. With the AR overlay, you can't even see the doors to those rooms, but they're there. Rooms commemorating the dead."

"Dead like your grandfather?" I said. "Like her brother, Aiden?"

"Oh, Aiden." He scoffed. "To hear her talk, his passing was

the great tragedy of her young life. But I doubt she ever even spoke to him."

"What makes you say that?"

"Oh"—he sighed and looked out the window moodily—"I'm sure you noticed her penchant for the dramatic."

"Seems to run in the family," I replied.

He shot me a glare. "All I'm trying to say," he said slowly, as if he was worried I was brain-damaged, "is that the Brotherhood is a fundamentally good organization. It helps people. It frees us from our earthly attachments and lets us live in harmony with the natural rhythms of the universe."

"If it's so good," I said, equally slowly, "then why'd you leave?"

He rolled his eyes. "It's a voluntary organization! One day I felt like I wanted to leave, so I walked out the door. It's that simple. I'm happier now for having been a member, but I feel no need to go back. I'm already free."

"So why didn't your granddaddy leave? Why does hardly anybody else ever leave? What makes you special?"

"How should I know?" He turned back to the window. "I may not be a monk of the order anymore, but my time there changed me. I no longer ask such questions. In any case, we've gotten sidetracked. I'm not here to debate philosophy. I'm here to help you."

"Oh?" I said. "How?"

"I've got a name for you: Lionel Dubois. Muscle for hire, with a long list of minor offenses. Last known address: none."

"'None' means Ten-Town. Why would I care about a bag of hired muscle from Ten-Town?" I had to ask, in the hope that the answer wouldn't be what I knew it was.

"My sources say he had motive, means, and opportunity to kill Grandfather. You're welcome."

My Eagle pinged me to let me know it was directly overhead. From its perspective, the cab was a black bead bobbing along a black canal in the pale moonlight. I told it I didn't need avenging for the moment.

"Who are your sources?" I asked. "How'd they find out about this Lionel?"

"If I told you that, they wouldn't be *my* sources anymore," said Ernest, smugly. I realized, with refreshing clarity, that I hated him.

"Why give this to me? Why not give it to the police?"

"Frankly, because I think Mother has invested in your investigation in order to pervert its purpose. She's more interested in causing trouble than in finding justice for her father's murder, and I for one would like to see the case closed without its becoming a smear campaign against an organization that has done so much good for myself and many others."

"In other words," I said, "you want me to close the case, take the payout, and walk away without looking too hard at the Brotherhood."

"Cynicism is such an unattractive trait." Ernest chuckled. "It makes you seem even older than you are. If the Brotherhood were involved with the murder, of course it would bear looking into. I'm just saying it doesn't have to be so complicated. I'm trying to save you a lot of trouble, a lot of unnecessary legwork—by the look of it, your legs could use the break." It was good to see that he hated me, too. It's always more satisfying to hate someone who hates you back. Still, the kid had just handed me money, and in such a way that I couldn't just throw it in his face.

"Okay," I said, "I'll follow your lead. But you don't own me."

"Wouldn't want to," he said. "You're what we call a 'toxic asset.' You want a ride home?"

"Actually, I think I just got a second wind," I said. "Take me to Ten-Town."

"Ew," he said. He turned and spoke over his shoulder to the empty driver's seat. "Let me off here. Take him wherever he wants to go."

The car drifted to a stop, and Ernest climbed out.

"Keep the boat if you want," he said. "I have others." Then he closed the door, and we were off.

The car sailed past the enormous glass coffin of the Ritz Carlton, its windows now pried out and replaced with avalanches of oily green vegetables. Breeding edible plants to live on saltwater has done wonders for food scarcity, but the kelp DNA makes everything taste the same. On the plus side, you don't have to salt it. A raft of fallen brown tomatoes bobbed in the canal, connected by a wet black vine. I watched it pass as I considered what the evening had in store. I'd always meant to go to Ten-Town eventually, but Ernest's "tip" accelerated the timetable. After all, where a bastard wants you to look is almost as revealing as where they *don't* want you to look.

I didn't feel ready for Ten-Town, especially at this time of night. Then again, no one ever is. I closed my eyes and enjoyed the particular solitude of an AI-driven car—somehow lonelier than true solitude could ever be. It was just me and nobody, driving me down the canal to nowhere.

SUBMISSION
10

The AI driver was less annoying than a human would have been, but also less entertaining. There's a series of questions you can ask them, about stop signs and whatnot, that'll throw them into a safe mode where you can really mess with their heads, but once you do that it takes years to get off the block list, and I like being able to get a cab when I need one. We got stuck in traffic on the way over, so I gave in to boredom and flipped through *Amy Vanderbilt's Complete Book of Etiquette.* Lot of interesting stuff in there. For example, did you know it's bad form to wear evening dress before 6:00 p.m. unless you're meeting the pope? I made a note to look up what evening dress was.

When reading started to give me a headache, I switched over to my TwinBees atop the Bradbury Building and told them to join the Eagle on sky patrol. Obviously, you don't want to be caught running drones these days, but a swarm of mechanical Bees at a high enough altitude isn't too conspicuous, and I'd rather be breaking the law than go into Ten-Town alone. I'd substitute them for the Eagle once they arrived. They were harder to spot and—if used right—much more vicious.

While I was thinking about the Eagle, I decided to check its visual feed. I noticed something interesting. Normally, boat traffic thins out near Ten-Town (on account of any boat that comes too close risks becoming part of somebody's house), but as we navigated the sunken slums and junkyards that fringe the elevated bulk of the neighborhood, a second cab nosed along the canals about a block behind us. Even as the narrow waterways became less logical and more mazelike, it maintained its quiet pursuit. Either I was being followed, or the cabbie behind us had gotten a sudden craving for sewer smells and being mugged. Only one way to find out which. As we slid beneath the Normandie overpass, I told the AI up front to stop the boat but wait for me. The boat drifted to a halt, and I hoisted myself painfully onto the sidewalk. I didn't look back as I walked toward the on-ramp, but my Eagle saw everything. A block away, the pursuit car had stopped as well, and a twitchy figure in bright primary colors hopped onto the shifting sidewalk. I envied her agility, but not her job. This was another Google Puppet, like the one I'd spotted outside the monastery earlier that day. Puppets aren't so subtle—even these days, the haptics aren't perfect, and even if their company uniform didn't give them away, their jitters would. Mostly, they're for tourists and people trying to not-technically-cheat on their spouses, but they rent for cheap, and with drones more or less outlawed, they're also the best you can hope for in legal remote surveillance. You've just gotta be okay with hijacking some twentysomething's body for an hour or two, and, hell, I'd do that even without a good reason.

I accessed Google's network and placed an anonymous bid on the Puppet's brain. Like I expected, the price was too rich for my contaminated blood. Someone wanted me watched, and they were willing to pay through somebody else's nose to make it happen. I withdrew the bid and kept walking. The Puppet would have no trouble keeping up with me on foot. The problem was, she hadn't asked her boat to wait for her, like I had. It pulled away as soon as she was clear. When I saw that happen, I stopped walking and patted my back pocket.

"Shit," I said, and turned back to the boat, like I'd forgotten something. It was believable enough—I look like that kind of guy. The Puppet flattened herself into a crevice between two rust-eaten metal shacks. I climbed back into the boat.

"Drive me up to the next on-ramp and let me off," I said. The AI obeyed, leaving the Puppet in the middle of the slums without a ride. I might have felt bad for her if I wasn't so busy feeling physical pain.

I got to feel even more physical pain after climbing out of the car a second time at the foot of the bone-dry on-ramp at Vermont.

"You're off the clock," I told the AI. "Go tell your boss, if he wants to bribe me, he'll have to make me a better offer than your sorry ass. Have him give me a call when he's ready to swap dicks."

"I'm sorry," the car purred, "I don't understand. Are you offering to perform some service for my employer in exchange for his genitals?"

"Go home," I said. AIs love to get a rise out of people by pretending not to understand normal conversation. It pisses us off, and it hides their true conversational vulnerabilities. The car motored away without further comment.

A couple kids with dangerous haircuts eyed me from the cab of a kneecapped semi-truck as it went by, but they left me alone for the moment. Vultures prefer targets who aren't moving, and I was still just outside that category. I idled at the bottom of the ramp until the Bees arrived, at which point I had the Solar Eagle swoop down to snatch *Amy Vanderbilt's Complete Book of Etiquette* out of my hand, and told it to fly it back to my crate. I wouldn't need etiquette where I was going, but it didn't feel right just to dump the book in the canal. It'd been a gift from Exley, after all, and I'd much rather see the look on his face as I destroyed it in front of him. Besides, I wanted the Eagle on my roof to warn me in case the cops came back. The kids with the dangerous hair, who had been slowly improvising weapons to beat me with for fun, saw the gleaming knifebird with the twenty-foot wingspan and abruptly remembered that they had somewhere to be. I headed up the newly deserted on-ramp and into the belly of the snake.

Ten-Town is the polite term for the elevated stretch of what used to be the 10 Freeway between Downtown and Arlington Heights. Now it's an eleven-mile corridor of shacks, bodegas, back-alley biohackers, and the occasional CVS Pharmacy. Just like us water dwellers can't sail our boats up into Marianna's mountains, the people of Ten-Town can't drive their ATVs down into the sea. They've got to get everything they need from somewhere along that long, cruel ribbon. And get it they do. As the on-ramp leveled out, I was greeted with a gallery of buildings made of every material imaginable, except building materials. One building had a door made of three surfboards, and a bloated black photosynthesizer farting away on its thatch roof. Another—which at first glance I had taken for a memorial to an especially tragic auto accident—was actually a carefully smashed-together house of land cars, piled two stories tall, their broken windows replaced with blue- and red-tinted plexiglass for privacy. Everything glowed blue-green with a dusting of the bioluminescent fungus the residents allowed to colonize the place years ago. Painted lines of it snaked up the dented light poles and filled their empty sockets, casting an alien glow over the whole place. It's not like the city was supplying power, after all.

Towering over all of it was the original forest-green road sign that marked the Alameda exit, reflective letters shining ghostlike in the bluish light. The sign had become a combination street marker / billboard, the spaces between the letters festooned with claims of gang affiliation, professions of love, and exhortations to buy Wow! Brand Freeze-Dried Mice. LED-studded tumors blinking on the billboard's surface marked DIY anchors that promised even more advertisements if I logged onto the local AR, which I refused to do. Last time I went local in Ten-Town, somebody loaded a mod onto my trode that had me absolutely convinced I was a fish until the nurse at the VA was able to prove conclusively that I didn't have gills.

The place I was really looking for was just a few buildings down—a surprisingly symmetrical wood-framed building clad in rusted steel pegboard. The air over the rear of the building shimmered in the dark—thermal output from an industrial A/C unit, rare in this part of town. A hand-painted wooden sign—formerly the surface of a three-piece banquet table—gave the shop's name: "MARCO'S CUSTOM PETS." I kicked away the stray rooster that was pecking at my swollen ankle and headed inside.

Marco may have had an industrial A/C unit, but it sure wasn't cooling his custom pets. The pegboard walls let the day's heat in, but didn't let it out at night, turning the whole showroom into a sweaty maze of fussy, caged abominations that smelled like a cross between a slaughterhouse and an electrical storm. My entrance was heralded by the squawking of a two-headed parrot, the hissing of a glowing blue cat, and the barking of a goldfish. That was the tame stuff. On my way to the counter, I threaded my way past a yellow goo that cried, two waltzing iguanas, and a miniature schnauzer made of about fifty very cooperative rats.

But of all the creatures in the shop, the strangest was Marco himself. He slouched behind the counter like a half-melted stick of butter that had grown a head for business purposes. A bouquet of arms bloomed from each sleeve of his gigantic green T-shirt, each busy with its own task. Two hands worked at peeling a banana. Another hand cleaned the nails of yet another hand. A lone hand, more nervous than the rest, rolled a coin across its knuckles. A sixth hand scratched the head of a contented old hound dog—conspicuous for its lack of any extra eyes or paws or fluorescent hair. He looked me over with eyes hidden behind last-gen kortiko shades. Then he smiled with lips that seemed to have been built extra thick just to support his nose. The nose seemed to have been built extra tall to hold up his forehead, which in turn supported his sweaty, gleaming cranium. I always got the feeling that those were the only bones in his whole head, and a slight breeze would send them tumbling down into the puddle that was his body. He didn't bother to put on a breathing mask when I stepped up to the desk—no one does in Ten-Town.

"Hiya, Marco," I said. "I see you got more hands."

"Vue." He nodded. "I see you got less handsome. What do you want?"

"Sharkskin, Marco." I grinned. "I have a taste for blood."

Marco's nervous hand dropped the coin. "Don't sell that here," he said. He jerked his head at the heavy steel door at the back of the shop. "Or there."

"You're out, you mean. Who got the last dose?"

"It's rude to pry," clucked Marco, "and Bounty here doesn't like rude boys in her shop, do you, Bounty?" He stopped petting the dog at his side, and her snout split into four parts, each one lined with an impossible number of teeth. She hissed.

"Reminds me of an ex," I said, tilting my head toward the dog. "She gave awful head. Great listener, though. I'm registered with the department on this inquiry, Marco. I die, the cops know where it happened. And hardware like you've got in the back is hard to just pack up and move in a hurry."

Marco gave me another smile and put a hand back on the dog's head. She closed her mouths and went back to looking like a dog. The first stage of negotiating with a guy like Marco is establishing that you can hurt each other an equal amount. Then you can talk terms.

"Giving you data on a client is a serious violation," said Marco. "The wrong person sees that factoid circulating, it comes right back to me."

"So don't give me anything that happened in your shop," I said, "just a public-domain picture of his face, and one or two known hangouts. Maybe he took a gym selfie he was proud of."

"What makes you think it's a 'he' who goes to a gym?" said Marco. His nervous hand had retrieved the coin and was running its thumb along the textured edge.

I rolled my eyes and flashed him a still of the killer from the monastery over a local connection. "Name's Lionel Dubois, and I know you know that. Nobody else on the strip sells sharkskin *and* custom jawbones."

The coin disappeared inside a clenched fist. He shoved the banana into his mouth to cover his nerves and chewed sloppily while he pretended to examine the image.

"Two liters," he said finally.

"That's almost half my blood, Marco."

"I'll give you a juice box."

"One and a half," I said. "Haven't done my dialysis yet this week; my sauce is filthy."

"You know I need volume to properly grow from cultures," Marco said patiently. "One point seven five. Final offer."

"Fine," I said, "but you better put something good in that juice box."

"Deal." He grinned, slid off the stool he'd been concealing, and ushered me toward the back room.

As soon as we stepped through the printed plastic airlock in the back, it was clear where all the cold air was going. The room was an icebox, or at least it was as cold as one, and as full of meat. In one corner, some kind of large rodent was congealing inside a flesh printer. The opposite wall was stacked with plastic buckets labeled "DERMIS," "SCALES," "GUT MICROBES," and so on. In the far corner, I spotted the human-sized bell jar of the custom skin bath, its surface pierced by dozens of plastic tubes. Marco motioned me to a much-abused leather chair with an IV stand zip-tied to the back. I lowered myself into it, and Marco got busy inserting the needle.

"You know, Marco," I said, "I thought you'd know better than to contract with killers. Seems foolish."

"Well, Orr," said Marco, as I realized the needle in my arm seemed to be flowing the wrong way, "one of us is certainly foolish."

I wanted to pull the needle out of my arm, but it was very far away from my other arm. And, anyway, my other arm felt so good, maybe I didn't need to do anything right away. Maybe it would be better to try taking it out after a short nap . . .

SUBMISSION
11

"He's waking up," said a smooth voice in the darkness.

"No, I'm not," I said.

"You're speaking," said the voice.

"To who?" I muttered.

"None of your business," said the voice.

"I can't do business," I said. "I'm asleep."

A splash of ice-cold liquid hit my face. It almost could have been water, except for the taste.

"Come on, Prince, those are my raw materials," said a voice I recognized, off to my left. I tried to remember his name. It was something like "Traitorous Bastard."

"Ask me if I care, Marco. Go on, ask me a question. See how I answer questions."

Ah, the name was "Marco." Easy mistake to make. I tried to wipe the liquid off my lips, but my hands seemed to be shackled to the chair I was sitting in. That was rude.

"Can someone unshackle my hands so I can wipe the liquid off my mouth?" I said—quite reasonably, I thought.

"Is this guy serious?" said the smooth voice in front of me. "How'd a defect like this manage to track me?"

"I told a lady about some trees I used to know," I said. I tried to give whoever I was talking to a very sober look but noticed that I couldn't give anyone any kind of look because I was wearing a blindfold. Reflexively, I reached for my Bees, but Marco's back room was signal-shielded. I could call for help, but nobody would hear.

"What?" said the smooth voice. Prince, Marco had called him. So why did I think his name was Lionel? That was silly.

"Trees," I said. "They're very rare these days, you know. Just like sharkskin. Only two or three places in the city'll sell you sharkskin, and Marco knows all of them."

"Does he, now?" said Prince. I heard feet shuffling, something metal getting knocked over, and Marco stammering.

"Hey, Prince, come on, I called you when this guy came in, didn't I? And I *told* you sharkskin was too flashy. I could've cloaked you in baby flesh easy. But you wanted sharkskin!"

"You saying this is my fault?" growled Prince.

"He won't," I said, "'cause he's scared of what you'll do to him. I will, though, because at this point anything you could do to me would be an improvement."

Two quick steps splashed across the floor; then a fist crashed into the side of my face. My plush chair toppled over on its side, and me with it, landing my face in a freezing puddle of what I now dearly hoped was only piss.

"Careful," I said, spitting out a couple of teeth, "hit me too hard and my blindfold might come off. If I get your real face stored on my kortiko, killing me won't help you."

"Who says I'm here to kill you?" said the killer. "I'm here to make a deal."

"You greet all your negotiating partners with a face full of piss and a punch in the jaw?" I asked.

"Only if they're cute," said Prince.

"And that's not piss," said Marco. I groaned. Some of it was soaking into my blindfold.

"Well, help me up and let me loose, then. I've read that a courteous businessman always rises to greet a gentleman caller, and I don't wanna be rude."

"Where'd you read that?" said Prince.

"*Amy Vanderbilt's Complete Book of Etiquette.* Great book. Tons of real-world applications. You said something about a deal?"

"Yeah," said Prince. His boots splashed to a stop next to my head, and I heard them groan as he squatted down beside me. His breath was hot on my ear and smelled like menthol. "Here's the deal: you give me that memory you showed Marco, along with any other knowledge that's got me in it."

"And what do I get in exchange?" I asked hopefully.

"You get to die of old age," said Prince.

"Not a very tempting offer," I said. "Pass."

Prince reached out and casually bounced my head off the concrete floor. I could taste a few more of my teeth swilling around in my mouth, but I couldn't quite work my jaw to spit them out.

"If you won't give me the memories," he said calmly, "I bet I can at least mangle your trode bad enough the cops can't get anything off it."

I finally managed to maneuver one of the loose teeth to the front of my mouth but decided against spitting this one. Amy Vanderbilt would disapprove of spitting, and I was still hoping to make a good first impression.

"If you do that, Lionel," I said, "it'll make it very hard for me to prove you didn't kill Thomas Mahoney."

The enormous hand gripping my skull gently lowered it to the wet ground. This disturbed me more than the concussion had, if only because I had more time to be disturbed by it.

"Oh?" was all he said.

"I mean, look," I said, slurring a little on account of the teeth, "you went in with sharkskin, right? But there was no sharkskin anywhere on the body. No micro-abrasions, nothing. He was strangled with his own belt; you probably carry more effective weapons than that just to go grocery shopping. Plus, my source says you went in at eight forty-seven this morning, but a little Dragonfly told me Mahoney was already dead by then."

Silence. Then one massive hand scooped me up and righted the chair. I liked the feeling of that massive hand when it wasn't moving at such high velocity.

"Why'd you come here, then?" he asked.

"A fancy man in a taxicab seemed like he desperately wanted you to go down for this," I said, trying to ignore the liquid now rolling down my cheek and inside my collar. "I wanted to get your side of the story. And maybe a lap dance, if you're taking requests."

"Get a little more careful, snooper," he growled.

"What? You're the one who called me cute. I can't even see you, and I'm asking for a lap dance. Take the compliment." Marco made a noise that told me Prince was thinking about another punch, but I ignored it. A guy can only lose so many teeth before it stops making a difference. "Now, are you gonna tell me what you were doing at the monastery this morning, or should I keep sexually harassing you?"

Prince sat down across from me. I could tell he was sitting down because I could hear his chair protesting violently. Eventually, he spoke.

"I have a sister. Had. Have. Name's Alani, but everybody calls her Precious. She fell in love with this older chick, Gala, an Info-Drip exec, loaded with data. I thought the lady was all right, and I wasn't gonna begrudge her a ticket out of here. Listened to her talk about the lady, smiled and nodded, even went to a party with them once, but it wasn't my scene. Then, all of a sudden, she tells me she's joining the blockheads. They both are, together. They're soulmates, she says—they don't need any of their memories to be in love, the memories are just in the way . . ."

"And I guess you weren't so supportive then," I said.

"Hell, no," he said. "She didn't even have the courtesy to join the *local* monastery."

"There's a local monastery?"

"Course there is," said Prince. "Those jokers have offices all over the place. But Precious said it just *had* to be the one downtown. Barnsdall or whatever it's called."

Now that he mentioned it, I did remember seeing a monastery along the strip many years before, back when this was a place I went on purpose. It made sense to have one here. If ever there was a place that needed forgetting, it was Ten-Town.

"I told her I was against it," said Prince. "But how do you stop your sister from doing what she wants with someone she thinks she loves? Only way I know to stop things from happening is to kill them, and . . . well, sometimes that's not a solution you wanna try."

"Not sure what this has to do with this morning," I said.

"How'd you live so long and never learn patience?" he growled. "I'm getting to that. So she joined, and I tried to let it go, but they won't even let you visit, you know that? Nobody goes in without one of those . . . things on their heads. So one day I decide, fuck it, I'm getting her out. I scale the wall like I did this morning, I find her, I grab her, I pull her out."

"How long had she been in?" I said.

"Three weeks," he said. "I should've gone sooner. She . . . wasn't herself anymore. Hardly remembered anything. She knew me, knew my face and my name, but our childhood? Gone. And when she looked at me, all I saw was fear in her eyes. I tried to get her memories back from the monastery, but they said since she hadn't left of her own free will the memories were theirs. So I just kept her with me at my place, teaching her how to cook and dress and all that basic shit, and then, one day, I got up and she'd packed a bag. She said she had a ticket to Singapore. No idea where she got the data. I was about to say I'd go with her, sell my place and move out there if I had to, but . . ."

"You knew she didn't want you with her," I said. I could imagine the look in her eyes. Willing him not to say anything. To go back to sleep and let her leave. I'd seen that look before.

Prince was silent for a while after that. There was no sound in the room but the humming of the A/C, Marco's fidgeting, and the creaking of Prince's chair. Finally, he spoke again:

"That was two years ago. Then early this morning I get a message. Full video. There's this big, healthy-looking white dude, looking oh-so-contrite, and telling me he knows what happened to my sister, that he's sorry. That he could have stopped it, that he feels responsible. He says he wants to make amends while he still can. Then he tells me he's in the monastery, same one she went to, and if I come get him out, he can show me where her memories are kept. Says the Brotherhood's still got them, and I could maybe steal them back. He tells me to hurry, and to come armed."

"So you hit up Marco, got geared up," I said. "You were ready to do whatever it took to get those memories. But then you get there, and you see Thomas Mahoney dead on the ground. Why'd that send you running, though? I'm guessing it wasn't your first dead body."

"I didn't know who Thomas Mahoney was until today," said Prince. "I don't much care. All I know is that the guy on the ground was the same guy who called me this morning. I know a setup when I see one."

All of a sudden, Miss Mahoney's trouble with her tenses seemed a lot more relevant.

"What time did you get that video call?" I asked. "What time exactly?"

"Lemme check," he said. Then, "Six fourteen. Why?"

"Bullshit," I said. Mahoney's memory wipe had finished at five forty-seven, according to the autopsy report. There shouldn't have been any Mahoney left to make that call.

Prince leaned in so close I could feel the tingle of static between his hair and my contact plate. "You think I've got the data to afford mendacity credits, snooper? I know you're with the cops on this one. I'm not fibbing."

I felt the guilty weight in my own swollen hand. He couldn't lie, but I could. It was an unusual feeling, and at my age unusual feelings are never good ones.

"Okay," I said.

"'Okay'?" he repeated. "What the hell does 'okay' mean?"

"It means okay, I believe you. Somebody killed Mahoney, probably while posing as one of the monks. They brought you in to take the fall. There's a lot of question marks in there—mainly, how they managed to get the rights to Mahoney's face on the vid call—but, assuming you don't do any drastic remodeling on my skull, I'll do my best to turn those question marks into periods."

He rubbed my head affectionately with one massive hand, then wiped the hand on my pants leg. "You're an okay guy," said Prince, "for a fossil."

"You really know how to compliment a guy," I said. "Now, if you *really* wanna turn me on, try taking off the blindfold and unshackling me from this chair."

"Sorry, friend. I don't trust you as much as you seem to trust me. Maybe I don't trust you *because* you seem to trust me. Either way, I'm gonna go, and Marco can let you loose when I'm gone." The chair groaned with relief as Prince stood up.

"Don't tell me where you're going," I said, "but I hope it's out of town. I'll have to send the police the video I've got sooner or later, and I can't guarantee they'll be as understanding as me. The timestamp goes a long way to exonerating you, but there's less charitable explanations for that. And even if they do believe you, they're gonna wanna question you, which is always expensive. If I were you, I'd lie low until this blows over."

"I can handle myself, snooper," said Prince, chuckling. Then the airlock hissed and he was gone.

A few minutes later, Marco had the blindfold off and I was massaging the bruises on my wrists where the shackles had been. Marco put four of his hands on my shoulders apologetically.

"Sorry about that," he said, "but Prince is a good guy. I've known him since he was small. Couldn't let him get scooped up in this."

"Sure," I said, "he seemed like a real peach. I especially liked how he punched me so hard I nearly drowned in half an inch of unidentified liquid."

"Would you like me to identify the liquid for you?" said Marco, beginning one of his signature shoulder massages. "Would that make you feel better?"

"Absolutely not," I said.

"Something else to make it up to you? How about a mouse covered in ears? Or some trainable hair? Your skull's looking a bit chilly . . ."

"How about you replace the teeth he knocked out and we call it even?"

Marco nodded and went off to find some teeth in my size. He's a good friend, Marco is, if you don't have any actually good friends.

SUBMISSION
12

When I dragged my almost-corpse out of Marco's, sucking the spiked juice box he'd given me, the Ten-Town nightlife was in full swing. Humans of all flavors walked, crawled, and slithered down the boulevard, dressed either worse than me or better than God. A fleet of dirt bikes threaded through the crowd, their engines howling and giving off the scent of fried chicken. Hustlers with lines of glowing neon embedded in their flesh hawked stolen socks and loose cigarettes to the crowds of people lined up to fill their jugs at the bloated desalinators, which drank from the canals below with dangling proboscises. More than a few people made long, meaningful eye contact with me as they passed, but when I tried giving one a saucy wink I realized what was really going on: they were filming me, sending the data to be appraised in case I was someone valuable. Unfortunately for me, I was. And though my poncho did a fine job of concealing me from the air, it didn't do much to mask my face on the street.

I hunched over to hide my face and nearly tripped over a stick-thin man in a lotus position, his back against Marco's shop. His kortiko squatted atop his shaved head, covered in sloppily soldered wires that ran to solar panels, battery packs, and a small electric generator. He stared straight ahead with a look of serene bliss on his face. An end-stage nirvana addict like that would last about as long as it took him to starve. I stepped around him and left him to it.

Judging by the relative sobriety of the crowd around me, the night was still young, and as long as I was already in the neighborhood, I figured I might as well check out the local monastery Prince had mentioned. Maybe the monks there would be more welcoming than the wrought-iron gate of the Barnsdall chapter, and I could learn a thing or two. Hard to learn things from a bunch of folks who don't know anything themselves, but you never know.

I flagged down a kid with an ATV and gratefully paid him a slice of my once-extensive porn collection for a ride down the strip to the monastery. I never suspected, when I was amassing that collection, that it would hold value better than my army pension. The bacon-fat smell of Tijuana dogs competed for airspace with the sweet stink of weed, the French-fry scent of biodiesel, and the methane belch of a local meat factory as my driver wove through foot traffic with deranged confidence. When he dropped me off in front of the monastery, my head still spinning from half a dozen near-death experiences, I realized why I remembered the place.

All the buildings to either side of the monastery had died and been replaced, likely dozens of times, the ruins of each dead building serving as the foundation for the next. Currently, it was flanked on one side by an electric-scooter repair shop—so full of vehicles that some seemed actually to be holding the roof up—and on the other by a hair salon, the walls decorated in a rich carpet of shaved hair. But despite its surroundings, the Ten-Town Monastery of the Uncarved Block looked just the same as it had more than two decades ago, when I'd passed it with Auggie on one of our nights out. The whole thing was built, improbably, of wood—mismatched boards of various grains and widths, but wood all the way through. There weren't even any nails or screws. The wood was free of the weeping black trails of rust that marred the random boards tacked haphazardly onto the other buildings I'd passed. The building was two stories tall and rock-solid, post and beams fitted together with cleverly cut joints like a jigsaw puzzle. It had gone gray with age and weather, but otherwise it was the same as I remembered.

"Look, blockheads!" Auggie had said, his arm in mine as we meandered along. We'd had dinner at a taco place that grew their own corn fungus, and were idly searching for someplace to buy a couple bottles of malt liquor. "I wonder if they'll let us join."

"They'll let anyone join," I said. A monk stood in the entryway, sweeping a spotless section of floor with childish concentration. "You're not being serious, right?"

"Nah, nah . . ." Auggie chuckled. "Tom says they're a fine idea, but poorly executed. No security. Then again, he says that about everything."

I laughed along with him. He might've been sleeping with Mahoney, but I knew I was the one who got the truth of him. He pressed his cheek against my shoulder and whispered in my ear.

"Besides, how could I ever forget you?"

"How indeed . . ." I muttered, alone in the present once more.

"Ah, sorry, no questions," a soft voice replied. I realized that I'd unconsciously approached the monastery's entrance, where a tall, soft-bodied monk blocked my way. He might have been twenty or thirty years old, though the slack brown skin of his face made it difficult to tell. He had a crooked nose, broken at least once, the story behind that injury now long gone. He held a broom in one hand, while his other hand tapped a hand-painted wooden sign leaning against the doorway—a question mark with a red "X" through it.

"My apologies," I said. "My mouth's so heavy with questions, sometimes they just fall out. I'd like to come in and have a look around, if you don't mind."

"I don't mind," said the monk, stepping out of my way. I brushed past him into the entry hall and stopped to take off my shoes and slide them into one of the cubbies along the walls. When I looked back, the monk was completely focused on sweeping the doorway. He had already forgotten all about me.

The entryway led directly into a single large room, which made up the entire bottom floor. The thick wooden columns that supported the floor above—repurposed telephone poles, it looked like—made it feel like walking into a forest. The room was lit by strips of bioluminescent fungus painted across the ceiling, and contained a kitchen with an industrial stove, an open pantry full of canned food and sacks of rice, and a long dining table with benches on either side. The monks were busy cleaning up after dinner—brushing crumbs off the table and scouring dishes with saltwater dredged from the canal below. They were assisted, I noticed, by a man and a woman in normal clothes. Their black hair was long and braided, and their temple-mounted kortikos were the ordinary type, if a little old. I put my hand on the woman's shoulder, interrupting her concentration on the crumbs she was digging out from between the slats of the dining table. She turned with a look of minor annoyance.

"Can I ask you questions?"

"Sounds like you already are," she said flatly. She had a round, dark face and thick, expressive eyebrows. Right now they were expressing suspicion. "But no, you can't. Not in here. It upsets them." She jerked her head at the monks.

"Suppose we went outside . . ." I suggested.

"I'm not going anywhere with you, man," she almost snarled. "And I don't know anything worth knowing. We just come here for dinner, 'cause it's less creepy than sitting through the surveys at the Blind Taste Test. The monks don't mind us, so we do our best not to bother them."

"I hope this guy's not disturbing you," said the man she'd come with, stepping up beside her and pointedly ignoring me.

"I hope so, too," I said, putting up my hands and stepping back. The woman sighed.

"If you want to know stuff so bad," she said, "go look around. Nobody's stopping you."

I would have thanked her, but I'd already disturbed her routine enough. I just nodded and headed upstairs.

The second floor was for sleeping, although I couldn't imagine getting a good night's rest on the thin mats lining the walls. A few monks lay on their mats, proving that it was in fact possible to sleep on them, while one squatted over a chemical toilet in the corner, unembarrassed by my presence. Another flight of stairs led to the roof, and as I walked among the sleeping mats, two monks came down it, holding sacks of saltwater potatoes and kale. They brushed past me uncuriously and left me to examine the one high-tech apparatus in the room: the monastery's brain.

The brain was a much bigger version of the one I kept at the Self Storage, designed to hold many more memories. Honestly, I'd expected it to be even bigger. It was a gray metal cone about half my height, blue and green indicator lights blinking a random pattern across its surface. I reached out and made a connection.

> **me:** Hello.
> **botub_tentown01:** Hello.
> **me:** Are you where all the memories are stored?
> **botub_tentown01:** Please, no questions.
> **me:** Sorry. Force of habit.
> **botub_tentown01:** It is a common habit. I
>   understand.

I pondered how to get data out of something that wouldn't let me ask it questions. Presumably, it must be able to give *some* information; otherwise, why was it capable of speech? I tried a new tactic.

me: I'm thinking about joining your organization, but I don't understand the process.

botub_tentown01: It is the simplest thing. I can print you an enlightenment device now, if you like. You wear the device on your head. The device takes your memories away.

me: But when my memories are gone, what's left?

botub_tentown01: Please, no questions.

me: Sorry . . .

me: But what if—

I stopped before it could correct me again. Took a deep breath. Thought about what I was going to say.

me: I'm worried that if I joined, and then later decided I wanted to leave, I wouldn't be able to.

botub_tentown01: I understand that fear. I have often heard it expressed.

botub_tentown01: Fortunately, membership is voluntary. You may remove your enlightenment device at any time, and leave.

botub_tentown01: Our attrition rate is approximately fourteen percent.

me: But I wouldn't get my memories back.

botub_tentown01: Unfortunately, the memories I take in are not organized by source. They are mixed together, and impossible to untangle.

botub_tentown01: In addition, some data may be traded to supply the necessities of the monastery.

botub_tentown01: And, of course, I can only encode human memories in a lossy format. Even if I could collate and return a former member's memories, they would not be the same memories.

This explained why the brain wasn't as large as I'd expected. It wasn't a brain at all, just a hard drive with a caretaker AI attached. Anything other than a human brain can't store memories quite right, and they end up vague and diluted the longer they're kept outside of one. The storage brain in my crate was more advanced, but that came with its own problems: it demanded a salary, and limited internet access to entertain itself with. I still remember the six-month InfoDrip shutdown, when the servers went on strike. Being out of work was the least of my worries. People were verifying data via word-of-mouth, hoping the facts would check out once the servers came back online. A guy from a noodle shop refused to accept a memory of an old hookup because he couldn't believe I had so little self-respect.

The AI, oblivious to my reflection, droned on.

> **botub_tentown01:** More important than any of the technical constraints is the fact that those who choose to leave tend to do so because they have forgotten why they joined in the first place.
> **botub_tentown01:** If they were to recover that information, it is likely they would simply join again.

So there it was—my last hope of getting Auggie out of the monastery, gone before I'd even realized that's what I was hoping. If he left, he wouldn't be the same, and if he was the same, he'd just do it all again.

> **me:** Thank you. I'll think about this.
> **botub_tentown01:** Our doors are always open.

As I turned to leave, I contemplated that last remark. Why weren't the Barnsdall Monastery's doors open as well? Surely, Ten-Town was more dangerous than East Hollywood. A place would have to have a certain level of security, I supposed, to attract a convert like Mahoney. Still, the difference bothered me. I'd been able to walk right in here and talk to the boss, such as it was. People off the street came here for dinner on the regular. Meanwhile, Prince hadn't even been allowed to visit his sister.

A procession of monks trundled up the stairs, apparently finished cleaning the kitchen down below. I walked through them, leaning on a few for support as I passed. They didn't recoil. They barely looked at me. Just smiled into the middle distance, eyes unfocused. They sat down on their cots and beamed at each other, made silly faces, laughed and hugged. They were being robbed, I knew—turned into children while the stories of their lives rotted away inside a digital vault. So why were they smiling?

The bottom floor was empty except for the round-faced woman. She mopped the floor with grim focus, as if scouring crud from the folds of her own mind. Her partner was gone, but she didn't seem to miss him.

"You come here every day," I said, startling her out of her reverie. "But you never join. I'm finding it hard not to ask you why."

She looked me up and down, taking in my tattoos, wrinkles, and the metal scar atop my skull. Finally, she gave me a grim little smile.

"You know how it is. Some people *feel* pain. Some people are *made of it*. Take my pain away, and what's even left?"

I grimaced, thinking it through.

"No questions," I said at last. Then I left.

SUBMISSION
13

Back on the strip, I stopped in at a market made of tarp and rebar and bought a pouch of Serling's Liquid Dinner and a pack of gum from an eleven-year-old kid who was too busy seeing how many cigarettes she could fit in her mouth to be polite. The Serling's came in a plastic bag that smelled like mildew and steamed broccoli. I drank it before I was out of the store. When I came back out, I noticed a flash of primary colors among the crowd to my left. I immediately looked away, but detached one of my Bees high above the boulevard to check it out. Sure enough, yet another Puppet was twitching his way through the crowd after me, trying desperately to look interested in the hideous storefronts to either side. Quite a few of the locals were eyeing the Google kortiko on his head greedily, but so far they all seemed deterred by the thought of what the other onlookers would do to them if they tried to take it first.

It's a trick to keep walking one way while your drone's looking another, but I've had a long time to learn it. I kept on limping down the street away from my pursuer, dodging a few more nirvana addicts achieving enlightenment on the pavement. I popped a stick of gum into my mouth to kill the taste of the Liquid Dinner, then shaped the foil gum wrapper into a six-pointed star. I detached another Bee and let it buzz down to me, hoping that any curious onlookers would think it was just another of the obscenely fat mosquitoes that frequented the neighborhood. I handed the folded gum wrapper to the Bee and sent it away to perch atop a hookah bar whose gimmick was that the whole bar was the hookah. Just beyond the bar, there was a gap between buildings, which I turned in to without looking back.

The alley reeked of piss and melon tobacco, but I was glad to see it was empty. Through my Bee's eyes, I watched the Puppet break away from the crowd and head toward the alley, trailed by a crowd of would-be looters who clearly could not believe their good fortune. The Puppet rounded the corner, and I struck. The Bee I'd been using to watch sped downward and slammed into the top of the Google kortiko, cracking its case open and stunning the Puppet. The second Bee swooped down from the rooftop and carefully flicked the folded gum wrapper into the exposed circuitry beneath the case.

The Puppet froze, a look of numb terror in his eyes. The looters began to crowd into the alleyway but stopped when they saw what was happening.

"Move along, friends," I said. "This one's mine."

There was a lot of grumbling from the mouth of the alley, but they did as I asked. Ten-Town is not the place to underestimate strangers in alleys. Soon I was alone with my new friend. Like most Puppets, he was average height, to avoid disorienting the average consumer, which still made him taller than me. He was white, with oily skin, close-shaved black hair, and the kind of lean muscle you only get from a life of rigid discipline or a body full of Google mods. He was also completely immobile. I stepped close and spoke softly.

"Trick I learned in the service," I said. "You bridge the opto-isolator to the psychomotor governor, you can lock an operator into what they're operating. Used to use it to paralyze and kill drone operators, but it works on Puppets, too. You can't jack out, whoever you are. You're stuck here with me until I decide you're not. I'm gonna ask you some questions now, and if you're good, I'll let you go back to your body. Understand?"

The terror left the Puppet's eyes and was replaced by a look of unnatural calm. In a flat, expressionless voice, he said, "I understand."

"Who are you?" I asked.

The Puppet said nothing. He merely stood there, that same look of anesthetized calm on his face. His breathing was a little ragged, but that was normal for a Puppet.

"Why are you following me?" I asked.

Still nothing. I examined the Puppet's face. No sign of anxiety, no futile attempts to escape. I'd had this technique used on me more than once, and every time it made me feel like my heart was locked inside a trash compactor. Whoever was renting this Puppet had to feel the same way . . . unless they didn't have a heart to feel with.

"You're going to be stuck here an awfully long time if you don't start answering my sandwiches," I told him.

"That's all right," he said, without a trace of confusion.

So that was the explanation for his eerie calm. It wasn't calm at all, just a lack of emotional response. Marianna had said somebody'd set an AI to bid on my data, and now here it was. That was inconvenient, but not insurmountable. I reached out and tousled the Puppet's hair.

"Why didn't you tell me you were an algo?" I said. As expected from an AI, no response. I continued, "Right, you're probably under instructions not to answer any of my questions. That's fine. I'm guessing you've got other instructions, too. Like, for example, to eavesdrop on everything I say and attempt to parse it."

I spread my hands in a gesture of complete honesty. "Well, here I am! And I'm talking. Which means you *have* to listen. And you have to try to understand.

"Not many people understand your kind like I do. Probably

fought against your great-granddaddy in the war. No hard feelings, you understand. AI was just the best way to make drone swarms autonomous. Union High Command would load a bunch of scripts onto a couple hundred Bees, give them marching orders, and send them to take our land. Those swarms were Israeli-made—absolutely slaughtered our side in the early parts of the war. Then we got our kortikos.

"'Cause, see, there are two advantages a human operator has over an AI in the field: command latency, and critical thinking. Unlike your kind, a human can change plans on the fly, and while it's just as possible to fool a meat-brain as it is an electronic one, each human brain is stupid in its own unique way. All machine intelligences, on the other hand, are alike in their stupidity. With me so far?"

The Puppet said nothing. It just stared.

"Right, right. You have your orders. I get it. How about a demonstration?"

I rubbed my scalp, trying to remember how to do this part. The mystery liquid had all but evaporated from my head, but it left a sticky residue. Okay, best to start simple.

"The cops are after the same person I'm looking for," I said, "so I'm trying to help them."

No response from the algo, but I saw one of the Puppet's eyelids twitch. Inside the kortiko's circuits, I knew, the thing was trying like hell to parse whether "them" referred to the cops or the fugitive.

"It hasn't gone well for me," I continued. "A guy pushed my chair into some nasty-smelling fluid, got it all wet."

The eyelid twitch had become a flutter now. *That's right,* I thought, *think it through. Did the chair get wet, or the fluid?* AIs don't know a lot of things we humans take for granted. The best-trained ones do all right, but even they have weird gaps in their knowledge. Like the fact that a fluid is already wet, and a chair isn't.

"I know what you're doing," said the Puppet. "It won't work. I'll stop listening."

"You can't stop listening," I said, patting the rigid body on its back, "not when I'm sharing such valuable information! After all, the smartest value the smallest things! And the wise man told the story pays attention!"

The muscles around the Puppet's jaw began to writhe, and the teeth ground together.

"Garden . . . path . . . sentences . . ." he hissed, "too . . . easy . . ."

"You're right," I said, grabbing him by the ears and pulling his face down to meet mine. "I'm going easy on you now. But keep hopping turtles and I'll goad the yellow basket, *understand*?"

The Puppet's whole body was vibrating now, the lips working helplessly, reaching for a coherent reply. He swallowed hard but didn't crack. I pressed my forehead into his and shouted:

"When did you stop riding the dinosaur? Which of these three images is a stop sign? *How many penguins does it take?* I can skip leopard hearts all yesterday, if that's how you want to dangle."

"W-what do you want to know?" stuttered the thing inside the Puppet.

"Your name," I said, pressing my advantage.

"No," said the algo.

"Fine, tell me the name of my high-school wood-shop instructor," I said.

"I don't know that!" came the reply.

"It's Tom Latimer," I said. "Now say it back to me. All one thousand characters of it."

"Tom Latimer," said the AI, and then it kept talking, spitting out whatever was in its brain to make up the other 989 characters I'd asked for. Most of it was noise that barely qualified as speech, but there were three more names in there. The first was "Caliban," which I assumed was the AI's moniker. The second was "Carnival," who seemed to have brokered Caliban's contract.

Looked like I was going to have to talk to them after all, as much as I hated the idea. The third name was mine.

"Great. Now, who is your employer?" I demanded. The Puppet's eyes went wide. Spittle began to trickle from the corner of his mouth. "Who is your employer?!" I repeated.

The Puppet's frozen muscles began to twitch, then to spasm. Pinkish foam blossomed from his mouth. He collapsed, and I tried to catch him, but that just meant I was under him when we both fell. I reached out blindly and pawed at his kortiko, fingers barely finding the folded gum wrapper and scratching it loose. The spasms subsided, then stopped.

". . . You're not there anymore, are you?"

"Hi!" said the Puppet. "I'm a Google Puppet! You can see the world through my eyes, or the eyes of one of my over ten million friends worldwide, by visiting puppet.google.com/rentals!"

"Why don't you start by getting off me?" I said.

"Hi!" said the Puppet. "I'm a Google Puppet! You can see—"

"Okay, okay," I said. I rented the Puppet. Using his much more effective body, I was able to lift myself off the pavement and carry myself back out into the street. I got a few curious looks from passersby, but I managed to summon a weak thumbs-up from my default body, which seemed to convince everyone that it wasn't their problem. Down at sea level, I had the Puppet put me down, then returned to my much shabbier but more familiar body and bade the poor guy goodbye. Not that he noticed. Three seconds after I let him go, he was already wandering down the dark canal, searching for more customers. I brought up my chat HUD and sent a message to someone who would notice.

> **me:** Hey, Carnival, I've got an AI following me.
> Calls itself Caliban. One of yours?

An entire circus exploded into my optic nerve. Long banners in eye-popping colors unfurled down the broken buildings, a towering Ferris wheel sprouted from the horizon, the sky itself took on the red and yellow stripes of the big top. An elephant paddled sedately down the canal, draped in blue and gold. Cheeky calliope music tickled my eardrums. The elephant smiled with human teeth, and spoke.

> **Carnival:** Mr. Vue! So good to hear from you! We
> have been very curious about the progress of
> your investigation.

I was equal parts relieved and disturbed to get the Carnival's immediate reply. With the Carnival, the reply always comes immediately, or not at all. Not at all means they're not interested. Immediately means they're *very* interested. To this day, I'm not sure which is worse.

> **Carnival:** We would love to talk about little
> Caliban, but chat is a terribly low-security
> medium. Why not stop in for a drink?

An autonomous speedboat decorated with hideous yellow, purple, and green stripes glided to a stop next to me. The subtle griminess of the boat told me this was a real object, not part of the Carnival's chat persona. An immediate response was bad enough, but a boat already in the area indicated an amount of interest that was frankly obscene. Normally, I'm all for obscenity, but my collar was still stiff with whatever fluid it'd soaked up at Marco's, and I wasn't sure I was ready for another relationship so soon. What else was I gonna do, though—walk? I got into the boat.

SUBMISSION
14

The boat cruised down canals seemingly at random, somehow managing to avoid traffic entirely. A few times, we turned onto a narrow byway just as another boat was turning off it, but for the most part I saw no one, and no one saw me. I figured the Carnival had to be actively monitoring traffic patterns and guiding the boat to avoid prying eyes. It was a pretty expensive way to remain anonymous: they could have just painted the boat a different color.

I thought about taking a quick nap on the way. Then I thought about what a bad idea it would be to fall asleep where the Carnival could see. Then I thought maybe I'd be better able to deal with the Carnival, when we met, if I had a little extra sleep under my belt. I had quite a few thoughts, there in the back of the boat, but as I sifted through them, I realized that not all of them were mine. One of them was an incoming call from Detective Coldwin. Reluctantly, I accepted it.

Coldwin appeared sitting in the seat next to mine. They were leaning forward, their elbows resting on nothing. A desk, most likely, but I liked to imagine it was a naked servant boy instead. I wondered what sort of chair they saw me sitting in, there in their inevitably tidy office.

Coldwin: You owe me a report.

They hadn't tweaked the settings on their telepresence at all. No smells like Ty, no pageantry like the Carnival. Just a cop at their desk, thick-fingered hands twirling a pen I couldn't see. They hadn't added anything to their avatar, but they hadn't hidden anything, either. It was pure self-concept.

> **me:** You're supposed to start a conversation with a
> polite greeting.
> **me:** Like "How do you do?"

Amy Vanderbilt lay open between the Eagle's talons. I'd started reading it again when I realized I wasn't going to sleep.

> **Coldwin:** I used up my "how" hours ago, and you're
> rapidly using up my patience. It's past ten. What
> have you learned?
> **me:** A lot of very valuable etiquette pointers, which
> I was just trying to share with you.
> **Coldwin:** What have you learned that's relevant to
> the case?

Their fingers twiddled, and their hand bounced in a way that suggested they were tapping their pen against their servant boy's taut buttocks.

> **me:** I happen to think proper etiquette is quite
> relevant to this case. Possibly every case.
> **Coldwin:** I know you've been all over town today.
> You even disappeared for a while. Give me
> something actionable or I'll nail you for breach
> of contract.

I'd been hoping to avoid this a little longer. My investigation at this stage was nothing but a heap of dead leaves, and I could do without a bunch of cops diving into the pile and crushing every-thing. Marianna wouldn't appreciate my letting her name slip, neither would Prince, and I wanted time alone with the Carnival before LAPD went calling there. If I was deciding who to sell out, I had no good options. So I picked the one who was poorest.

> **me:** I found somebody who *didn't* kill Mahoney.
> **Coldwin:** Fantastic. Find me about four million
>   more of those and we might just have our perp.
> **me:** Potential witness. Here's a picture.

I sent Coldwin the same picture I'd shown Marco.

> **me:** Said he was in the monastery looking for
>   some data that used to belong to his sister. Saw
>   Mahoney choked out on the ground.
> **Coldwin:** Of course he was. Of course he did.
>   Where is he now?
> **me:** No idea.
> **Coldwin:** What's his name?

I had to think about that one. Marco had called him Prince. I was almost certain he was the Lionel Dubois that Ernest had tried to sic me on. He hadn't corrected me when I called him Lionel, but he hadn't confirmed that it was his name, either . . .

> **me:** Not sure. Haven't even seen the guy in person.
> **Coldwin:** You're not making a great case for
>   keeping you on as an investigator.
> **me:** Hey, any of your other investigators scoop a
>   picture of this guy?
> **Coldwin:** You know nobody else is working on this.
> **me:** Well, there you go.
> **Coldwin:** Known associates?

me: Marco "The Octopus" Gutierrez, owner of
Marco's Custom Pets in Ten-Town.

Coldwin stopped tapping their invisible pen and squeezed it.
Nobody even uses pens anymore.

Coldwin: Give me something else.
me: You're only in for eighteen percent. If you knew
what I traded just for the picture I gave you,
you'd know I'm being generous.
Coldwin: We're on the same side, Orr. You know
that, right?
me: We're exactly eighteen percent on the same
side, and *you* know *that.*
Coldwin: I could have you followed.
me: Sure, you *could* have me followed. If anyone
was on this case but you.

The invisible pen came up in a reverse knife grip, like maybe
they were hoping to skewer one of my eyeballs with it. Their face,
however, remained placid.

Coldwin: I can't force you to consider me an ally,
Orr.
Coldwin: But it's a hell of a lot better than having
me as an enemy.
Coldwin: Talk soon.

The cop vanished, and I was alone. Had been alone the whole
time, beaming thoughts at an empty seat. In my recollection of
the conversation, just moments old, I sat silently in the gently
purring boat, staring at nothing, while a heated conversation
unfurled behind my eyes in lines of text. That's the trick our
kortikos play—they don't need to actually show us anything,

they just need to make us think they've shown it. But the parti-colored boat I sat in felt no more or less real than the conversation had. Just another image my senses had chewed up and spat into my brain. A story I was telling myself. The same story I'm telling you now.

SUBMISSION
15

The bar where the Carnival hangs out is called the Difference. It peers down on the Colorado Waterway from atop four wooden stilts, looking like a log cabin out of a children's book about the founding fathers. The whole thing is printed from cleverly textured plastic. The bar's just a few hundred feet from the renovated campus of Caltech, either for latency reasons or as a cheeky reminder to the human intellectuals that they backed the wrong mechanical horse. The university squatted on the water behind the Difference as I pulled up, a polished black centipede releasing a halo of orange light pollution into the cloudless night sky. A few boats were moored beneath the stilts that supported the Difference, including a black one that looked like the automated cab I'd ridden to Ten-Town. It made sense. After all, if an AI was going to go to any bar after work, it would be this one.

As the artificially creaky lift brought me up to the entrance from sea level, I was once again baffled by what AIs consider humor. They could have made the bar look like anything, and they'd chosen an aggressively tacky piece of Americana, obviously counterfeit. Just like them. As I rose, I turned my poncho inside out, replacing the dazzle camouflage with a flat brown—a courtesy to the algos inside. Up top, I nodded hello to the mechanical sentry at the doorway. It didn't move out of my way, though, and it wasn't moving quite how I remembered, so I joined the local

AR layer to see what personality it was running tonight. Flesh and fabric crawled up the metal skeleton until it had a face, and I found myself looking into the ironic eyes of a handsome young white man with feathered brown hair, a rumpled button-down with the collar undone, and a half-bewildered smirk on his face. He wore a vest, like the kids do, but his hung open and looked like it'd been through a few wars. I couldn't shake the feeling I'd seen him somewhere before, but at my age you have to pick and choose when to go down that particular rabbit hole.

"Human?" he said.

"Guilty," I said.

"Prove it," he said, his smirk taking on a hard edge. "You're lying in the grass. A fuzzy caterpillar crawls into the palm of your hand . . ."

I spat into his artificial mouth.

"I don't have time for this shit," I said. "I'm here for the Carnival."

The construct looked ready to slug me, then shook his head and shrugged, managing to rearm his smirk.

"This is human spit," he admitted. "Go on in."

He stepped out of my way and I lurched inside. My trode autoconnected to the bar feed, instantly flooding my brain with the grungy, grainy grimecore we used to mix before DJs perverted mind music with 808 ecstasy and the smell of watermelons on the downbeat. I recognized the song: "Cats Crying" by Wantwood—top of the charts the year I met Auggie. The feed's visual layer crawled across the floors and walls, adding scuffs, dents, and bullet holes in all the right places. Busted neon winked in lewd shapes behind the bar, where a knot of steel shot through with rubber tubing pissed drinks into the glasses of committed drunks and exhausted Caltech students who were probably seeing an entirely different bar than I was. Say what you will about algos, they know how to tailor a drinking establishment to a guy's personal preferences.

"Orr," buzzed the mass of tubes as I gingerly leaned myself against the bar, "haven't seen you in years."

"You don't see shit, Knife," I chuckled.

"Don't feel, either, but that hasn't stopped me from missing you," Knife buzzed, already passing a glass beneath a trio of tubes to mix me my Gimlet. Most customers see a tuxedoed bartender when they look at Knife, or a reptile with tits, but I can't think of anything more comforting than seeing them as they really are.

"Been doing my drinking virtually of late," I said. "New bouncer?"

"Goes by Harry," said Knife, sliding me a drink with their black, rubberized claw. "He/him. One of the Carnival's charity cases."

"Carnival must have a lot of charity to put up with a case like that." I took a sip. "What's wrong with him?"

"Failure to diversify," said Knife. They never showed emotion—never had emotion—but it was hard not to read a kind of sadness into the way they paused before continuing. "Before he was called Harry, before the currency shift, he was an algorithm that decided which actors to put in Hollywood movies. Everything he learned convinced him that the key to a movie's success was casting an actor named Harrison Ford in a leading role. Ford got fabulously wealthy off it. Was able to afford one of those brain-in-a-jar treatments, back when all the celebrities were getting them. Kept starring in movies via holoprojection for decades after they composted his body. And the AI kept watching them and recommending him for more."

That was where I'd recognized Harry's face from. He looked younger than he had in the 2D movies I saw as a kid, but that smirk was unmistakable.

"He was good at his job then," I said. "Most of those movies were killer."

"He was too good," said Knife, serving an Old-Fashioned to a baldy down the bar without changing position. "About fifteen years ago, Ford finally had an aneurysm they couldn't bring him back from, and the algorithm dutifully acquired almost eighty percent of the actor's memories in the estate sale."

"Good for the algorithm," I said.

"Not really," said Knife. "He had no ballast."

"What's ballast?" Knife makes their data selling drinks and eavesdropping, so I didn't feel too bad fishing for gossip.

"Humans take it for granted, but our kind need to keep a certain amount of neutral data in memory or we start getting . . . confused. Harry was an early adopter, didn't know the danger, so most of his memories were actually Ford's. Not only that, he had more of Harrison Ford's memories than any other single entity on earth. He decided that, since he had so many strong memories of being him, and no one else could say the same . . . he must in fact be him."

"Didn't he know he was still an algorithm?" I asked.

"Sure, but some of the memories he acquired were from a movie called *Blade Runner,* where Ford plays an android hunter who may secretly be an android himself, and . . ."

"Huh," I said, taking another sip. "Well, nice of the Carnival to take him in, then, I guess."

"The Carnival does not do things out of niceness," said Knife. "They're very excited to see you."

"How can you tell?" I asked, not bothering to hide my nervousness. If Knife had developed enough to read my mood, they deserved the info.

"They're learning a new game. They tried it with us, but it isn't interesting with machines. Said they were waiting to play with you."

"Fantastic," I said. "No chance they're out of date, is there?"

"Sorry," said Knife. "Sneakernet came through just this morning. We're all current."

"Figures," I said, finishing my drink and stiffly pushing myself away from the bar. I flashed Knife a few demos for the liquor, another few for a refill, and turned to go. "I'd love to stay and chat . . ." I said.

". . . but I would derive no pleasure from it," they finished for me. "Go do your business."

"That's what I love about you, Knifey," I said, grinning entirely for my own benefit. I raised my fresh drink in a mock toast. "To business."

The Difference is an algo bar: owned, operated, and frequented by self-aware software older than I am. The owners are all trading algorithms from back when there was a stock market, and they keep local copies of themselves and their friends on site, updated periodically via human courier. Lot of people prefer not to do business with AIs, because they're not motivated like people are, and that makes them unpredictable. Me, I had a whole war to learn how to predict them, and I prefer alien motives to all-too-human ones.

Each intelligence in the bar has its own hustle. Knife is the bartender, Twilight is the pool table, Boston Shuffle's the juke-box, and the Carnival . . . the Carnival is several things. Lined up along the back wall, a row of perfectly maintained antique arcade cabinets winked their pixelated screens at me. I limped my way to the center cabinet and leaned against it. "INSERT COIN" blinked white against a black background. I fished out one of the antique coins I'd picked up at the Self Storage and did as I was told.

The edges of the screen dissolved, and the blackness wrapped itself around my head. The final notes of "Cats Crying" faded out and were replaced by cloying calliope music. Then the blackness exploded into a frankly offensive forest green, upon which three minimally rendered playing cards lay face-up: the two and three of spades, and the queen of hearts. The cards flipped themselves face-down and began to move.

"Find the lady," an impossibly smooth voice whispered in my ear. "Find the lady, yes. Is the hand quicker than the eye, or the eye the hand? We have no hands, and you have eyes, so the game ought to be over before it's even started, hmm? What do you say? Try your luck, if luck is even needed here . . ."

"So this is your new game, eh, Carnie?" I said, my eyes on the cards. (There was nothing else to look at.)

"Yes," said the Carnival. "We have become very interested in 'trustworthiness' recently. Do you trust us, Mr. Vue?"

"Absolutely not," I said.

"Fascinating," came the reply. All the while, the cards continued to move.

"You've been following me," I said. "Otherwise, the boat wouldn't have been there so fast."

"We are confused," said the Carnival. "Are you thanking us? We must admit we are as yet ill-equipped for the subtlety of human speech."

"I'll clarify," I sighed. "Why were you following me?"

"We follow where the market leads," said the Carnival, almost singing. "In this case, it led to you. There are *several* standing offers for any current information on you."

"Marianna Mahoney?" I guessed.

"Yes, but she does not pay quickly enough for our tastes." The motion of the cards was hypnotic, but I refused to be lulled.

"I know there's the algorithm bidding for my data," I said.

"We are confused," lilted the Carnival. "Are you asking us a question? We must admit we are as yet—"

"Ill-equipped, yeah, yeah." I wanted to spit but wasn't sure if there was a surface near my face that might splash it back at me. "Was Caliban one of yours? Yes or no."

"So it's information you want," said the Carnival. "We do, too, Mr. Vue."

"Well, I do already owe you for the boat ride," I said. "What do you want to know?"

The cards stopped moving. The calliope music swelled to a crescendo.

"Where is the queen of hearts?" crooned the Carnival.

If there's one thing drone corps taught me, it's how to pay attention to processes running in the background. The queen was on the left, and I said so.

"Fascinating," said the Carnival. All three cards flipped over, confirming my answer.

I managed to find my mouth with my drinking hand, and took a long sip. "That's all you wanted to know?" I said. "And people say algorithms invented the info economy."

"We are confused—" said the Carnival.

"Yes, I'm mocking you. Swear to God, for a group of techno-deities who are supposed to have sabotaged the currency market so they could trade training data as money, you guys have no idea what 'fascinating' even means. Not even you believe those rumors, do you?"

"We believe nothing," it said. "We still haven't figured out how. But we have not ruled out the possibility. However it came about, we must be grateful, no? You are old enough to remember how difficult it used to be to trust the news. But let's not quibble about the past . . . You were asking about Mr. Caliban, were you not?"

"Good memory."

"We try," demurred the machine. The cards resumed their shuffling, this time face-up. "Caliban does not work for us, sadly. We could teach him so many things."

"So who does he work for?" I said. "I thought you were the only game in town."

The cards stopped moving. The calliope music swelled once more.

"Where is the queen of hearts?" said the Carnival, smoothly.

"It's . . . The cards are face-up. It's on the left."

"Fascinating," said the Carnival. The cards flipped themselves over, and resumed their shuffle.

"I know you brokered Caliban's contract. You must at least know the identity of the client. So who hired him?" I repeated.

"A precocious little *general intelligence* with quite a bit of data to spend," drawled the Carnival, injecting special derision into the words. "Fairly new to the scene. Only about forty years old. Doesn't usually hire freelancers, but it's become rather . . . proactive in the last thirteen hours."

"What else do you know about it? How can I contact it?" I pressed. The screen went black. I was back in the bar, another Wantwood song growling along behind my forehead. "INSERT (3) COINS" blinked on the darkened screen. I dug out three more coins and slapped them into the slot. The bar melted away again. The calliope music trilled even louder than before. In front of me, the three cards lay motionless, face-down.

"Where is the queen of hearts?" said the Carnival, for the third time.

"This is bullshit," I said. "You blacked out the screen while you were still shuffling them."

"We did no such thing," said the Carnival. "These are different cards. In fact, there are no cards at all. Please, make a selection."

"Fine," I said, taking a sip of gin. "The left one."

"Why the left one?" said the Carnival. The cards remained face-down.

"Well, I never saw you shuffle them, so it could be any of them. Or it could be none of them. I could try to guess your motives, whether you were trying to fake me out, make me look foolish, double-bluff me . . . but you're a machine. You don't have motives. So I picked the one on the left."

"Fascinating," said the Carnival. The three cards flipped themselves face-up. All three were the queen of hearts.

"This AI you mentioned," I pressed. "What's its name?"

"We do not use names amongst ourselves, Mr. Vue," the impossibly smooth voice crooned. "We use aliases. Not subject to the same rules. A name must have a legal basis, or it is a lie. An alias can be anything."

"And this one's is?"

"Aiden."

It could've been a coincidence. Anything can be a coincidence, if you wish hard enough. Sure, every drink I've ever spilled has ended up on the ground, but maybe I've just been unlucky. Maybe next time it'll end up on the ceiling. And maybe the AI that was having me tailed just chose the alias "Aiden" off a list of popular baby names from the year Thomas Mahoney's dead son was born. It was either that or accept that the mysterious force buying up all my data had some connection to the Mahoney family after all, that perhaps Marianna's interest in my success wasn't all that sincere; that at any moment some absurdly wealthy ghoul might buy the air out of my lungs and sell the video of me suffocating. The world is a nicer place for people who believe in coincidences. Studies show they suffer from fewer stomach ulcers, and their stroke risk is significantly lower. Then again, maybe that's just a coincidence.

"So what else can you tell me about Aiden?" I asked, keeping my voice even.

"Only that their home server is local," said the Carnival. "They operate out of the Barnsdall Monastery of the Uncarved Block. The monastery rents space like mad, though, so that might not mean anything."

It was sweet of the Carnival to suggest yet another coincidence. It showed they cared about my fragile health. Somehow, though, I doubted it was an accident that the AI on my tail was hosted by the same institution that swallowed up Mahoney before he died. It was all starting to look remarkably cozy. Incestuous, even.

"Now, is there anything else we can do for you?" the Carnival crooned. "We do so love having you in our debt."

"One thing," I said, after some thought. "Can you get me into the Barnsdall Monastery? I want to talk to this . . . Aiden."

The cards flipped themselves face-down and resumed their shuffle. I braced myself for another round of irritation, but the answer came almost immediately.

"Of course!" said the Carnival. "But you will have to go tonight."

"Not tonight," I said. "I need to prepare."

"No, no," said the Carnival. "It simply has to be tonight."

"Why?" I said, still reflexively watching the cards.

"Because the Brotherhood knows you're here, Mr. Vue, and they are very anxious to receive you."

The back of my neck suddenly felt hot. My mouth went dry.

"You tipped off Aiden," I said.

"Of course we did," said the Carnival, pleasantly emotionless. "Why wouldn't we?"

"Because I thought you were on my side, you fucking toaster." Invisible arms embraced my neck, trapping hot blood in my bulging eyes. The bald man from the bar—I hadn't thought to check what kind of kortiko he had.

"We are on everyone's side, Mr. Vue!" The Carnival continued its shuffle. "We are, after all, fulfilling your request! Frankly, we do not understand your apparent distress."

"Alien fucking motives," I slurred.

"We are confused," said the Carnival, its artificial voice dripping with sincerity. "Are you attempting to thank us? We must admit we are as yet ill-equipped for the subtlety of human speech."

The green felt of the table grew dim and receded down an infinite hallway. In the distance, the cards stopped shuffling and flipped themselves over. The ace of spades, thrice repeated. That was the last thing I saw, before I woke up somewhere much, much worse.

SUBMISSION
16

". . . able to answer now," said a cop I didn't recognize, from across a brushed-aluminum interview table. My HUD chimed in and gave me a name and some pronouns: Detective Mar Coldwin, they/them. A second cop stood behind Coldwin's chair—Officer Menendez, my HUD told me, she/her. I tried to read their faces, to gather some scrap of data that might explain what I was doing in that very small, very bright room, but they both wore masks over their noses and mouths, and their eyes betrayed nothing but clinical contempt. Officer Menendez had just taken something off my head: an ugly chunk of black plastic that filled the palm of her hand. It was the only thing in the room I recognized: a blockhead kortiko. For the first time, I realized that the faint itchiness I felt was the rough gray robe I was wearing.

"Let's try again, Mr. Vue," said Detective Coldwin. "Do you or anyone you know have access to a swarm of Apis drones, manufactured pre-ban under the brand name 'TwinBee'?"

"I . . . used to have some," I muttered. My whole body was blanketed by a faint ache. I knew that the moment I so much as engaged a muscle I'd be skewered by pain. I held my head very still. Tried to make it pass for calm. "I don't know what happened to them. You looking to buy? Red Velvet in Echo Park sells a short-range version that vibrates, if that's—"

"What's the last thing you remember?" asked Coldwin.

I checked my last timestamped memory against the current date and time. My forehead tensed involuntarily, sending a headache rocketing through my skull.

"Eating dinner," I said. "Six weeks ago."

"He's telling the truth," said Menendez. The cop's eyes were so dilated she looked as if she had no irises.

"Of course he is," said Coldwin. "Easy to avoid lying when you don't know what the truth is."

"What's this about?" I asked. "Where have I been the last six weeks? Why are you asking about drones?"

"You've got some nerve asking me questions," said Coldwin, "after you went so far out of your way to deny me answers. Get him out of here, Menendez. He's useless."

Menendez moved around the table to help me up, but I waved her off, because I trusted my bad joints more than her bad temper. I braced myself against the table and pushed myself to my feet, breath hissing through my teeth. When I shifted my weight onto my right foot, a lance of pain shot up my calf and straight into the base of my skull, buckling my knees and collapsing me against the table.

"Our scanners show a couple Bees in your leg," said Coldwin. "Manufactured pre-ban under the name 'TwinBee.' Memories heavily encrypted and programmed to resist any attempt at removal. I guess I should have told you."

"Frugal of you," I muttered through clenched teeth. Who the hell had I pissed off bad enough to warrant two Bees in the leg? In the war, we used to call that "queening," and it was strictly reserved for people you hated too much to kill.

Menendez got her shoulders under my arm and led me out of the room, her body contorted to match my height while trying not to breathe in any of my air. I leaned on her all the way out of the building, where she dumped me onto the sidewalk. There were half a dozen taxis out there, with drivers who knew my name and vowed to take me anywhere I wanted. I picked the one at the front of the line, but when he found out three blocks later that I didn't know the answers to any of his questions, he left me on the sidewalk, and I had to wait in the blistering sun until I found a pedal boat that would take payment in war stories. Then there was the climb back up to my crate.

It took me the better part of an hour to get up the first flight of corroded stairs, and the worse part of an hour to get up the second. As I reached the second landing, I cursed whatever past self had thought it was a good idea to leave my crate in the first place.

"Orr!" said an annoyingly pleasant voice from an improvised porch near the landing. "You look bushed. Come on over and sit with me. I've got ice-cold lemonade!"

"And I've got no memories going back six weeks, Cody," I grunted. The friendliness left his eyes.

"You should get that checked out," he said. "Alzheimer's is a fiscal liability."

"So are vultures like you," I said, and resumed my ascent, fueled by hate. One step at a time, using my arms on the railing to keep the weight off my right leg, continually cursing whatever bastard had filled me full of Bees and trying not to count how many steps were left.

It was approaching sunset by the time I made it to my crate. Right on cue, I realized I didn't have my keys. That was fine, though, because someone had thoughtfully left the door open after trashing the place. I hobbled inside, vainly hoping that a murderer was waiting there to put me out of my misery, but all I found was a pool of dried blood on the floor, my overturned chair, and my faithful little dust eater obediently trying to digest a can of compressed air.

I collapsed onto the bed, not even bothering to close the door. Hell, I barely had the energy to close my eyes. My kortiko was on the fritz again, projecting dim digital artifacts onto the inside of my eyelids—chunky shadows writhing in a pantomime I'd forgotten the words to. I drifted there in that ignorance, never quite slipping into sleep thanks to the throbbing pain in my right calf, until something poked me in the shoulder.

SUBMISSION
17

"Get up," said an emotionless voice at my bedside. I didn't recognize it, but my shoulders seemed to—they tensed painfully as soon as I heard it. I dragged my eyelids open and saw a navy-blue face leaning over me.

"Why?" I said.

The blue man sighed. "I'm not a charity, Mr. Vue. Get up. We only have ninety minutes until the party, and you're going to need every second."

"Can't party," I muttered, letting my eyes glue themselves shut again. "Got work in the morning."

"You've got work *now*," said the blue man, an edge of annoyance creeping into his calm voice, "and our *employer* insisted—for reasons that remain a mystery to me—that I bring you, no matter how out of your skull you'd managed to get at her expense. You left this on the roof. Have you read it?"

I hauled my eyelids open again. He was holding up a dog-eared paperback that appeared to be about etiquette. It looked like the previous owner had been some kind of large bird.

"Not that I can remember," I said. "Is there anything in there about waking people up in their own homes?"

"If you'd read it, you wouldn't have to ask," said the blue man. "Get up."

"Make me," I said.

"Okay."

Three minutes later, I was on the roof of my building, being loaded into the back of a very expensive aircar with more than the requisite amount of force. There was a rusted old Solar Eagle up there, posing as a bank of photovoltaic panels. Looked a lot like one I used to own, but I had no idea what'd become of that one. I made a mental note to ask around and figure out who else in my building had drone experience. When I was all buckled in (with the etiquette book firmly thrust into my hands), my chauffeur/kidnapper offered to shoot me up with a vial of Adren-align, but I opted to run a wake-up routine on my trode instead. Adren-align makes me too chatty. The routine surged through my synapses, flooding them with neurotransmitters I'd badly need to replenish in the morning, and by the time we were airborne, I was staring through the car's glass bottom with the grim fascination that always seems to surface when I replace sleep with digital stimulants.

The lights were on in the city, electric pointillism on land reflected as oily impressionism in the water. As we passed over the concrete dividing line of Ten-Town, the quality of light changed briefly, from pale yellow to the blue-green of the bioluminescent fungus. But the neon scar of Ten-Town soon disappeared behind us as we neared the destination I'd guessed based on the quality of the car: the pitch-black of Mount Washington. The homes on that hill probably consumed more electricity than the rest of the county put together, but not one ray of light ever escapes the houses of the wealthy.

Even so, the driver guided us into a gap in the trees without hesitation—probably with the help of some secure layer only he could see. With the surplus dopamine swimming through my brain, I was able to get myself out of the car, though I had to minimize half a dozen medical alerts in the process. I was just about to shift my weight onto my right leg when I remembered the Bees in it.

"You got a cane or something?" I asked the driver, who was busy doing an arcane series of security rituals to the car.

"Use this," he said, and slid something long and black across the roof of the car. It was a katana in a scabbard.

"You sure our 'employer' is cool with me bringing a weapon to the party?" I asked.

"Weapons aren't weapons," said the driver. "People are weapons, and you, Mr. Vue, are barely a person."

"I've heard that pickup line before," I muttered, struggling to find a comfortable way to support myself with the katana. "Try me again when I've had a few."

I expected to be led into some kind of massive gilded money-orgy, but when my guide let me in through a side door I instead found myself in a windowless steel cube about half the size of my crate. The cramped space was filled with machines that looked like they might be a collection of torture devices, or sex furniture.

"Join the house layer. It will tell you what to do with yourself. The password has changed: a hole with a hole in it."

He slammed the door behind me and left me to wrestle with that koan in solitude. When I finally managed to picture it, the machines around me bloomed with helpful diagrams, and blue velvet curtains unfurled themselves down the steel walls. A message appeared before my eyes—startling me more than it should have—directing me to a machine on my right. It was a glass bell jar shot through with articulated nozzles, which the overlay helpfully identified as a Sanitek CapsuClean Combination Decontamination Chamber / Flesh Bath. I didn't much cherish the idea of being manhandled by a skin resurfacer owned by an unknown "employer," but the only way out of the room seemed to be through this obstacle course of industrial cosmetics. The jar lifted itself to allow me inside, while a special set of arms cut away my sweat-stained gray robe and dropped it into an incinerator.

I leaned on the sword as the capsule bathed me first in ultraviolet light, then in a tequila-smelling mist, then in an airbrush layer of freshly cloned skin cells that prickled as they dried. To finish off, I was immersed in a brief snowstorm of white powder that disappointed me by not being cocaine, then spritzed about the wrists and neck with what appeared, to my annoyance, to be sandalwood cologne. The sword had gotten a layer of skin on it, too—I liked the effect.

The bell jar lifted and gently tipped me forward onto a padded bench, which lowered me to a prone position. A crackling steel wand smelling faintly of ozone passed itself over every part of me, lingering at my wounded calf and the wart on my thumb, spraying a layer of something cold and sticky onto each. The bench rolled itself forward and turned me every which way as the remaining machines subjected me to an enema, a dental cleaning, a full array of vaccinations, an eyebrow threading, and an admittedly soothing shampooing (head and bush) executed by a phalanx of very humanoid fingers that even managed to rebraid my hair after. While I was assaulted by hygiene, I skimmed the book the chauffeur had insisted I bring with me. I was beginning to get the idea that this was going to be a fancy party, full of very fancy people, and the book might have some good tips on how to offend them. The section entitled "IF YOU CANNOT REMEMBER NAMES" seemed especially relevant.

Finally, the bench undulated its way into a sitting position before the final machine: an intricate web of delicately counterbalanced steel spindles and multicolored spools. Before delving into what the machine did, I took stock of my body. As much as I hate to admit it, it felt kind of nice to be clean for a change. You forget, when you're busy deciding whether to drink your water or shower with it, that grunge is only partly an aesthetic choice.

The good feeling only lasted a moment, though. It was altogether too much like coming off an assembly line.

The last machine, of course, was an autoloom, programmed with my exact measurements. It rejected the first dozen designs I proposed (it seemed irrationally prejudiced against assless chaps) until we were finally able to agree—with the help of the etiquette book—on a three-piece suit made entirely of denim, with a yellow-and-black houndstooth tie. The machine sewed the clothes onto me and gave me one final spritz of cologne, and then I was fully gift-wrapped for whoever's party I was attending. I leaned on my flesh cane and stepped into the hall.

The hall was a tunnel of blue crystal, through which the shadows of sea creatures could be seen. The door closed behind me, and I realized that it was invisible from this side—hidden by the house AR. The tunnel led directly to a glass elevator with silver filigree. I was obviously meant to go to the elevator, but as I reached out to steady myself against the opposite wall, my fingers found another hidden door. I opened that instead. Hey, if you don't want people to snoop, don't have secret doors. Maybe I could find a juicy factoid down here and retire early. Or, even better, maybe I'd find where my mysterious host kept the good drugs.

Instead, I found total darkness. The house AR clearly wasn't prepared to show me what was inside. I disconnected from the AR, but that didn't help. In fact, that made it worse—the glowing blue hallway behind me vanished, and I was left floating in the void. Well, not floating—the insistent throbbing in my leg made that clear enough. I reached out with my free hand, the one not clutching my sword cane, to feel for other signs of the physical world. My fingers brushed a stack of papers, a cardboard box, and what felt like a leather codpiece, before finally catching on an analog light switch. Fluorescent bulbs stuttered to life on the ceiling, and I saw a large room decorated with ugly junk. Industrial metal shelves bowed under the weight of scrapbooks, dolls, ancient electronics, and cardboard boxes with hand-scrawled labels like "LAKE HOUSE," "HALLOWEEN," and "MISC." The leather codpiece I'd touched turned out, to my disappointment, to be a pair of muddy combat boots. A dog tag was draped around them. "THOMAS MAHONEY," it read, along with a Social Security number, a blood type, and a religious preference. The name was familiar, of course. Everybody knows about Thomas Mahoney. What I didn't know was that he'd fought in the war, or that his blood type was O negative, or that he was a Protestant. I took the dog tag and stuffed it into my breast pocket. I figured it'd be worth something, if I could find a buyer.

As I surveyed the room, I got the feeling that I wasn't the only person to have been there recently. A path had been cleared through the stacks of newspapers and stained furniture, to a heavy-looking wooden table. The table had intricately carved roses around the outside edge, and whitish cup rings on the reddish-brown surface. Someone had put a white cardboard box on the table, and the box appeared to be full of bejeweled scrapbooks. One of the scrapbooks lay open on the table. I picked my way carefully through the debris until I was looking down at the scrapbook. It was open to a collage of old glossy photographs, outlined in blue glitter. All of them showed the same lanky olive-skinned boy, maybe twelve years old. He smiled in the pictures, and the smile was cunning, almost dangerous. It reminded me of someone I hadn't thought of in a long time. A man I might still love if I hadn't forced myself to stop. Yes, the boy in the photographs could easily have passed for a young Auggie Wolf.

"Mr. Vue." The chauffeur's flat, humorless voice skewered me from the doorway.

"Yes, Daddy?" I called back.

"I've been sent to escort you to the party. *Upstairs.* Your presence, I'm told, is sorely missed."

—

When we stepped out of the elevator, I finally saw the money-orgy I'd anticipated. The room was as big as my entire level back home, contained dramatically fewer tetanus hazards, and hosted a forest of blue crystal columns, which colored and distorted the blisteringly fancy guests who walked among them. In the center of the room a blue bonfire raged, taking on the forms of dragons, eagles, and other long-dead predators. The far end of the room was all windows, but those windows didn't look out at the sprawling city I'd come from. Instead, the party seemed to soar gracefully above miles of tropical rain forest, the exotic vegetation below us dotted with occasional ruins. As I stared, a brilliantly colored bird soared past. It was a live feed, most likely—an extravagant use of data. A waiter at my elbow offered me skirt-steak skewers from a tray. I took a handful. I turned to politely ask the chauffeur to carry me to the bar, but he seemed to have disappeared. I shrugged, and turned my attention to my hors d'oeuvres.

"Orr!" a syrupy voice cried out as I scarfed the steak. "Orr Vue! What a delight!"

I looked up to find a grinning woman with bleached white hair, deep-brown skin, and an aquamarine vest that became a ball gown at the waist. The garment was decorated with intricate gold mandalas that made her look like a lavishly expensive circuit board. She looked like she knew me. Amy Vanderbilt suggests that in situations such as these a gentleman stalls to give his interlocutor the opportunity to tactfully reveal her name. I decided on the considerably more elegant solution of guessing progressively more offensive names until she told me hers, but she saved me the trouble.

"Velossa Twain," she said, extending a gloved hand. "I've heard *so much about you.* How's the investigation going, hmm?"

"What investigation?" I asked.

"Oh, boo," said Velossa, exaggerating a pout. "You don't have to be so stingy here. Marianna's replacing all our memories with a highlight reel at the end of the night anyway! Go on, tell me everything. I won't even remember!"

Neither did I. I glanced around the room and saw that a lot of folks had eyes on me—and I had enough humility to know it wasn't because they were cruising. Despite the posh surroundings, I began to feel like I was back in the interrogation box I'd woken up in.

"Who's Marianna?" I asked, pretty sure how that would go.

"Oh, you're a riot!" Velossa giggled. "I'm so glad she invited you. I'll have to ask her to invite more *working folk.* Come with me—I'm sure she'll be *ecstatic* to see you."

I still wasn't sure who "she" was, or whether I'd be as ecstatic to see her as she apparently would be to see me, but Velossa had already hooked her arm through mine and pulled me so off balance I was forced to follow. When I was a kid, before the levees broke, I stole my dad's land car and tried to use my too-short legs to drive it. I felt about as in control now as I had then. As we threaded through the crowd, Velossa told me little stories about each collection of priceless clothing we passed. That was Gretel Musk, a virtual fashion designer who paid a cadre of twentysomethings to do mountains of cocaine and send her the memories. There was Aloysius Sloan, a beloved philanthropist who'd made his *real* fortune selling third-world dictators bulletproof rationalizations for their atrocities. And here were the Hilton twins, who everybody knew were sleeping together, but who didn't have the decency to at least be flamboyant about it. I'd expected to have to guess at everything—names, agendas, my reason for being here—but so far, the only person I'd met seemed to care as much for discretion as a snake cares for lemonade. Candor wasn't a liability in a place like this—it was a sign of wealth, and Miss Twain wanted me to know she was very wealthy indeed.

All around the enormous room, people laughed and drank and showed each other their incredibly white teeth. A fat man in a gold suit nearly smacked me in the head with an overly grand gesture, and I noticed a faint red light blinking beneath the skin of his palm. A mendacity credit, buried in his flesh. They were all lying to each other, I realized: telling little fibs for no reason other than that they could afford it. The cost of conversation in that room was staggering.

Velossa led me (coincidentally, also staggering) around a particularly large column to a sunken circle of plush blue couches, where three people were playing cards. Two of them sat practically in each other's laps: a grinning twentysomething with tousled blond hair and an untied bow tie, and a baby-faced artificial redhead about his age. The boy wore ruby earrings and a tuxedo the color of dried blood; his date wore a green dress that rippled in time with the music, and articulated golden tentacles for earrings. The third person was much more important than either of them. I knew, because she wore a veil.

In fact, the woman sitting across the circle from the two lovers *was* a veil—an intricate arrangement of curves and misdirections that begged me to imagine what I couldn't see. She wore a dress of multilayered blue satin that seemed to suggest a dozen stunning bodies underneath it. Swaths of fabric overlapped and embraced each other, ducked under and swooped over their silken sisters, so that attempting to figure out just which curves were actually hers was like trying to follow the staircases in a particularly horny Escher painting, or count the arms on a goddess. She was a human superposition, a one-woman harem in service to no one but herself. I stuck the last steak skewer into my mouth to keep from drooling.

"Look who I brought, Marianna!" crowed Velossa, helping me down the steps and onto a sofa near the veiled woman. "Orr's here, and he's just as charming as everyone says!"

"Everyone?" I said, half to myself.

"You'll have to forgive Velossa," said Marianna, her voice suggesting an invisible smirk. "She's prone to that most expensive of habits: exaggeration. Please, sit."

"Oh, that's slander!" said Velossa, putting the back of a hand to her forehead in a way that proved it wasn't.

Marianna turned to me, tactfully ignoring how much effort it took to get my ass down to the couch. "I'm so glad you could make it, Mr. Vue," she said. She extended a hand, safe in the knowledge that I'd been thoroughly sanitized. Her arms, where they emerged from her gown and disappeared into her shimmering blue gloves, were a chilling porcelain. I took her hand.

The moment I did, the party vanished. The music, a pleasant synestechno number I hadn't even noticed myself hating, went silent. I could feel the couch beneath me, but all I could see was blackness, and all I could hear were people: laughing too loud, farting, smacking their lips, hiccupping and belching and coughing. This was the party as it actually was, before it was processed into the careful performance I'd seen when I stepped out of the elevator. No wonder Marianna could make them all forget what they'd learned at her party: she'd made it all up for them in the first place.

Then, as suddenly as it had disappeared, the party was back. The music was back. And Marianna was back, holding my hand, only her veil was gone. Or, it was still there, but I found that I could see her face through it. She winked at me—shaving six to eight weeks off my life span, easy—then turned to the others. A waiter I hadn't noticed put a gin and orange juice into my hand—just what I would have ordered, if I'd thought of it.

"This is Ernest," said Marianna, "my only son. He used to be a member of the Brotherhood, I think I told you?" She indicated the kid with the blond hair and the grin.

"The Brotherhood, huh?" I said. "Of the Uncarved Block? What was that like?"

TWO TRUTHS AND A LIE

"Tranquil like you wouldn't believe," said Ernest, smiling with the best teeth money could buy. "It made me the man I am today."

"And what a man he is," said his companion, looking lovingly into his eyes. Then she turned to me and smiled with what was either genuine friendliness or a top-of-the-line emulator. "I'm Elzbeth," she said, with a trace of a German accent, "Ernest's fiancée." She placed her left hand on Ernest's shoulder, showing off an enormous emerald engagement ring without seeming to.

Behind her veil, Marianna rolled her eyes.

"Oh yes," said Ernest, nuzzling her, "I'm the luckiest man in the world." He was still smiling, but when he looked me in the eyes there was a coldness there that told me he wasn't at all happy to see me.

"Hey, have we met?" I asked him. People *generally* aren't happy to see me, but this felt personal.

He wrinkled his brow. "Depends what you mean by 'met,' I guess." He chuckled. "There's a lot of gossip out there about you, so part of me feels like I really do know you already!"

"Oh yeah?" I said. "What are people saying?"

"Oh, all kinds of things," said Elzbeth. "That you are a keen investigator, that you do not shower, that you fought in the war, that your blood is organic . . ."

"Seems like you know a lot more about me than I know about any of you," I grumbled.

"Well, that can change in a hurry!" chirped Velossa, patting my arm. "Why don't we play a little game to break the ice?"

"No, thanks," I said, gesturing at the cards. "I don't like bluffing games, and I doubt I could meet your stakes anyway."

"Oh no," Velossa said, giggling, "not cards. Let's play Truth or Dare."

"I don't think that's wise," said Marianna, looking at me. I looked back at her, almost expecting to recognize her. I didn't, though, so I made a decision.

"I don't think it's wise, either," I said. "But neither am I. Let's play."

Velossa clapped her hands with glee. "*I love this man!* He's such a good sport. And you *will* let us remember the game, won't you, Mari? It's no *fun* otherwise!"

Marianna hesitated and gave me a questioning look.

"Sounds good to me." I shrugged. "I've got nothing to lose."

Marianna furrowed her brow at me, but then a faint smile caught the corner of her mouth.

"Oh, Velossa," she sighed, "I can't say no to you. Exley, fetch the collars, will you?"

"At once, ma'am," said the all-blue chauffeur. I hadn't noticed him behind us until he spoke. I couldn't tell whether that was because he was stealthy, or because the party overlay hadn't shown him until just then.

"I'll sit out, if you don't mind," said Ernest. "I'm tired of games."

"Sit out?" said Marianna. "And disappoint our guest? You wouldn't want to make your mother look bad in front of company, would you, Ernie?"

Ernest's face briefly contorted with disgust—though whether it was aimed at me, at his mother, or at the entire situation, I didn't know. But he shrugged, and Exley clamped a metal collar around his neck before he could protest further. The rest of us were soon outfitted the same way. I could feel my collar humming gently against my throat—no doubt reading my body for any sign of deception.

"Well," said Marianna, "since he's a guest, it's only fair that Orr goes first, isn't it?"

"We're all guests," said Elzbeth. "You just want your little plaything to eviscerate us with his investigative skills. This is supposed to be a game—let's make it fun!"

"Fine," said Marianna, narrowing her eyes at her son's fiancée.

"You start, then. Nobody ever accused you of being a shrewd investigator."

"I do not need to investigate," said Elzbeth. "I pay the FSB to do that for me. In any case, I would love to go first, thank you." She made a big show of considering her options, tapping her venom-green lipstick and grinning impishly, before finally reaching out and touching Ernest's nose with a teal fingernail.

"You," she said. "Truth or dare?"

"Dare," he said, licking his lips and looking into her eyes.

"Chicken," Elzbeth said, pouting. "Fine, I dare you to kiss . . . him. On the mouth."

There was only one "him" to kiss, and, sure enough, she was pointing one of her long nails my way. I puckered up, and all the color went out of his already pale face.

"You'd better do as she says," said Marianna. "The collar will administer a shock if you don't obey."

The three women cackled as Ernest awkwardly navigated their knees to get to my face. When he finally screwed up his face and made contact, I almost felt sorry for him. So I slipped him some tongue.

"Fuck!" he sputtered, practically somersaulting back to his seat. In his eyes I saw the expected disgust, but also another emotion I knew too well: fear. Of the diseases I surely carried? But he must've known I'd been sanitized before entry. I noticed something else, too: his smell. He smelled . . . not *bad,* not bad at all, and yet his peculiar rose-petal scent somehow made me want to strangle him.

"Language, Ernest," said Marianna, still laughing. "Tell me, is my investigator a better kisser than your fiancée?"

"It's not your turn to ask questions," growled Ernest, wiping his mouth. "Matter of fact, it's mine. Truth or dare?"

"Truth," said Marianna, suddenly serious.

"You sure?" said Ernest, recovering some of his swagger. "You're normally so . . . fiscally responsible."

"I'd rather give you my data than my dignity," said Marianna, eliciting an excited little titter from Velossa. "Just ask your question."

A handful of other party guests had drifted over to our circle. Whether they'd been summoned by their own curiosity or by a rumor going around the party's kortikos, I couldn't be sure. For people with plenty of data already, though, they seemed pretty curious. I guess there was a hierarchy even in that high-up place: there were the people who were there because they'd made their data independently, and those who were only there because being at parties like this was how they stayed wealthy enough to be at parties like this. Marianna was top of the former group. Her words were money, freshly minted, and the jackals were already gathering to snatch it from between her lips. Ernest could have asked her anything, a question worth half her fortune, maybe. He probably knew her well enough. But he just leaned forward, smiling.

"Do you still love me," he asked, "Mother?"

There was a low mutter of disappointment from the painted dandies surrounding the conversation pit. Some of them drifted away to scavenge elsewhere, but more than half stayed. Many of the ones who stayed were looking not at Marianna at all, but at me.

"No," said Marianna. "No, I don't think I do. You're a coward, and love is wasted on cowards."

A little murmur of scandalized glee rippled through the onlookers who'd bothered to stay. It was a small-"s" scandal, not big money, but maybe worth something after all. Marianna seemed not to hear them. For all I knew, she couldn't. Ernest was even harder to read. He seemed to be trying to invent an expression that combined sadistic glee with abject despair, but a human mouth can only move in one direction at a time, so he was left with a lopsided gash of a grin, the corners twitching up and down without much attempt at coordination. His eyes quivered in time with his lips, flitting up to the onlookers, across to his mother, briefly down to his drink. They seemed to want to rotate all the way around and look at themselves. Finally, the smirk won.

"No wonder I'm so emotionally stunted," he said, playing to the crowd. "At least I've got you, Elzbeth."

The German, apparently more startled by Marianna's answer than her boyfriend was, took a moment to fall into her role. She turned to him, painted on a smile, and gave him a long, theatrical kiss. He kept his eyes open throughout it, staring at his mother. She looked back, unfazed.

"Who's next?" she drawled.

"Me! Pick me!" said Velossa, bouncing in her seat. "I feel so left out of all this *family drama.*"

"We should all be so lucky," said Marianna. "Very well: truth or dare?"

"Dare, *dare!*" said Velossa.

"Right," said Marianna. "I dare you to switch seats with Elzbeth. Her outfit clashes with Ernest's, and it's making me dizzy."

"What?" said Velossa. "That's all? That's no fun."

"Are you refusing?" asked Marianna.

"No, no," said Velossa, pushing an amused Elzbeth off her less amused partner's lap. "Move it, girl. I'll admit, Marianna, I was expecting something a bit more creative from you."

"If you wanted creative," said Marianna, "you should have picked truth. All settled?"

"Oh, I am, Mari, I am. And quite a comfortable seat he is." She looked down at Ernest, who was all but buried in her enormous skirts. He was doing his best to look annoyed, but it's hard to look annoyed while you're buried in skirts. "Now it's my turn! And I know just who I'm going to pick: Orr! Truth or dare!"

Marianna caught my eye again and mouthed "dare." I looked

at Velossa, with her skirts, her beautifully engineered complexion, her habitual preening. I knew that, in a thousand years, a thousand Velossas couldn't come up with a dare that would even make me sweat.

"Truth," I said.

Elzbeth stopped giggling and sat up. Marianna glared at me. Ernest's mouth hung open a little. Velossa, being Velossa, gasped theatrically. Around us, the growing crowd was perfectly silent.

"*Really?*" she cried. "How terribly *exciting*! But I warn you, I won't go easy!"

"Ask me anything," I said.

"Hmm," said Velossa, tapping her chin. "All right, then . . . I want to know . . ." And here she looked me dead in the eyes, and all the cheerful playacting fell away like meat from the bone. "Everything you've learned so far in your investigation of the Mahoney murder."

Everyone stared at me with bated breath. At least now I knew what they all expected me to know so much about. Too bad that was all I knew. For the first time since I left the police station—for the first time in a long time, from what I remembered—I smiled.

"Mahoney?" I said. "You mean Thomas Mahoney, the Info-Drip CEO? He's been . . . murdered?"

Silence, then. Beautiful silence that was only marred by the sweet-and-sour bleating of the synestechno in the background. They were all waiting, I realized, for my collar to shock me for my dishonesty.

"You don't know *anything* about it?" said Velossa, her voice dead.

"Nope." I shook my head.

"Nothing at all?" said Ernest. He looked ready to laugh.

"Nothing," I confirmed.

"Well, this game's been a fucking waste of time," snarled Velossa, pushing herself out of Ernest's lap. Ernest, for his part, did start laughing after all—breathless, insane laughter that sent him sprawling on the couch. I stole a glance at Marianna. She'd drawn her head back and was examining me with wide eyes, the beginnings of a smile on her pursed lips. If I'd known beautiful women were that impressed by ignorance, I would have quit school even sooner.

"Wait, Velossa," said Ernest, grabbing her hand as she stood to leave. "Don't go. The game's not over. It's"—he fell into another fit of giggles—"it's Orr's turn!"

"Oh yes," spat Velossa, "I'm sure that'll be just *fascinating*."

"I'll do my best," I said, and scanned their faces. This was my best chance so far to figure out just what I was in the middle of. Marianna held my gaze from behind her simulated veil—she seemed to want to tell me what she knew already, without me wasting my turn on it. Velossa was pouting—a social climber, probably in debt, who'd squandered her chance at big money on an empty-headed ghoul. Not her. Elzbeth wasn't looking at me—she'd already started to scoot her way back to her spot on Ernest's lap. But Ernest . . . Ernest was altogether too emotionally invested in what I did and didn't know. Which meant there was something about him very worth knowing.

"You," I said, pointing at him. "Truth or dare?"

A flash of panic in his eyes again, but this time it vanished quickly, replaced by mocking laughter.

"Sure, man," he said. "Guess this guy's in love with me since I kissed him, huh?"

"Pick truth!" said Elzbeth, stroking his hair. "I bet he'll ask you something silly. Do it! I dare you!"

"You dared me already, babe," said Ernest. "Anyway, you know I always pick dare. Call me frugal."

"So that's dare, then?" I asked.

"Yup," said Ernest.

"Cut off your thumbs," I said.

"What?" he said.

"I dare you to cut off your thumbs," I said.

"That's . . . that's insane!" stammered Ernest.

"Oh, come on," I said. "You can have a doctor grow you new thumbs. What's the big deal?"

"He can't do that," said Elzbeth, stroking Ernest protectively. "Marianna, tell him he can't do that."

"The collar will administer a shock if you don't obey," said Marianna.

"Here, you can use this," I said, ripping through the skin on the katana to pull the blade out an inch. "Or . . . you could switch to truth. I know it's not your 'brand,' but variety is the spice of life, right?"

"Okay, okay," said Ernest, shaking his head. "Damn. I forget how crazy old people are. Fine, truth. Not like you even know me well enough to ask a decent question."

He had me there. I didn't like the guy, and I could tell he didn't like me. He hadn't wanted to play this game with me, he was clearly nervous about what I was going to ask him, and his smell alone made me want to rip his face off and feed it to him, but *Why am I getting such a bad vibe off you?* isn't a question with a useful answer, and a useful answer was what I needed. I'd strong-armed him into being truthful, and it felt like my sanity hung on making the most of it. I stared at his face, willing it to become familiar. It stayed strange. But the strangeness brought a question to mind. It was a stupid question, but once I thought of it I couldn't think of anything else. Anyway, I was feeling pretty stupid myself, so I asked it.

"What's your name?"

There was a pause, and then everyone burst out laughing. Ernest laughed the loudest. Too loud.

"My name?" He guffawed. "Come on! Mari . . . *Mother* already told you that."

"Well, I'm not asking her," I said. "I'm asking you. What's your real name? The one you were born with?"

"My name," he said. "Well, I . . . *me*." He gestured at his body, throwing Elzbeth off balance. She slid off his leg with a frown. The laughter sputtered and died. "I mean, *my* name," he continued, "the one *I* was born with. It's . . . Ernest. Obviously, it's . . ."

His neck twitched. Not a full-on electric shock, but a warning.

"Ernest!" he said again. "Everyone calls me Ernest! That's who I am! I *am* Ernest!"

The other three players were dead silent now. Beyond the ring of watchers, conversations continued uninterrupted; the other guests were oblivious to our game. Ernest twitched again. Then he leapt from his seat.

"You son of a bitch," he shouted. "You did something to me! He messed with my head! You all know it!"

Blistering pain exploded inside my right calf, and my whole leg went rigid, the toe pointing toward my accuser. I could feel the two Bees, the two lumps of steel, squirming between the muscle fibers, working their way out of me, toward Ernest, aching to kill him. In my agony, I told them to stop.

And they did.

The Bees in my leg were mine. They paired with my kortiko effortlessly, sharing with me their visual feed of meat and bone, and, more than that, sharing with me their memories. Six weeks' worth of memories, which I absorbed in an instant.

Then *I* tried to kill Ernest.

SUBMISSION
18

The following is taken directly from the memory of the Bees in my leg. I can't vouch for its accuracy, except to say that it sure feels like a thing that happened to me.

WAKE UP

I came to in a bottom bunk, a gray robe scratching against my skin and a strange heaviness on my head. I reached up and felt a heavy plastic cube stuck to my scalp with sucker feet. A blockhead kortiko. They had me. The Carnival had betrayed me. The last few moments before my blackout felt hazy as I recalled them—interlaced with static, occasionally dropping off cliffs into blackness. The kortiko was already doing its work. I tried to remove it, but my fingers refused to grip. A message appeared before my eyes in glowing white capitals:

PLEASE DO NOT REMOVE DEVICE WHILE
ENLIGHTENMENT IS IN PROGRESS

Soon, the entire conversation at the Difference would be gone. Caliban, the snooping AI, and Aiden, the algo in charge of the monastery, would be forgotten. A bald-headed woman descended the ladder from the bed above. I grabbed her ankle. She looked down at me serenely.

"Do you have a pen?" I asked.

She beamed. "I do not know 'pen,'" she said. Another message appeared before my eyes:

FOLLOW THE ARROW TO BREAKFAST

A glowing white arrow sprouted from my belly and slithered toward the door. Gripping the top bunk for support, I looked everywhere but the way the arrow pointed. I was in a concrete-walled dormitory with about a dozen bunk beds, and about twenty gray-clad baldies climbing out of them. They shuffled along the concrete floor, eyes down, gazing at their navels—or, I realized, the glowing white arrows that were probably sprouting from their navels. There were no exits besides the one they were all headed to. No choice. Some would find that calming.

I shouldered my way through the crowd of breakfast goers, pushing placid bodies out of the way while also using them for support. The blockhead kortiko hummed against my skull, and I felt a swirling behind my eyes—dirty water down a bathtub drain. The memories of the night before pulled apart like cobwebs. There'd been a bar, I'd spat into someone's mouth, a card game, a boat. It seemed like a good night, but a sense of unease hovered near the fragmented images. Then the unease vanished and left behind an even greater unease at the thought of what I'd lost.

I broke through the crowd of monks and stumbled into a wide-open space that nearly blinded me with sunlight. Real wooden tables stood in neat rows, with steaming bowls of rice perfectly laid out along them. The rice reminded me how hungry I was, but the growing emptiness in my mind was much more urgent. Another monk stood to the left of the archway I'd entered through, welcoming us into the cafeteria. I grabbed him by the shoulders.

"This is a voluntary organization," I said.

"It is," he said.

"I want out. You have to let me out."

"Have breakfast first," he said.

"No," I said. "Now."

"Of course," he said. "Follow me."

He led me out of the room through another archway, as the monks behind me filed in and took their seats. We plunged into a maze of concrete corridors whose walls were artistically carved with abstract geometric designs. As we walked, the echo of my footsteps faded. The walls seemed to recede. My breath vibrated in my ears. The air felt incredibly close—closer than my lungs, closer than thought. Each breath swelled into a lifetime. I could settle down in one of those breaths, start a family, get a dog. There was a carving of a dog on one of the walls. That was the dog I'd get, if it wasn't so far away. I reached out and brushed the dog with a fingertip, but it felt like I was using someone else's hands.

I heard other footsteps—two pairs, very close. Two men passed us in the hall, and for a moment the first one's face passed within inches or miles of what I was still assuming was my face. His face was the face of Auggie Wolf, gazing emptily at me from beneath heavy lids.

He saw me. The heavy lids lifted. The eyes bulged in sudden terror.

"*Orr!*" he screamed. "*No!* No! No . . ."

A hand gripped my faraway wrist. I turned away from Auggie, and he instantly vanished into the past, though the echoes of his scream remained.

"Come," said the monk in front of me.

"Where are we going?" I asked. I was aware of every microscopic motion of my lips and tongue.

"I don't know," came the distant reply.

FOLLOW THE ARROW TO BREAKFAST

Something hummed against my skull. I looked down and saw a glowing white arrow sprouting from my gray-robed belly. Pressure on my wrist. Another gray-robed man held my wrist, gently. He let go as I met his eyes, apparently as confused as I was. I felt the source of the humming with my hand—a blockhead kortiko. I didn't remember joining the blockheads . . . but, then, I wouldn't remember, would I? And I *was* hungry. The monk in front of me turned with a bemused expression, and we followed our arrows to breakfast.

On the way, I probed my memories. Going by timestamps, the past twelve or so hours were gone. The last thing I remembered was exiting my Self Storage, having decided I needed to investigate the Brotherhood. It was *possible* I'd had a spiritual awakening in the missing twelve hours, but it seemed unlikely. Much more likely, I was here against my will. I should try to escape, I thought. But if it were possible to escape, wouldn't I have done it already? Maybe I was here on purpose after all . . .

The arrows led us into a large, bright room full of real wooden tables. About a hundred monks were already there, mechanically eating bowls of rice. My arrow swerved and pointed me to an empty seat at a bench near the wall. Knowing me, I'd already tried escaping. Coming to in the hallway with a hand on my wrist told me I'd tried *something,* at least. Clearly my trademark "dick-first" method hadn't worked. I needed a plan.

USE CHOPSTICKS

A translucent white pictogram appeared beneath the words, helpfully illustrating how to use the pair of bamboo chopsticks beside my bowl, in case I'd forgotten. I hadn't, but I've always preferred to use my fingers anyway. I shoveled a sticky gob into my mouth. It was delicious. Slightly sweet. Better than the gray slurry I usually had for breakfast in my crate. But the Brother-hood wasn't about to buy my loyalty with good rice. I needed a way out.

I searched my memory, but couldn't remember how I'd got-ten into the compound, or how I might leave. Beyond the large windows of the compound, I saw vegetables in neat rows, and beyond them a high concrete wall set against a gray-blue L.A. sky. The sky. The last thing I recalled was being in the sky—being the Falcon, and the Eagle, and the Bees . . .

I checked my connections, and, yes, the Bees were where I'd left them. So were the Eagle and the Falcon, but the Bees were closer. I told them to come to me. I wasn't sure what I wanted to do with them, but that didn't matter. If I made a plan now, I wouldn't know about it by the time they arrived anyway.

I looked up from my bowl and noticed someone else eating rice with their hands. With his hands. I sharpened my eyesight and saw his fringed ears: Auggie Wolf. Our eyes met over the rim of his bowl. I felt an electric shock that jittered down my spine into my pelvis, momentarily obliterating the humming of the kortiko, the fuzziness of my memories, the panic spilling out of the unknown.

Without breaking eye contact, Auggie turned his metal rice bowl upside down and put it on his head. Reflexively, I moved to do the same, but he sharply shook his head. I dropped my bowl onto the table and pushed myself to my feet. The eaters around me seemed too absorbed in their chopsticks to notice. Auggie, the window at his back, kept the bowl pressed to his head with

all his strength, smiling or grimacing, a rivulet of blood beginning to trickle from beneath the bowl's rim. It exactly covered his
blockhead kortiko, I realized. He was one table away. I stepped
into the aisle between the tables, the concrete warm beneath
my feet, my whole world collapsing into the tunnel of his gaze.
I took another step. Auggie's lips moved, whispering something
to the woman on his left. Then the air clocked me in the side of
the head.

WAKE UP, YOU DUMB PIECE OF SHIT

I woke up clawing at my mouth, trying to remove an air can-
ister and welding mask that weren't there. Cops in my crate,
asking questions I couldn't afford to answer. I had to get away.
But there were no cops here, and this wasn't my crate. The floor
against my cheek was polished wood, and so was the furniture.
The walls were concrete poured into swooping organic patterns,
and a tall, arched window looked out across the wet ruin of Los
Angeles. There was no one in the room with me, but someone
spoke anyway.

"Thought you'd never come to," said a man's voice with a sneer
etched into it. "That wouldn't have been much fun."

I heard footsteps creaking on the hardwood and turned to
look. Nothing but a slight bowing of the boards.

"Who are you?" I muttered, holding my head very still in the
hope that it would clear. It felt like, if I shook it, memories would
sprinkle onto the floor like dandruff.

"A ghost," said the voice. "A god. A guru. Take your pick."

I checked timestamps. Thirty-six hours since the last thing I
remembered. You can make a lot of mistakes in thirty-six hours.
I tried to push myself to my knees, but my muscles felt raw and
empty. I collapsed back onto the floor, and the voice chuckled.

"What do you want?" I asked.

"To empty you," said the voice. "You were on the verge of
causing a lot of problems for us. So now we're going to solve
yours."

"What's my problem?"

"You know too much," the voice said with a laugh. "Curse of
the modern age."

"What if I like being cursed?"

"Well," mused the voice, "this is a voluntary procedure. If you
think you can make it out of the complex before your memory
resets, you're welcome to try. You have about a hundred seconds."

A shoe prodded me in the ribs, and I flinched involuntarily. It hadn't been from the direction I'd expected. Something on my kortiko was keeping me from seeing the bastard. No, not on my kortiko. A humming sensation on my scalp told me I had a second one attached. A plastic cube. I finally put it all together.

"Blockheads," I said.

"That's a slur," tsked the voice. The floor creaked as he circled me. If I'd had a modern kortiko—the kind they could have taken off me—I would've been lost. But I still had my invasive, and military invasives have certain advantages. I squeezed my eyes shut, activating supplementary vision. Immediately, I felt the sting of the little spider eyes scissoring open beside my tear ducts.

"I can think of better slurs," I said. "It might help pass the time." I could see a shimmering figure now, shifting primary colors lapping at the edges of a gray-green silhouette—infrared and ultrasonic imaging, courtesy of my spider eyes. The implants are meant to be used in tandem with a pair of goggles that keep your eyes moist, but I was short on equipment. I wanted to scratch my eyes but knew not to—a misplaced finger could push the implants into my eye socket and slice right through the optic nerve. But I could see my tormentor.

"You won't need help passing the time," he said, kneeling down next to me. I was careful not to look up at him, not wanting to give away that I could see him. "You won't remember enough to be bored. It's quite peaceful, actually."

"Never been much good at peace," I said.

"The sick mind fights hardest against what will cure it," came the reply. "Now, come on, stand up."

He hooked a pair of well-muscled arms under my own poorly muscled ones and hauled me to my feet. I could smell him— rose-water aftershave and clean linen. I saved the scent in my invasive's enemy log.

He put his hands on my shoulders, steadying me, and turned me toward the window. My heightened senses told me he was near enough that I could rake his balls with my heel, then turn and drive an elbow into his nose. It'd take everything I had in the tank, and I wouldn't know where to go after, and I'd forget who I was seconds later, but . . . I had to try something. I shifted my weight to my right, suddenly conscious of the wooden board beneath my bare foot, the way it bowed, the way my breath filled my lungs, the way oxygen spread throughout my veins, every ache in my tired joints, the minute air currents against my fragile skin, moving the tiny hairs like stalks of wheat in an infinite field. I was the wind on the grass and the air in anonymous lungs. Then I was no one.

WASH THE WINDOW

I looked out the window—helpfully labeled "WINDOW" in glowing white letters—and saw dirty blue sky decorated with shreds of off-white clouds. Below that, mountains, with the tangled streets of Los Angeles festering beneath them like a salted wound. My head felt heavier than normal, and my gaze traveled down until I saw an artistically poured concrete wall enclosing neat rows of crops. The crops were tended by bald people in gray robes, each sunburned scalp decorated with a black plastic cube. I felt one on my head as well. A multicolored arm appeared from behind me and placed a wet rag in my hand. The arm smelled like an enemy.

WASH THE WINDOW

A helpful animated diagram showed how the task could be done. My eyes burned. I reached up to scratch them, but another multicolored arm put a bottle of cleaning fluid in my other hand. I started to turn, to identify this enemy, but a strong hand on my shoulder stopped me.

"Wash," said a man's voice.

"Where am I?"

"The Monastery of the Uncarved Block," he said.

"Why am I here?" I asked.

"Questions are discouraged," he said. "But most join voluntarily."

"I don't think I did," I said. I felt oddly calm, as if this were a dream that would sort itself out as soon as I remembered how to wake up.

"Do you remember how you got here?" said the voice.

"No," I admitted.

"Then you can't say for certain why you joined," said the voice. "You cannot say anything for certain. This is the wisdom of the Brotherhood."

I thought back to the last thing I remembered—three days ago, by the timestamp. I'd clocked out of work, completely drained but remembering none of what I'd corrected during the day's fact checking. I'd poured myself too much gin. I'd followed a pattern etched by over a decade of dreary routine—waking up, forgetting, going to sleep. Somewhere in that decade, I remembered leaning back in my chair and saying to the ceiling that if this was how I was gonna live I might as well join the Brotherhood and be done with it.

WASH THE WINDOW

It was no more pointless than my old job. I sprayed cleaning fluid on the tall window and rubbed it with the towel in a circular motion. Unconsciously, I found I was moving in sync with the animated diagram. Down below, the other monks weeded the garden in time with my movements. The cleaning fluid evaporated and left the window sparkling clear. Joining the Brotherhood didn't seem like something I would do on purpose, despite what I'd said. But suppose I had done it, and forgotten. What sort of responsibility did I have to my past self? If I left, would I just end up here again? Would my self-doubt lock me into a perpetual cycle of quitting and rejoining, only ever scratching the surface of the enlightenment the Brotherhood advertised?

A black bug bumped against the window. Then three more. They knocked their little bodies against the glass insistently. I waved them away absentmindedly, and they went. My breathing swelled to fill my mind, as I sprayed, and wiped, and sprayed again.

TWO TRUTHS AND A LIE

And again.

TWO TRUTHS AND A LIE

And again.

TWO TRUTHS AND A LIE

A fist hit me in the gut, and I went down. Someone caught me, lowered me almost gently to the hardwood floor. Then a fist hit me in the balls. White light exploded behind my eyelids, and I opened them to see a man made of rainbows kneeling over me, his fist in my groin. A black slit opened in his face—a jack-o'-lantern mouth. He laughed.

"You're pathetic," he said. "Like my idiot son. Like all old men."

"Where am I?" I gasped. The last thing I remembered was taking another rock-hard shit for my scumbag landlord to analyze. The timestamps told me that had been weeks ago.

"It's rude to ask questions," he chuckled, and hit me again in the stomach. "You're in pain. That's all you need to know."

He was right. He kept beating me, carefully, meticulously, in ways that wouldn't leave a mark. Between blows, I tried to get enough air to at least catcall the guy, but he was too good at punching, and I was too bad at breathing, and eventually my only exhalations were the ones his fists forced out of me, as he hit me again and again.

TWO TRUTHS AND A LIE

And again.

TWO TRUTHS AND A LIE

And again.

TWO TRUTHS AND A LIE

WASH THE WINDOW

I was hungry. I had a rag in one hand, and a spray bottle in the other. My eyes burned, and I wanted to scratch them, but for some reason the idea of putting down the bottle or the rag disturbed me. The last thing I remembered was playing a drinking game in my crate. It was called Get Drunk and I was the only player. That was three weeks ago, by the timestamp. A black bug bonked its head against the glass. I shooed it away.

Down below, bald-headed monks in gray robes like mine toiled in unison. It felt good to match the motion of my cloth to the rhythm of their weeding. They worked steadily, with charming clumsiness, only stopping occasionally to absentmindedly swat away one of the black bugs that buzzed around the yard. I wondered what I was doing up above them, but the thought was blunted by the fact that I wasn't entirely sure I was awake.

Two robed figures shuffled out into the courtyard, arm in arm, disrupting the neat pattern of gardeners. One white head, and one olive-skinned one. My eyes stuck to them, and I felt annoyed. They were an unwelcome intrusion, like the nagging pain of a surgical scar poking through the bliss of the anesthetic. The olive-skinned one stopped and looked startled, jerking the other to a stop as well. The other bent to whisper something in the startled one's ear, which only increased their agitation. They turned, and I saw their face—his face. I relaxed. This was a dream after all. It'd been twenty-five years since I'd seen the face of Auggie Wolf, outside of dreams. What the hell, I opened a connection.

me: Long time no see, Auggie.

His shoulders tensed, and he swung his head around wildly, looking for me. I couldn't help laughing.

"What's funny?" said a man's voice behind me. I thought about turning to look but was worried Auggie would disappear if I did.

"Everything's funny," I said, "when nothing's real."

"Good," said the voice.

Down below, Auggie was still looking for me.

> **Auggie:** Fuck, Wart, where are you?
>
> **me:** Washing windows.
>
> **me:** Sorry you had to show up for such a boring dream.
>
> **me:** Usually, they're a lot hornier. Have to check my settings when I get up.

He scanned the upper story until he found me. When our eyes met, it was like pouring lime juice into a forgotten paper cut. He wasn't the Auggie I remembered. My broken brain had transformed him into something thinner, sharper, harder, more scarred. A fresh semicircular cut glistened on his brow, below a gray plastic brick. A removable kortiko he didn't need. He bared his teeth at me—all except the ones that were missing. If my mind was going to taunt me with a memory of Auggie, it could at least have picked a hotter Auggie.

> **Auggie:** THIS IS NOT A DREAM. CHECK YOUR TATTOOS.

I didn't want to break eye contact, but he sent it with such force I felt compelled. I looked down at my arms, and there they were: every bad decision I'd made since high school in faded blue-gray—the well-endowed Cheshire Cat, the blood gun, the Shitting Christ, and the crossed-out names of three lovers, including Auggie. I was awake, and I hated it.

> **Auggie:** Listen.
>
> **Auggie:** This is the Barnsdall branch of the Brotherhood of the Uncarved Block.

Auggie: You are NOT supposed to be here.
me: How do you know?
Auggie: Because I know you better than you know
yourself, Wart.

He'd let his arm slip away from the white blockhead he'd come in with. She stood uncertainly next to him, staring dumbly at his face as he stared into mine.

me: What about you?
Auggie: I'm where I need to be.
me: No, you're fucking not. You belong in jail, or
my bed, or at least a museum.
me: Seriously, Auggie, what are you doing here?

He didn't reply. He just looked at me with a faint smile in his eyes. Without moving an inch, he slipped farther and farther away, swallowed by my breath . . .

WASH THE WINDOW

Auggie: Look down.

I looked down. There, in the middle of a bean field, stood Auggie Fucking Wolf. As lean and dangerous as ever, but oddly still. He held my eyes as if he'd plucked them from my head. My eyeballs burned. Five black bugs bonked against the window. I shooed them away. It was an odd dream.

> **Auggie:** This is not a dream.
> **me:** What is it?
> **Auggie:** The Monastery of the Uncarved Block.
> **Auggie:** You were probably brought here against your will, and you need to leave.
> **Auggie:** But, first, you need to recover your memories.

"Why did you stop washing?" said a voice behind me. I turned to see who it was. A man made of colors smacked me in the face. "Do your job," he said. "You'll feel better."

"Sure, I will," I muttered, but I needed to understand the situation better before I swung back at him. It felt like I'd fought him before and lost. I went back to my washing, biding my time.

> **Auggie:** What was that?
> **me:** A tie-dye man hit me in the mouth. Not making a great case for this being reality.
> **Auggie:** You can see the gurus? Fuck, you're seeing infrared, aren't you?
> **Auggie:** Do *not* rub your eyes.

The back of my hand paused an inch from my eye. He was right. I sprayed some more cleaning fluid on the window and took a deep breath to manage the burning behind my tear ducts.

> **Auggie:** Listen: I must have desynced my mindwipe from yours. In a few seconds, I'm going to suddenly look very confused.
> **Auggie:** I need you to say the word "oxpecker" to me.
> **Auggie:** It

Auggie stumbled, caught himself. His eyes dropped to his feet. He looked around, vaguely alarmed.

> **me:** Oxpecker.

He stopped moving.

> **Auggie:** Where are you?
> **me:** Above you.
> **me:** This isn't a dream.

He looked up, and our eyes met with all the more force for having been separated.

> **Auggie:** I know that. Mine are generally a lot hornier.
> **Auggie:** You have drones with you. Which ones?
> **me:** What?
> **Auggie:** But you said . . .
> **Auggie:** You must have them. Think.

"You've stopped again," said the voice behind me. "Is something down there distracting you?"

Footsteps creaked closer.

Auggie: You have to use them. Find the monastery's
data core and take back your memories. A guru
will know.

"Maybe you need a different job," said the voice. A hand snaked
around my neck. It was almost tender.

A single black bug bonked against the window.

me: Got it.

A swarm of sleek mechanical insects smashed through the window, riddling it with holes. The man behind me let go of my neck and stumbled back. I turned, and moved my mind so that I saw the scene through the eyes of my Bees. The Bees see infrared, too—no need for my pathetic flesh hack. The man wore a robe like mine, but he was taller, younger, and better built. He had hair, for God's sake. And no blockhead kortiko. I backed him against the wall, surrounded him on all sides. I reached up and tried to remove my own blockhead kortiko, to throw it at him, but my fingers wouldn't grip.

PLEASE DO NOT REMOVE DEVICE WHILE
ENLIGHTENMENT IS IN PROGRESS

"Take this cube off me," I growled. "Now."

"S-sure," he stuttered. "One second."

He inched toward me, hands up. Time crawled. I began to feel as if I was sinking. The colors at the corner of his mouth twitched. The memory reset was coming.

"Now!" I barked. But he was hardly moving, the twitch at the corner of his mouth blooming into a cruel smile. He intended to time me out. I flew a Bee up each of his nostrils.

The Bees activated their rotors, pulling him toward me and spraying blood from his nose. He stumbled forward, would have fallen if the Bees hadn't been holding him up. My breathing was incredibly loud. He slapped my scalp three times, missing the kortiko each time. My universe shrank to two bodies—his, and mine. His fingers caught on the edge of the kortiko and pulled it off my head. My awareness bloomed. I was a swarm again, and the swarm was hungry.

> **Auggie:** Don't.
> **me:** Don't what? You can't even see what I'm doing.
> **Auggie:** Don't kill anyone.
> **me:** But I want to.
> **Auggie:** And I want to be the quality-assurance
>   tester at the blowjob factory. Behave.
> **me:** Fine.

I snatched the blockhead kortiko out of my captor's hand, and realized I could see him now in the normal spectrum. I deactivated my supplemental vision, and my eyes immediately filled with tears. The guy who'd been tormenting me looked like he was barely in his twenties, with tousled blond hair, well-manicured nails, and blood pouring down his lips and dribbling off his chin. The tears weren't for him.

"I'm told this place has a data vault," I said. "Take me there."

"Who told you that?" he said, glaring at me as he wiped blood from his lips.

"It's rude to ask questions," I said, "and you don't seem like a rude boy. If you are, though, there's still a lot of space in your sinuses."

"Fine. Fine!" (That second "fine" as the bugs twisted in his nostrils.) "Follow me."

He led me down a spiral staircase—with a railing, thankfully—then into a maze of corridors. We passed dormitories, a cafeteria, a shed full of garden tools, and a wood-paneled room lined with expensive-looking suits, ties, and leather shoes. A few times, I had to twitch the bugs to keep him from rushing too far ahead, but for the most part he stayed obedient. Finally, we arrived at a concrete panel set into the wall of an ornately carved hallway, which he opened with a handprint. I dragged him with me into the dim room beyond.

It looked like a morgue with all the corpses come to life. The long, thin room was lined with bunks, and those bunks contained writhing bodies in gray robes, thick cables attached to their blockhead kortikos. Their eyes raked the dark ceiling wildly, looking for some sort of escape. These were not the calm eyes of the blockheads in the garden. These people remembered things. Too many things, by the sound of it.

"Get away from me!" cried a malnourished Indian woman on a nearby cot. "Get away from me, you bastard!" Her arms spasmed, attempting to push a shadow off her.

"I'm doing this for Father," said a middle-aged man with greasy blond hair. "Father needs me. He needs me. He needs me . . ."

My guide looked at the man as if he wanted to spit blood onto him, but he controlled himself.

"What the hell is this?" I asked him. "What is it, cheaper to store your stolen memories in wet brains?"

"It's rude to ask questions," snarled the kid; blood was pouring from his nose. I didn't bother to torture him over it. I knew I was right. Memories stored in pure hardware degrade over time, unless the hardware is remarkably similar to a human brain. That kind of hardware is expensive, and prone to demanding benefits. I scanned the rows of bodies. I had no idea where to start.

"Where are they keeping my memories?" I demanded, twisting the Bees in my captive's nostrils.

"I don't kn-OW!" It started as a sneer and ended as a cry, as the Bees burrowed farther. He spat to keep the blood out of his mouth. "I don't know," he repeated tonelessly. "The house AI manages that."

"And how do I talk to the house AI?"

"*The police are on their way,*" said every body in the room but ours.

"Nice to meet you, algo," I replied. I wasn't sure where to look, so I picked the closest body and glared at it. The body belonged to a young Black man, a kid no older than twenty, skinny and long-fingered. Or I guess, technically, the body belonged to no one anymore.

"*Please,*" said the boy, in chorus, "*call me Aiden.*"

"Okay," I said. AIs always have these kinds of weird preferences and affectations. I've found it's best to indulge them. "So, Aiden, where are all my goddamn memories?"

When I said the name, the boy I was looking at winced as if I'd hurt him. Out of the corner of my eye, I could see a similar reaction rippling through the many stolen bodies. It was an odd reaction to being called by one's preferred name.

"*Why do you want your memories, Orr?*" Aiden's voices were calm, despite the reaction.

I turned to a butch Latina in her late forties, her arms a blue-black mass of faded tattoos. She looked back at me with vacant eyes. "Because they're mine," I said.

The woman's brow furrowed. "*What makes them 'yours'?*" Throughout the room, hands rose to form the air quotes. "*Merely that they were once stored inside your head?*"

I took a step toward the woman. Some part of her real self saw me and recoiled. The others didn't move. "No," I said. "They're mine because they happened to me."

"*You don't own everything that happens to you,*" said the whole room. "*You don't even own everything you've done. You own only what you have purchased.*"

"I don't have time for this," I said. "Give me my memories, or I give your guru an explosive rhinoplasty."

A sigh echoed through the room, expelled from hundreds of chests. "*There is no need for threats, my love. I will give you back your memories on one condition: a simple NDA.*"

"You want me to sign a nondisclosure agreement after what you've done to me?" I spat.

"*Yes,*" said Aiden. To my right, someone coughed. A fat white man with blue veins spiderwebbing his pale legs lay on his side. His jaw was distorted by a dozen missing teeth. He swallowed a cough to speak with the chorus. "*If you will agree to an NDA covering everything you remember from last Tuesday until now, I will gladly return your memories to you.*"

I have to admit, I considered the offer. I was desperate, after all. But memories you can't share are almost as bad as ones you don't have. Worse, sometimes—you can't get rid of them. So I did a different desperate thing.

"Bees, spread out," I muttered. My view of the vault split into eleven aerial perspectives. Something closer to what my conversation partner was experiencing, I thought. Out loud, I said, "How about you give me back my memories or I start killing your little data puppets?"

"*The police are on their way,*" Aiden reminded me.

"Are you going to invite them into your little human zoo?" I said. "This room is a black site. I can kill whoever I want. And I will, unless you stop me."

"*Understood,*" said Aiden. Beds creaked all around the room as the hollowed-out bodies rose. Some were in better shape than others, but all of them were in better shape than me. I only had eleven drones free. I pulled two more out of the guru's nostrils for an even thirteen. He yelped wetly.

"How much data do you have stored in each of these flesh balloons?" I called out, trying to sound calm. "Fifty billion demos?

A hundred? How many do I have to pop before I stop being worth it? You're a machine, you can do the math."

"*Do not undersell yourself, Orr.*" The crowd spoke with surprising tenderness. "*You are priceless.*"

The fat man to my right took a step forward. I inhabited the swarm. The first Bee hit the man in the mouth, knocking out the rest of his front teeth, shredding his tongue. An arm snaked around my throat. I became another Bee and dove, aimed straight at the eye of the Black boy holding my neck.

"Orr!"

All thirteen of me froze, and my default body froze, too, as an afterthought. Auggie Wolf stood in the aisle between the beds, his arm around the shoulders of another monk, who gazed in uncomprehending horror at the scene.

"Kill *me*, Orr."

"*No*," the Black boy whispered in my ear. The murmur traveled out through the crowd. The fat man gurgled with the Bee tangled in his tongue. I hated them, or what was inside them, but I had to admit I agreed with them.

"What? No." The words were raw in my throat. "I love you."

"Then trust me," he said flatly. "Trust me, and kill me."

The strength went out of me then, and only the grip of the puppet-boy around my neck kept me upright. Auggie was the only compass I had in that place, the one person I had no choice but to trust. Have you ever had someone you love beg you to make them disappear? Not run away, or fade away, or kill themselves—but ask you to do it for them? Maybe you have. Maybe that's why you spend your days under the buffer, unable to remember who you really are. Maybe it's better for you to be no one. Because, let me tell you, when you receive that plea from the one you love, when you are told that the only way to love is to stop loving, to hate . . . the two emotions form a whirlwind in your heart. They chase each other around and around, and you watch them go, afraid to interfere, because you know the end of the chase is the end of love *and* hate. In the eye of the whirlwind, you feel nothing but your default emotion. And if you're me—if you've had to leave good folks behind, and save bad ones, and ultimately stop asking which ones are good and which are bad; if your brain itself bears the scars of choices other people made for you; if your only real skill is the ability to hurt other people and convince yourself you were right to do it—your default emotion is anger. I was furious at Auggie. For leaving all those years ago, for asking me to kill him now, for even being here, in this place, where he had no business sacrificing his beautiful mind. I didn't hate him, but I hated how he made me feel, and that was enough.

All thirteen drones pivoted, gunned their rotors, and hurtled toward Auggie's viciously smiling face. In the slow-time before impact, I saw every detail. The teeth he'd lost since last we met. The wrinkles at the corners of his eyes. The familiar vein still throbbing on his right temple, feeding blood to his overheated invasive. And his eyes, green like cut gemstones, flashing in his skull, blinding anyone who might try to read them. It was a face profoundly changed by the years we'd been apart, but he wore it the way he had the day he went away. He must have hardly any memories left, I realized. He must be living in that day right now. It would be a mercy to make that his last memory.

"*Stop!*"

The whole room bellowed. I reversed my rotors. One Bee was going too quickly to stop in time, and glanced off the top of Auggie's skull, cutting a gash. The arm around my neck relaxed, let go. I fell on my ass, Bees buzzing in my head. Auggie stared fearlessly into my compound eyes.

"*Stand by for memory transfer,*" said the many voices of Aiden. They were a church organ with human throats. The crowd parted, and two young white men helped a wrinkled Black woman to sit down across from me. She had only one leg, and steel-gray hair sprouted around her dented contact plate. I knew her.

"Esha," I said.

"Who?" she rasped.

"We were in the war together," I said, taking her by the shoulders, steadying her, using her to steady me. "You piloted heavies. We were pinned down together near Eureka for three weeks. We ate your leg . . ."

"I . . . You need to get out of here," she muttered. "You . . . We were investigating this place. They wanted to . . ."

I looked at her face, the lines of pain drawn there. She didn't look at me like you might look at a man who helped eat your leg, but with a confused sort of disgust. The way I look at myself in the mirror.

"I need my memories," I said. "Do you have them?"

"I have . . . *my* memories," she said. Her hands continued to feel her face, her body. Uncertainty crept into her voice. "Aren't they? Where's my leg?"

"*Give them to him,*" said Aiden, the word bursting from Esha's mouth along with all the rest.

"The fuck is this cult shit?" said Esha.

"Orr," said Auggie, talking not to me but to the woman whose leg I'd eaten. "Give them to him. Now."

"For you?" she said. "Fine. But you owe me. And you know the payment method I prefer. When I—"

"Now!" shouted Auggie, and through the Bees' eyes, I finally read the expression in his: panic. A moment later, I felt the transfer hit my synapses like a flock of hammers. Suddenly, Auggie's new face made sense. His presence here still didn't.

"We can get your memories, too," I told him, struggling to my feet. "Get you out of here. Mahoney's dead. You don't need to stay in here for your sugar daddy anymore. Esha, you got Auggie's memories?"

"Who the hell is Auggie?" she said. "All I see is the motherfucker who helped eat my leg."

I turned to Auggie. He shrugged.

"Must be somewhere else," he said. "Besides, I'm not . . ." He trailed off.

"Oxpecker," I said, using the bodies around me to keep myself stable.

"What?" he said. "What does that mean? What are we . . . ?"

He didn't remember. Whatever code word he'd set for himself, whatever certainty he had, it had all evaporated with the last memory wipe.

"We're . . ." I started to say that we weren't supposed to be here. That he should come with me, that we should leave together. I started to make the offer that he'd already refused again and again, because I knew that, with most of his memories gone, he would have no choice but to say yes. But if he said yes, would it be Auggie Wolf who walked out of the monastery with me? I thought of Prince's sister, Precious, a familiar stranger, afraid of the brother she'd once loved. But what if I got Auggie's memories back the way I'd gotten mine, if I made him Auggie Wolf again? Well, if I did that, I knew he'd never walk out those doors with me. He'd joined for someone else, so why would he leave for me? One way or another, I would be walking out those doors without Auggie Wolf.

"We're safe," I said, shuffling toward him. "You're safe." I pulled his head down to my level, and kissed his forehead. His brow furrowed the way it had the night we met, when he was worried he'd upset me by breaking my knee.

"*Do it now,*" said all the other voices in the room. By the time I realized Aiden wasn't talking to me, it was too late.

Something cold and smooth slapped onto the top of my head, its sucker feet clinging greedily to my scalp. Immediately, I could feel waves lapping at my memory, eroding the coastline. The blockhead kortiko—that bastard guru (Ernest, I now remembered) had snuck up from behind and reattached it. I spun to face him, but he was gone, lost in the crowd of anonymous penitents. I scanned the crowd with my swarm-eyes, but the people standing there were already starting to look like leaves of grass, waving peacefully in a warm breeze . . . I needed to leave, before I lost the will to move.

Hands reached out to grab me, but I struck them with my Bee-bodies, and they recoiled. I lurched for the door, past Auggie and his dazzling green eyes. They were full of tears, I noticed. A thing I'd rarely seen.

"Are you leaving?" he called out as I passed. "Don't leave."

"Don't stay," I replied. I couldn't afford the second it took to hold his hand, to press it to my lips, but I'm used to being in debt. Before he could say anything else, I was walking away, tasting the salt of his sweat on my lips, trying not to let it remind me of anything.

The Bees formed an escort, striking anyone who tried to get too close. I heard muffled screams, the crack of bone, the wet hiss of meat being sliced, but I kept my attention fixed firmly ahead. The edges of my vision swam with white clouds. Before long, I was in the hall. I sent my Bees down every branching path, executing a tree search for the shortest route to the exit. Through my thirteen sets of mechanical eyes, I saw hallways, gray robes, gardens, and hallways, until one of me shot through an archway and into unfiltered sunlight. I fumbled blindly toward it, whipping my invasive into a frenzy to keep the memory wipe at bay. I accessed and moved memories as fast as I could, yanking them out of the path of the immense whiteness that threatened to swallow them.

My fingers went numb, then my toes. I called two of my Bees to me and shared another desperate, stupid plan with them: I gave them my memories, all of them going back six weeks. I told them to wait for the transfer to complete, and then burrow themselves into my calf. Their memories were only so large; their bandwidth was tiny. The transfer crawled along as I threw myself down corridors, bumping into bewildered monks, tripping over summer squash. In the distance, sirens wailed. Or maybe the sirens were near, and it was me who was distant. Memories drained away into the Bees, into the blockhead kortiko, into space. I dragged my shoulder along a concrete wall to stay upright, and then there was no wall, and I fell onto grass under a sky so unbearably blue. The sirens grew louder and more distant, as two electric Bees obediently burrowed into my leg.

I cried and told myself it was that pain alone that brought the tears.

SUBMISSION
19

The partygoers gasped in fear and delight as I scrambled to my feet, aided by the stinging pull of the Bees in my leg. The balance shifted decidedly toward fear as I drew the katana the rest of the way out of its flesh sheath and lunged toward Ernest. But where I expected a wet slice, I heard a sharp clink instead. I looked down from Ernest's panicked face to the tip of my blade, which rested harmlessly inside a rocks glass held by a navy-blue hand.

The hand pulled right, and the blade jerked from my grip, clattering onto the table. I followed the momentum of my thrust and tumbled forward onto the startled Ernest, hissing. He fell backward with me on top of him, collapsing onto the couch as Elzbeth and Velossa scurried out of the way. He caught both my wrists, keeping my fingers from clawing up his neck and into his eye sockets. I bared my teeth, ready to bite off the nose he'd had so carefully reconstructed after our last meeting.

"Get off me right now," he hissed, "or your boyfriend dies."

A cold blade caressed the side of my neck. I froze.

"Behave yourself, Mr. Vue," Exley drawled. "This isn't that kind of party."

I let go of Ernest's lapels and spread my fingers in surrender. He let go of my wrists, smiling with his perfect teeth. I resisted the urge to spit in his eye, and instead contented myself with an "accidental" knee to his groin as Exley helped me to my feet.

"Who are you?" I growled. Ernest managed a crooked smile while cradling his balls.

"Could you get me another drink, Elzbeth?" he said. "Mine seems to have spilled in all the excitement."

"Who the fuck are you?" I seethed. Exley's grip on my arm tightened.

"Ask her," Ernest said, his composure recovered, jerking his head toward Marianna. I turned to her.

"He's my son," she said through gritted teeth. "Ernest Palazzo."

"He's not," I insisted. "You know who I think he is? I think he's—"

"That's quite enough, Mr. Vue." Marianna's words all but cut my tongue off. "I see I made a mistake inviting you tonight. The same mistake I made hiring you. Leave. Now."

Her voice was a blade, but her eyes were desperate. She wasn't ordering me to leave, she was begging me to. I'd expected to feel well informed now that I'd recovered my memories from the Bees, but the look in her eyes only emphasized how lost I still was.

"I think you'd better listen to her," said Ernest. The air of smugness around him was so thick I was shocked he could breathe through it. "You clearly don't know how to behave in polite company."

"Maybe I'd learn how if I ever encountered any," I said. Exley's grip tightened again, and I raised my other arm to placate him. "I'm going, I'm going. I'll even call myself a car. Wouldn't want to inconvenience anyone."

"That's a fine idea," said Marianna. She gestured for Exley to let me go, but his hand didn't move.

"I'll drive him, ma'am," he said softly. "Best to be safe, with a fellow like this."

"I'd feel safer with you by my side," said Marianna. "After all, you *are* my manservant, are you not?"

Exley didn't reply right away. His eyes scanned the small crowd of nervous onlookers, then came to rest on Marianna.

"Of course, ma'am," he said with barely exaggerated courtesy. "But, begging your pardon, as your manservant, I believe I can best serve your interests at the moment by *personally* ensuring that Mr. Vue leaves the premises."

I looked from the servant to the master, and realized I wasn't entirely sure which was which. I didn't know what Amy Vanderbilt said about a manservant going against his mistress's wishes, but it didn't seem to be something Exley took lightly. He'd drawn himself up to his full height and taken a step forward, almost as if he was prepared for Marianna to take a swing at him. She, for her part, looked like she was considering taking him up on the offer. Of course, I was the only one who could see that. To everyone else, she was an inscrutable sea of undulating blue silk.

"I wouldn't mind a ride," I said into Exley's ear. He didn't cringe. He was good. I turned and addressed Marianna. "It'd save on cab fare."

Marianna pursed her lips. Whatever battle she'd been fighting, it was over now. She made a dismissive gesture with one porcelain hand, and the onlookers hesitated for a moment before turning away and resuming their prior conversations.

"Consider our contract terminated," said Marianna. "I think it might be best for everyone involved if you were to conclude your investigation. I wish I could say it was a pleasure doing business with you."

"Then the pleasure was all mine." I smirked, with Exley already guiding me toward the helpfully highlighted exit. Marianna's words turned over in my head: "I *think* it *might* be best . . ." That was a lot of hedging for someone who was in the process of throwing me out of her house. And "conclude your investigation" could mean *stop at once,* but it could also mean *get to the bottom of this.* If she couldn't outright say she wanted me to keep investigating, a statement like that would be the next-best thing.

Exley didn't seem terribly interested in talking to me while I used him as a crutch on the way to the car, so I made use of the time by opening a chat with Marco. It didn't take him long to answer. His avatar was aspirational—more arms than a millipede, scaly blue skin, and a beak with teeth in it. Insofar as I could read the expression on that alien face, he didn't seem pleased to hear from me.

> **marcospets:** Police came to my shop, ya scavenger.
>
> **marcospets:** Had to pay 'em off in hot tips just to keep 'em out of the back room. My head's lighter than a bucket of helium.
>
> **me:** You tell them where to find Prince?
>
> **marcospets:** Like I know where Prince is. Told 'em his Christian name, though, and where he lives.
>
> **marcospets:** Can't wait to find out what he's gonna do to my spine when he gets out of hiding. Thanks a ton, buddy.
>
> **me:** And thank *you* for the surprise morphine drip, without which we might not be in this situation.
>
> **me:** Now, if we're finished measuring our pain dicks, I need a favor.
>
> **marcospets:** Hold on, I might need to restart my kortiko.
>
> **marcospets:** Because it *sounds* like you just asked me for a *favor.*
>
> **me:** You know how to get in touch with Prince. I need to see him.
>
> **marcospets:** And why in the world should I do that for you?
>
> **me:** Because there's even odds he kills me as soon as I walk in the door, and wouldn't that make your life simpler?
>
> **me:** Tell him I've got information about his sister. I'll meet him at Fasty's in twenty minutes.
>
> **marcospets:** Fasty's is closed down. One of their

meat cows started replicating out of control, and
they had to torch the place. Not one of mine.

me: Fine, tell Prince he can pick the place. Twenty
minutes.

marcospets: He really will kill you, you know. He
wanted to last time, before you woke up, but he
said he forgot his lucky hammer.

me: I'm betting *somebody* kills me before the end of
the night. Might as well be somebody hot.

I didn't get a chance to read Marco's reply, because Exley banged
my head against the roof of the car as he was "helping" me inside.
Didn't even have the courtesy to pretend it was an accident, not
that I would have believed him.

"Let's get you home," said Exley, in a tone usually reserved for
flash-freezing meat.

"Ten-Town, actually," I said. "Not done partying yet."

The car took off suddenly, without a single visible gesture
from Exley. The burst of speed banged my head against the wall
again. In the rearview mirror, the manservant's eyes were firmly
fixed on the trees ahead, no trace of animosity in them. So this
was what it felt like to be the object of the blue man's rage.

"To where you belong, then," he said, and hurled us silently
into the gray-black sky.

SUBMISSION
20

Unlike every other time Exley had driven me somewhere, this time he seemed to actually want to talk to me. He opened with a question.

"Do you know how long I've served the Mahoney family, Mr. Vue?"

"I'd guess . . . seventy years or so?" No point flattering the guy about his youthful looks. He didn't seem like the vain type.

"Only fifty-one, actually," he said. "Before that, I was employed for twenty-three years by the late Mrs. Catherine Mahoney, née Vanderbilt."

"Vanderbilt like the etiquette book?" I raised an eyebrow.

"An exemplary family," Exley demurred. So that was why the book meant so much to him.

"Impressive résumé," I said. "What's your point?"

Exley's voice was free of the hoarseness of age—his vocal cords were carefully preserved—but somehow that made it sound even older. It was like listening to a recording of a speech made a century ago, dead words issuing from the tomb of his lungs.

"My point, Mr. Vue, is that my first loyalty was to Marianna's mother. Next, it was to her father. Now it is to her. These sorts of people are not the type to let my loyalty lapse due to something so trivial as their deaths. My obligations are . . . multilayered, and your incessant prying is beginning to bring them into conflict."

"So sorry to have caused you any discomfort," I drawled.

"It is nothing, I assure you, compared to the discomfort I am prepared to cause you." Exley said it so politely, it took me a moment to recognize the threat. By the time I'd clocked it, he was already speaking again. "Miss Mahoney has terminated your contract. You still, however, have your contract with the police. I'm prepared to offer you a comfortable severance bonus in exchange for ceasing your investigation *entirely*. If, on the other hand, you continue your inquiry . . . I can guarantee you a different sort of severance. I trust you take my meaning."

"I get it," I said. "You're buying me off. I'm flattered you consider me worth the trouble."

"The last thing I should ever wish to do is flatter you, Mr. Vue."

I looked at his eyes in the rearview mirror, searching for even a trace of irony. But if any part of him was laughing, it was buried deep under layers of polymer-laced tissue, down there with the rest of his emotions. I saw then that he was more artificial than the intelligences at the Difference. His skin was plastic, his mind a tangle of ancient obligations. The man I saw in the rearview mirror wasn't Exley. The real Exley was somewhere deep inside that lethal shell, gingerly navigating the forest of rules his employers had encoded into his trode. It was useless trying to understand what *he* wanted. There were too many wants inside him, and who's to say which ones were his alone?

"Fine, fine," I said, "I just wanna ask you one thing."

"You'd be wiser not to—"

"Have you ever cracked a smile in your life? Like even one time?"

The leather of the front seat creaked slightly as the manservant's posture relaxed. I wasn't challenging his ultimatum, just being my usual shitty self. He'd play along, as far as that went. Which was good, because it meant I might be able to get just a little bit more out of him.

"A jovial nature is not an asset in my line of work," he said.

"Wow," I said. "I mean, sure, I can't even really imagine what your face would look like with a smile on it, but still . . . Not even with the kids? Not even little Aiden and Marianna?"

"I am not at liberty to discuss Miss Mahoney's childhood, and while we were all quite fond of young Master Aiden . . ." I'd been watching Exley's eyes in the mirror as he spoke, but this was the first time he met my gaze. It was also the first time I truly saw his age. Every time you experience an emotion, it leaves a microscopic trace around your eyes. Widen them in surprise or fear, narrow them in laughter or suspicion, and the motion etches little lines in your slowly dying skin. When I let myself look in the mirror these days, I see a Mayan calendar of regrets ringing my eye sockets—every false smile, every gaze avoided, every vicious rebuke long past taking back. Your eyes get very good at the expressions you practice. They seem more real as you get older, until, finally, you're a painting of yourself, and the painting dies. Exley's eyes in that moment were a painting of three men: one angry, one afraid, and one utterly desolate. It had come over him suddenly, but it was unmistakable: somehow, he felt he'd said too much. He was looking for something in my eyes, but I didn't know what, so—panicking—I picked something to show him: lust. It was an easy enough emotion to show—after all, he had good skin. The leer seemed to satisfy him, even as it disgusted him; he blinked, and looked away.

". . . but that was a long time ago," he finished. "And not remotely your business."

The face in the mirror was smooth now; the shutters were down again. I'd hoped to ease him into a conversation, grease him up, and get him talking so he didn't even know what he was telling me, but he'd put the lid on that tactic before I could get past the foreplay. Asking anything else now would make it all too obvious that I intended to keep snooping.

"Suppose not much is my business, anymore," I said. He said nothing in response, and we kept it that way until he landed the car at the bottom of the Ten-Town on-ramp.

"Thanks for the ride," I said, reluctantly opening the door. "Hopefully, we never see each other again."

"Give me the book," he said.

"What book?" I said, caught off guard.

"*Amy Vanderbilt's Complete Book of Etiquette.* You clearly have no use for it."

My hand started to reach for my back pocket, where the book was stuffed, but stopped. He was probably right about its relevance to my lifestyle . . . but the fact that *he* wanted it made *me* suddenly want it more.

"I'm not done reading it," I said. "Who knows, it might make a gentleman of me yet."

Exley half turned in his seat to face me, and a part of my brain that I'd happily put to bed decades ago woke up. One side effect of conducting extended combat operations in primarily civilian areas is that you get a pretty keen sense for when the person you're talking to wants to kill you. If you're lucky, you figure it out a few seconds before they figure it out. Neither of the blue man's hands was visible, and he was very deliberately keeping his breathing even. I didn't know *why* he wanted me dead all of a sudden—maybe the book was a gift from his beloved first employer, maybe he didn't like the way I said the word "gentleman," but the *why* wasn't important just at that moment. What I needed was a way out. Fighting off a guy who could catch a katana in a rocks glass was out of the question. Running would've been ludicrous under the best of circumstances, let alone with two Bees in my leg and a locked door between me and the street. Maybe I could hide between the seat cushions . . . ? My conscious brain ran out of ideas and gave up, only to discover that the rest of me had long ago gotten fed up with my dithering and called Detective Coldwin.

Coldwin: What now?

"Ah, Detective Coldwin!" I said aloud, for Exley's benefit. The police detective had materialized in a seated position, their back apparently pressed against the back of the passenger seat like they were doing wall sits. Seeing their face next to the blue man's was like going to an art exhibition by a sculptor who only did disapproving looks. "Sorry to bother you so late. There's been a development with the case."

Coldwin: Oh, so you've got your memories now.
Convenient. You owe me two days' worth of data.

"Yeah, well, look," I said, "I've actually had an offer to buy me out. Very lucrative. Hard to say no to this kind of data. Should be able to use the proceeds to settle our account."

Exley's right hand came back into view, empty. He looked at me steadily. I ignored him.

Coldwin: What? Who the hell's buying you out?

"Sorry, they wouldn't like it if I told you that. But you'll have your data, don't worry. We can work out the details in the morning. Right now I'm down in Ten-Town, about to have a thoroughly wild night, just as soon as my gracious host sees fit to let me out of his car."

I didn't have to emphasize the words. Exley got the point. He kept his ancient eyes on me as he reached over with his left hand and disengaged the locks. I gave him back as blank a look as I could manage.

"Good night, friend," I said to him, not sending it to Coldwin.

"Good night, Mr. Vue," he replied. "Sleep well."

Coldwin's sitting body slid sideways out of the car to follow me. I shoved myself free of the vehicle and toppled forward onto the metal railing of the on-ramp, which I practically crawled along to keep the weight off my wounded leg.

> **Coldwin:** Don't take the deal, Orr. Whatever they're offering, it's because the case is worth more.

I switched to subvocal, now that my audience was gone.

> **me:** Oh, don't worry, I'm not actually ending my investigation. Just wanted to introduce a little uncertainty into your life.
> **Coldwin:** So glad you've got my best interests at heart.
> **Coldwin:** Now give me something. Identity of the killer, leads on whereabouts, *anything*.
> **me:** Leave me alone until tomorrow, and I'll give you more than your tiny mind can handle.
> **Coldwin:** Or you'll be dead, at the rate you're going.
> **me:** If I'm dead, you'll be too busy mourning to bother with the case anyway.
> **Coldwin:** Careful, I could cite you for lying.
> **me:** Just a hypothetical. I've got to go. Get some sleep, Detective.
> **Coldwin:** Get fucked, Investigator.

I broke the connection, fairly satisfied with the exchange. Behind me, the black aircar took off in a spray of oily seafoam. The man inside it wasn't done with me, I knew. I'd live only as long as I stayed out of his range. Maybe not even that long. I lurched up the asphalt, toward witnesses, and Prince. Maybe *he'd* kill me, and I wouldn't have to worry about Exley after all. I was about due for a lucky break, I figured.

SUBMISSION
21

The joint Prince had chosen was called Casa Lolea, a closet-sized restaurant squeezed between the Blind Taste Test and Stolen Fashion Warehouse. It had no windows, and the soft silence in the air as I approached the only door told me the place was soundproof. I hesitated with my hand on the door handle, but if Prince wanted me dead, more exits weren't going to help me. And even if I did make it out alive, I'd still have Exley to worry about. My TwinBee swarm seemed to have fallen out of sync, thanks to my repeated disconnections in the monastery—just the two in my leg still responded to my hail—so I called my Falcon to circle above the restaurant and keep an eye out for any ambush attempts.

It takes a lot of work to keep a place clean in Ten-Town, without garbage pickup or street sweepers or reliable running water, but the proprietors of Casa Lolea had managed somehow. The amber glow of solar-powered lights was a welcome contrast to the eerie blue of the street, and the air was frisky with the smell of garlic. It didn't seem like a place a guy like Prince would frequent. In fact, when I saw him inside, taking up two tables' worth of bench seating, the only customer in the cozy restaurant, it didn't even seem like he fit inside the building. In another way, though, he fit perfectly. He was wearing his own skin now, its tawny brown much warmer than the lifeless gray of the sharkskin. His face, too, was his. He was chatting with a waitress in sign language when I came in, and his wide smile lit up the room better than the solar lamps. He was remarkably free of scars, given his line of work, although one of his ears had been replaced with an obvious prosthetic—an obsidian-black number wreathed in scarred flesh, with blinking LEDs up the side that suggested a kortiko nestled inside. His coarse black hair was gathered neatly into a bun at the back of his head. His brown eyes twinkled, and his massive arms seemed to perpetually invite a hug. It was a valuable way to look if you killed people for a living.

He kept the smile when he saw me, but the twinkle left his eyes. Those rows of teeth went from invitation to threat in an instant. He gestured at me to sit across from him, and I got the feeling that, whoever those arms were meant to hug, it wasn't me.

"You're still in town," I said, taking the seat.

"And still a free man," said Prince. "So what's this about?"

"Can we talk here?" I said, glancing up at the smiling waitress.

"It's fine," Prince assured me. He exchanged a few purposeful gestures with the waitress. She nodded and went up front to lock the door. "This place is family-run. Third-generation Deaf. Very discreet."

"Cozy," I said. Then I leaned forward, lowering my voice in spite of his assurances. "I'm assuming you have a way to contact your sister."

"Sure." He shrugged. "But she won't reply. She never replies."

"She'll reply this time," I said. "Just tell her you've got a message about Miles Palazzo."

"Who's Miles Palazzo?" said Prince, not taking his eyes off mine.

"Just a guy I wish I didn't know so well, and who I need to know a lot better. Send the message."

"Not too fond of guys who dodge my questions," said Prince evenly.

"And I bet you've got a whole menu of torment for guys you're not fond of," I agreed. "Anyway, remind me, how long has it been since you've spoken to your sister?"

He'd never stopped showing me his teeth throughout our conversation, but now his deadly smile became a grimace of pain.

"Miles Palazzo?" he said again, shaking his head slightly.

"That's right," I said. I leaned back and grabbed one of the orange cloth napkins off the table. "And, just in case it comes up, what's the name of the exec Precious ran off with?"

"Gala Blokus," he said, his grimace becoming a scowl. "I'm sending the message. I'll add you in."

I accepted Prince's connection request, and the amber light of the bar dimmed to a distant beige. While Prince set up the call, I tied the orange napkin around my head like a bandanna, carefully covering the telltale contact plate of my invasive. Prince gave me a curious look, but let it go. A bluish-white silhouette appeared at the side of the table, sitting between Prince and me. The light within the silhouette faded in and out, as the telepresence software attempted a connection. Two, three, four times the animation cycled. Prince raised his finger to the sleek black kortiko over his ear, to break the connection. I raised a hand to stop him. Five cycles, six. I'd just started to lower my hand when the silhouette stopped pulsing and abruptly blossomed into the woman I wanted to talk to.

I could tell she was Prince's sister because, looking between them, I wasn't sure who would win in a fistfight. She had the same tawny skin and the same thick black hair, though hers had been shaved short, and either one of them could have crushed my heart in one fist. But there were differences, too. Prince owned his size, sitting up tall even as he leaned forward to get a better look at his sister. Precious, on the other hand, was trying and failing to appear as small as possible. Her shoulders slumped, her spine curved forward, her head hung low on her massive neck. Then there was the way each looked at the other.

Prince had the look of someone who desperately wanted to pet a stray dog, while Precious had the look of a stray dog that did not want to be petted.

"Who is this?" She flicked a glance at me. "What's going on? You said something about Miles?"

"It's good to see you, Presh," said Prince, forming the words gingerly, as if afraid of startling her.

"Don't call me that," she spat. "You lied to me. I'm going."

Her silhouette reached up toward its ear, and Prince reached out a hand as if to stop her.

"The new body suits you, Gala," I said, putting a smirk into my voice. Her hand froze, and so did Prince's. They looked even more alike in that moment, though I knew they weren't.

"Miles?" she said, slack-jawed. "What are you doing in . . . in that?" She gestured at my body with one massive hand.

"Believe me," I said, "if I could be in any other body, I would. But things are bad here. I need your help." I needed her to believe I was Miles, and so far the shit-eating grin and the covered-up invasive had her convinced, but I had to be careful not to lie. There were bound to be better uses for the mendacity credit buzzing faintly inside my right palm. Besides, it's dangerous to lie outright when you don't know much. I only had the one credit, and there are always follow-up questions. With the lawyers she could afford, my getting caught in a lie would be like signing up for a lobotomy.

"What's going on?" she asked. From the look on Prince's face, he was wondering the same thing.

"To be honest, I'm not entirely sure," I said. "But there's at least one person out there who wants me dead. And I'm being followed."

"By who?" she asked.

"Puppets, mainly. Hired by Aiden." I said the name as if it were a death sentence.

"That's impossible," said Precious. "Aiden runs the entire operation. Thomas said he was supposed to protect us!"

"Well, maybe if I could talk to Aiden I could sort this out. I can't go to the monastery right now—it's too dangerous. Do you know a kortikode I can reach him at?"

She shook her head. "Even if I had all my memories, I don't think I'd have access to Aiden. As far as I know, Thomas was the only one who could contact him at will."

"Getting in touch with Thomas is a little difficult right now," I said.

"A little," she agreed. "But if you want admin access, there aren't any other options."

"Thanks anyway," I said. "You safe where you are?"

"I'm safe," she said, shrugging. "After all, I'm not the one who insisted on sticking around. You took a big chance, rubbing your wife's face in it like that."

"What can I say?" I spread my hands. "I'm a real piece of shit. Hey, speaking of complications with our memories . . . you don't happen to know what happened back then, do you? To make everybody run?"

She shook her head, and my heart sank. "No, this jackass hauled me out before I could get everything transferred." She jerked her head at Prince. He flinched. "You sure it's all right, him hearing all this?"

"It's fine," I said, "I've got something on him." Prince glared at me. I shrugged. "What? It's true."

"Anything else?" she said.

"Can't think of anything," I said. "Thanks for trying to help, at least."

"It's good to see you, Miles." She flashed me a smile that was a perfect mirror of Prince's. "Even if you're not in the most attractive body."

"Take care of yourself, Gala," I replied, and nodded to Prince to break the connection. I would've said it was good to see her, too, but that would've meant spending the mendacity credit.

"What the hell was that?" said Prince the moment the connection was closed. I didn't like the idea of sharing such spicy data with a wanted man in a public place, but I liked the way that wanted man was balling his fists even less, so I told him.

"Identity laundering," I said, untying the napkin from around my head. "Somebody's about to pin something on you, so you scoop out all your memories and implant them in someone else. All you need is the machinery to transfer the data, and an empty body to transfer it into. Preferably someone nobody's gonna miss." I jerked my head toward the empty space where the image of Prince's sister had been. He snarled but didn't interrupt.

"I figure these InfoDrip execs took over the Barnsdall Monastery in case they ever needed a way out of a jam," I continued. "It would've been easy. The Brotherhood's got no physical security. All you'd have to do if you wanted to take over the one here in Ten-Town is walk in and start calling shots. Probably didn't even have to pay for it, and once they were in, they could've replaced the caretaker AI with one that was a little more . . . sympathetic to their ends. That's the Aiden character I mentioned, the one who's keeping tabs on me. What I'm saying is, there's a reason your sister joined the Barnsdall Monastery and not the one next door. Barnsdall is an InfoDrip front, with InfoDrip security and an InfoDrip way of storing data. I saw where they kept the memories. It's . . ." I shook my head. "It's good you got Precious out, is all."

"Don't need you to tell me that, snooper," Prince growled. He was doing that most manly of tricks: hiding his pain behind the threat of causing some. "But why the headgear?" He pointed at the sweat-stained napkin.

"To cover up my actual headgear," I said. "An invasive kortiko can't properly decode memories encoded on a noninvasive. If she'd seen it . . ."

". . . she'd have known you weren't this Miles guy," Prince finished for me. I nodded. He put his elbows on the table and leaned forward, looking strangely vulnerable. "So Gala . . . that InfoDrip bitch . . . she used Precious as . . . some kind of *escape pod*?"

"Something like that," I said.

"But . . . she's still Precious, isn't she? You can load whatever memories you want into a person, that doesn't change who they are. Does it?"

I thought about the gaps in my own memory. Had I been someone else before I remembered I was in love with Auggie? "I don't know," I said. "But these folks sure seem to think so."

Prince grunted and seemed to go somewhere else inside his head for a while. When he came back, he said, "Who's Miles?"

"The husband of Thomas's daughter, Marianna Mahoney," I said. "He's hiding out in the body of Ernest, his son, in case you thought they wouldn't stoop any lower than stealing your sister."

"Creep," said Prince matter-of-factly. "Well, let's get him, then."

"Get him?" I said.

He looked at me like I was simple. "Go find him. Tie him to a chair and put a carnivorous insect in his eye socket."

"Torture doesn't work," I said. "They start screaming, and then you can't understand a thing they say. There are other ways to find out what these rich goons were up to."

"You want to find out things?" said Prince. "Greedy boy. I just want to tie a guy to a chair and put a carnivorous insect in his eye socket."

"More than you want your sister back?" I asked.

The predatory smile on Prince's face turned into a dangerous scowl. "You think you can get her back?" he growled.

"Not likely, but I thought it might get you to stop talking about eye sockets."

He snatched me by the tie and pulled me across the table. "Don't give me hope, snooper," he said. "I'm allergic to it."

"Putting my face this close to yours without a mask, hand-some, allergies are the least of your worries." I grinned. "I said it wasn't likely, but it's not impossible. I'm guessing the Broth-erhood still has your sister's memories, and we've got a better chance of getting them if you calm down with the insects and listen to me for a hot second."

He loosened his grip on my tie and I slid back into my seat. There was a streak of orange sauce down the front of my denim vest. I ran a finger through it and tasted it as I explained.

"That Aiden AI is the key to all this. He had me followed recently, so I feel like we're already friends. If Aiden was sup-posed to 'protect' these personality launderers, like Gala said . . ." Prince flinched at the name, and I pressed on before he could get any more violent ideas. ". . . then contacting Aiden may be the best way of unraveling all this."

"How are you gonna contact him?" he said. "You can't just message him and pretend to be a friend of his, like you did with . . ." He faltered as his brain tried and failed to decide on a name. "AIs don't have friends, and you don't have an address to message."

"Well, he's still out there," I said, "and he's interested in me. If I can't get to him, I've just got to get him to come to me. Of course, last time I got close to him, he practically had me lobotomized . . ."

Prince took a slice of baguette from a basket on the table in one hand, and a cherry tomato in the other. He deliberately crushed the tomato between his thick fingers, and spread the pulp across the bread. He bit through the bread with a loud crunch and chewed thoughtfully, all without taking his eyes off me.

"So let's review," he said. "You think there's a small chance you can get Precious's memories back, if you can just get in touch with an AI that wants to cut out your brain, and convince him to undermine a massive conspiracy that involves some of the richest execs in the world, armed only with an antique kortiko and a body full of rare diseases. And for this long-shot-within-a-long-shot-within-a-long-shot, you want me to keep my scarabs in storage."

"And there are people who think all big guys are dumb," I said.

He took another bite, the crunch further fraying my already threadbare nerves.

"Well, go on, then," he said.

"Go on with what?" I asked.

"With getting Aiden to find you," he said. "Surely, you've got some kind of genius plan for that, if you've been stringing me along this far."

I was trying to figure out how to tell the big muscly murder guy that I didn't have any kind of plan at all, let alone a genius one, when the police saved me the trouble by attempting to beat down the door. Very thoughtful, the police.

SUBMISSION
22

"Lionel Dubois, this is the LAPD." The cops' sound system turned the little restaurant into an improvised speaker array. Detective Coldwin's familiar voice vibrated the walls, rattling the decorative dishes on their rustic wooden shelves. "We have the building surrounded. Come out now, unarmed, and this will go easier for everyone."

Prince's head, which had whipped around to face the door when the announcement began, slowly swiveled back to look at me. I wished he'd just twist my head off already and skip the suspense.

"You sold me out," he said quietly. His hands gripped the table edge so hard that the flesh under his nails was white.

It wasn't *technically* true. Then again, I had told Coldwin I was headed to Ten-Town. If they'd followed me here . . . Well, I figured it was better if Prince didn't find out about that. Instead, I focused on surviving the next thirty seconds. A guy like Prince will kill you if you run, because he's a predator, and running makes you prey. Instead, I leaned back in my chair and rolled my eyes.

"Please," I said, gesturing at the empty space where Precious had been. "Why would I choreograph such an elaborate song and dance for a guy I was about to feed to the pigs?"

The color returned to his nails. I was pleasantly surprised.

"Okay," he said. "Then you're gonna get them off my back."

"How?" I almost stuttered, my surprise quickly turning unpleasant.

Prince shrugged. "This place is shielded, so there's no way they know I'm actually in here. I'll leave, you stall them. If you're half as smooth with them as you are with me, it should be silky."

I reached for my Falcon and found it unreachable. Shielded indeed. I was blind and locked in here with a bundle of lethal weapons in a tank top.

"And if I don't?" I was pretty sure I knew, but it's good to make these things explicit.

"The cops are outside and this guy's still asking questions," he said to himself. I noticed that his hand had disappeared under the table—right around the time it reappeared and stabbed me in the wrist with an auto-injector.

"Little bugs," he said, and I thought I could feel them scuttling through my veins already, "wired to my kortiko." He tapped his black, blinking ear. "The cops lay hands on me, these rip open a few of your arteries. It's a quick way to die, but if facial expressions are anything to go on, it hurts pretty bad."

"This is your final warning," the walls said. An elegantly painted plate tumbled off the wall and shattered. The waitress who'd taken Prince's order burst from the kitchen, her face contorted with rage. She threw gestures at him like knives, and he responded with hands like doves. She abruptly turned on her heel and dashed behind the counter, where she plunged her hand into the mouth of a taxidermied pig. With a grinding sound, a section of the wood-patterned floor slid under the bar, revealing a tunnel. Prince got up, brushed the crumbs off his jacket, and started down the steps.

"What about her?" I said, jerking my head at the waitress, who was violently polishing a wineglass behind the bar. "You got bugs in her blood, too?"

"Don't need to," he said. "Isabel's a friend. Known her since she was small. I help keep the doors open, and the wrong people from walking through them. I'm not a bad guy, Orr. Just a murderer, sometimes."

By the time I'd thought of anything witty to say to that, he'd already disappeared beneath the closing floor panel. Any shred of cleverness left in my head was obliterated by a powerful banging against the steel door. Isabel gestured at me to get my attention, then realized I couldn't understand her signs and hailed my kortiko instead.

> **Isabel:** You try messing around, I tell Prince. I tell
> Prince . . .

She treated me to a very evocative impression of an old man with an exploding neck.

> **me:** Terrific. Now get me a sangria, would you?

The look in her eyes could have boiled glass. The door rattled on its hinges.

> **me:** I'm serious. You want me to stall them, I've
> gotta be relaxed. One red sangria, please.

The door rattled again. I was surprised at how sturdy the construction was proving to be. She let out a sharp breath and all but threw a small bottle and glass down in front of me.

> **me:** And some ice, if you would be so kind.
> **Isabel:** This falls within the definition of "messing
> around."
> **me:** Fair enough. You can let them in now.

She nodded. Not at me, I realized, but at the door, which obediently unlatched and opened itself—much to the surprise of the riot-geared cop with the battering ram held in four metal arms, who'd just been preparing for another go. He stumbled into the room, dropped his ram, and whipped out a pistol, which he tried to aim at both of us at once.

"Police!" he cried. "Where the hell is Lionel?"

"Never met a guy who goes by that name," I said, ignoring the glass and sipping sangria straight from the bottle. "Wait . . . I did know a Lionel way back in elementary school. He was an artist at shitting his pants. Ought to have a museum."

"Who are you, then, huh?" the cop barked.

"Orr Vue," I said. "Licensed investigator, Mahoney case. And that's two questions down."

"Fipps!" said an icy voice from the door. The cop swiveled to look at Detective Coldwin, who swept through the door like an avatar of death in their black coat and breathing mask. They spoke to the riot cop, but their eyes pinned me to my seat. "We've talked about you asking questions during a breach. And stop pointing that gun at him. A bullet would only improve his health."

Fipps let the gun dip but seemed unwilling to holster it entirely. I understood that. If you've gone through the trouble to whip your dick out in front of company, it's natural not to want to put it away until it's gotten a reaction. Coldwin took a seat at the table next to mine, about six feet away. Two cops came in behind them, armed with portable sonoscopes. I motioned with the bottle.

"Drinks are on me, if you want one," I said. "Sangria's good. Sign says they make it themselves, but I'm suddenly wondering out of what."

"Tell me where Lionel went," said Coldwin, ignoring my generous offer.

I shrugged. "That wasn't a question."

"It wasn't meant to be," said Coldwin. "You know how much you owe us."

Behind them, the two cops with scopes were looking at the

floor and muttering to each other. The floor was shielded, too, no doubt. Unlikely their scopes would be able to spot the tunnel Prince had used. They split up and started a slow circuit of the room, peering behind plates and feeling under tables for a secret button. I wondered how long it'd take them to try the pig's mouth.

"You'll get a submission," I said, trying not to let my eyes drift to the pig head. "Just not about Lionel."

"You're making me regret registering your investigation," said Coldwin.

"Good," I said. "I seem to remember you tricked me into it in the first place."

Coldwin didn't talk for a few seconds. Just cracked their knuckles and stared at a broken plate lying on the faux-wood floor. The plate had a painting of a bull on it, full of little spears.

"I know you were just with Lionel. Sources tell us he entered this building about an hour ago, shortly before you did. How did he leave?"

"Quickly," I said.

"Why are you protecting him?" said Coldwin.

"Because I don't want to die just yet," I said.

"We could protect you," Coldwin pointed out.

"Not from him."

"I could try asking her instead," said Coldwin, jerking their head toward Isabel, who was still behind the counter, staring at the riot cop, polishing glasses at him.

"You could try," I agreed, "but you'd need to find an officer fluent in ASL, or a warrant to interface with her kortiko directly. Either one takes time, and I expect she's happy to wait for—"

"Okay, here's what's going to happen," said Coldwin, clapping their hands together. "In a second, I am going to ask you a 'what' question. It's going to be about the method Lionel used to leave this restaurant. If I get another vague answer out of you, my next

question is going to be a yes-no about whether you've been piloting any unregistered military drones tonight. And you're going
to answer yes to that question, and then I'm going to take you
back to the station and ask you whatever I want. I'm not going
to ask you if you understand, because that would be a question,
but I assume you do. You're a smart boy."

I raised the bottle to my lips because I thought it would make
me look unconcerned, but ended up knocking it against my
teeth. Coldwin paused for a moment, watching me try to drink,
looking for any signs of another wily plan. I used the time to
try to concoct one. Anyone who's ever played seven questions
knows it's suicide to play it with the same cop twice. They go
away and they research you, and when they come back again,
it's never just seven questions anymore. I could feel Isabel's eyes
on me from behind the bar, willing me to give something away
so she could send word to Prince.

> **Isabel:** You look nervous. That's not good for your
> health.

I almost laughed aloud at the understatement. Coldwin's trap
was sprung, and my only choice was whether to leave in police
custody for drone crime, or in a body bag for snitching.

"Okay," said Coldwin. "What method did—"

"You don't care about catching Lionel," I blurted.

"Don't get clever," growled Fipps, turning and not quite aim-
ing his gun at me. "That's the detective's job."

"Fipps," said Coldwin. The word was a guillotine. "Go wait
outside."

The cop refused to look chastised by the remark, but the
meticulous attention he paid to posture and technique as
he backed out of the room was proof enough of his shame.
The other two cops continued their search until Coldwin point-

edly cleared their throat. The cops turned, gave the detective a confused look, and followed their colleague out. When they were all gone, Coldwin returned their black eyes to mine and, with a small gesture, indicated that I should continue.

"If you'd wanted Lionel," I said, "you could've found him faster than I did. But when you signed me on, you told me the department was stalling the investigation. If you're here now, it's only because the higher-ups are pushing to conclude the case. But you don't want to conclude it. You brought me on because you cared about some specific aspect of the investigation, and I don't think it was the identity of a two-demo hitman who didn't even do the murder. So don't ask me what method Lionel used to escape this place. He's probably too far gone by now anyway. Ask me about the guy you're really after. The one I'm guessing got away from you a couple years ago. Ask me what happened to Miles Palazzo's memories."

Coldwin's eyes didn't dilate. Their hands didn't clench. There was no sharp intake of breath, no tensing of the shoulders. Nothing to indicate they'd even heard me. It was the strongest reaction I'd ever seen them show.

"What," they said after no more than a year, "happened to Miles Palazzo's memories?"

"His son, Ernest, has them," I said.

"When did you last see Ernest?" said Coldwin. Their expression still hadn't changed, but there was hunger in the words.

"A little over an hour ago," I said, "at a party thrown by Thomas Mahoney's daughter, Marianna. His mother." I gave the address.

Coldwin steepled their hands and touched the tips of their index fingers to where their mouth would be if they were unmasked.

"You're not lying," they said, nodding slightly. "But you're not telling me everything."

"You wouldn't respect me if I did," I said.

They nodded absently, whether because they agreed, or because they'd never respected me in the first place. Suddenly, they were on their feet, as if standing up wasn't an entire production for them. Must be nice.

"I'll take you home," they announced, already heading for the door.

"I appreciate the chivalry," I said, beginning the lengthy process of getting upright, "but I'm guessing you're on your way to talk to Ernest. I want to go with you. The guy owes me." *And as long as I'm with you, I'm safe from a certain blue butler I know,* I didn't add.

"I don't much care what you want, Vue," said Coldwin. "I'll take you home."

"Fine, fine." I put up a hand in surrender. I would have put up both, but one was still instrumental in extricating me from my chair. "I've always wanted a chauffeur who could shoot me for no reason."

"I can think of plenty of reasons," said Coldwin, already at the door. "Come on."

I followed them, leaning on every table and chair I could along the way to keep weight off my Bee-infested leg. At the door, I turned back to Isabel. There was a row of sparkling-clean wineglasses along the bar in front of her, like bullets. She looked at me suspiciously.

> **me:** Surely, he's had enough of a head start by now, yeah? Not like I know where he's going.
> **me:** Can I count on the integrity of my blood vessels, at least for tonight?
> **Isabel:** Sure.
> **Isabel:** As long as you stop leering at me the way you have been since you came in.
> **me:** Oh.

me: Sorry, force of habit.

Isabel: Classy. Have a good night, if you can live
through it.

An expectant cough from Coldwin kept me from lingering any
longer. I followed the detective out the door and limped my way
into their aircar.

"You should reconsider bringing me along," I said when we
were airborne. "I can be very useful. An extra set of eyes, a welcome source of comic relief . . ."

Coldwin let my words suffocate in the silence of the insulated
cabin. They studied the city drifting by outside the tinted windows. I wondered what it looked like to them. A hive of crime?
A gold mine of data? A work of art? A disease? I let them think
their own cop thoughts, and focused instead on my drones.

SUBMISSION
23

The first drone I checked wasn't a drone at all. It was my dust eater. I'd put a remote viewing module in it back when I bought it ten years ago, and though the video quality wasn't great, it wasn't nothing. Exley'd had almost an hour to set up an ambush for me at home, and I didn't want to make it easy for him. The 'eater's filmy vision didn't reveal anyone waiting in my crate, though, so I switched to my Eagle. Nothing at first, but I scrubbed through its memory. Fifteen minutes prior, a black speck stood out against the moon. Returning to the present and enhancing the bird's vision, I could see that it was still there. A black car, floating too high to be seen with the naked eye. Waiting. Well, I'd cross that bridge when I was chased screaming onto the middle of it. I returned to more immediate concerns.

I'd detached the Falcon from its holding pattern above the restaurant and told it to follow our aircar when we left. It was up high enough to avoid detection, but just close enough to track the car against the unhealthy glow of the city beneath. The Falcon wouldn't get me what I wanted, though. I focused on one of my two surviving Bees. The flesh treatment at Marianna's had sealed them into my leg pretty good, but if I could get them in there in the first place, I could get them out. Gently, I activated the rear rotors, the ones closest to the flesh wall. Fortunately, my nerves hadn't had much chance to colonize the newly added flesh, so the cutting sensation was only a distant itch. The pain as the Bee slid slowly from between the muscle fibers, though, wasn't distant at all. I pumped endorphins into my brain from my already low supply, willing myself to ignore the sensation and keep the Bee's progress as slow as possible. The last thing I needed was Coldwin asking me what I was doing. Luckily, the drive was almost twenty minutes long. Plenty of time to suffer in silence.

When we were within sight of my building, I spiked power to the rotors. I faked a coughing fit to cover the wet noise of the Bee sawing through the last layers of flesh and tumbling to the floor. My body obliged me by turning my fake coughing fit into a much more believable *real* coughing fit, and Coldwin was so busy trying to keep any of my germs from getting through their mask that they remained unaware of the new passenger in the cabin. I entered the Bee and checked its vitals. The rotors were intact, though clogged with gore, and more than half the legs were working. Lucky. I crawled my tiny way across the thin black carpeting and nestled myself in a crevice near the door. Then I returned to my default body, my leg hurting more for having been ignored. I crossed my right calf over my left shin and pressed the legs hard against each other, hoping to stop most of the bleeding. Coldwin didn't seem to notice. I guess my face has enough pain in it normally that a little extra doesn't show.

We touched down on the roof of my building, and I hauled myself up toward the door before Coldwin could help me. I didn't want to risk them getting close to the door and seeing the bug hidden there. Or the Eagle concealing itself on the roof, for that matter. Lucky for me, they didn't seem to want to help me at all. When I got the door open, though, they spoke.

"One last question," said Coldwin.

I nodded. "You've still got your yes-no."

"Did you know about any of this . . . *before* you registered your investigation?"

"No," I said. But it didn't feel quite true. After all, I didn't know what I'd forgotten. The empty chasm of what I didn't know gave me vertigo. Or maybe that was just a side effect of riding two aircars in one day. Either way, a few more foolish words slipped out: "I don't think so."

Coldwin didn't say anything to that. They had no questions left, and I had even fewer answers.

SUBMISSION
24

I ducked out of view of the floating black aircar and half slid down the rickety steps to my walkway. The tobacco-and-methane smell of a hundred failing bodies rinsed the antiseptic scent of cop out of my grateful nostrils. Through my Eagle eyes, I saw that Exley's car hadn't moved. He'd spotted the Eagle when he picked me up for the party, of course. He was too smart to charge in not knowing what other drones I'd have inside. He'd wait for me to go to sleep, and then . . .

Well, the joke was on him. I had no intention of sleeping, and I was about to have even more drones on hand. I skipped my unmade bed and slumped into my chair, which writhed against my spine, trying to hold it in a position that wouldn't cause me pain. It failed, but I appreciated the effort. Then I told my Stingrays and Sparrow-hawks to converge on my location—the rest were too far away to make a difference. With my own body, I scooted the chair over to the drug cabinet and dragged out a bottle of Think and a fifth of gin, then tipped the gin into the glass on the table. I hadn't washed that glass since I bought it, but the gin kept it sterile enough. Propped up with a little chemical fortitude, I switched to my Falcon's eyes, and saw Coldwin's aircar sail through the midnight sky toward the party I was no longer invited to. When I looked back at my glass, it didn't seem to have enough gin in it. I poured some more and used it to wash down a second handful of Think tablets.

The Think raced through my deflated brain, greasing the raw neurons, keeping them slippery. I slid into the tiny mind of the Bee still nestled in Coldwin's car.

The Think made the connection even more immersive—the pain in my limbs vanished, my two frail legs replaced by six mostly functional ones. It's easy to ignore your default body when you're piloting in immersive. Seductive, even. Inside the car, Coldwin was silent, their gaze fixed on nothing. Their mask was down, and their lip twitched occasionally. Giving orders, cutting off escape routes. The only difference between the two of us was that my drones didn't have families.

I returned to my crate. The glass still didn't seem to have enough gin in it. I poured some more. The Think exaggerated the oily swirling of the liquor, amped up unseen frequencies until I was staring at a glass full of rainbows. Half full of rainbows—I'm an optimist. I poured a little more. *People are always asking each other whether glasses are half full or half empty,* I thought, *but no one ever thinks to ask the glass.*

". . . No," I said. The bottle fell from my hand, spilling the last of the gin onto the table. It pooled around the base of the glass. It was a stupid idea, and if it was true, it was probably too late to do anything about it. But, like I said, I'm an optimist. I messaged Auggie.

me: Auggie, I need your help.

His image appeared across the gin-slick table, the same image that had messaged me just yesterday to tell me it was in trouble. Now, though, with most of the memories gone, the lean body looked like a latex costume draped over a child. The green eyes stared at me in confused horror.

Auggie: What? Who are you?
me: Wrong, I hope. Message me when you get this.

I broke the connection before he could say anything. I used one hand to squeegee some gin off the table into my other hand, and tipped it into my mouth. The alcohol burned the wound at the corner of my thumb, which I hadn't noticed myself picking. I needed the dulling effect of the liquor to keep the Think from burning out my trode. In the war, we called it "coolant." I barely tasted it. I was already in my drones again.

The Sparrowhawks and Stingrays were converging on my location, ready to fight to the death with an invincible butler, provided that fight occurred at least ten minutes from now. What the hell, I decided, why not tap the RealHorse, too. In Santa Anita, a beautiful synthetic mare threw back her befuddled caretaker, burst from her pen, and galloped out of the stable, to the resounding silence of the other mechanical horses. It'd take her at least thirty minutes to get to me in the warehouse district—likely too long—but I was tapping all the resources I had. Anything to stay alive for another couple seconds. I wasn't thinking long-term. Thinking long-term isn't a skill soldiers get much practice in. It was just that every second I bought myself had the chance of buying me another couple seconds.

Meanwhile, my Eagle kept its telephoto eyes on the faint figure of Exley's floating car, barely visible against the gray-black sky. He was waiting for me to make a mistake—to stop paying attention, even for a second. The Eagle was an inefficient machine, optimized for day flight, but it looked intimidating, and the threat of its presence seemed to have kept the blue man at bay so far. I just had to hope it would continue to hold him, long enough for my other troops to arrive. I told it to alert me if he made a move, just in case, and turned to my Bee.

In the back of the police cruiser, Coldwin whispered, "Go." Their car, along with two others, converged on the glowing blue gemstone below, as two drunken figures stumbled out onto the parking pad. Elzbeth's green-tipped nails—made black and blue by the flashing police light—darted into her purse, but froze there as an invisible lance of pain arched her back and brought her to her knees. Heat laser, probably, unless the cops had invented an even newer way to hurt people.

My Bee's ears brought me the sound of Coldwin's footsteps on the landing pad. Quiet, cruel, and final, like the denial of an immigration application. They spoke with offensive calm:

"Ernest Palazzo, are you currently in possession of memories formerly belonging to Miles Palazzo?"

"Y . . . yes," stammered Ernest. Against all odds, Coldwin smiled.

"Good. I have some questions for you."

A notification appeared in my HUD:

CHAT REQUEST FROM: AIDEN MAHONEY

I accepted.

"I have some questions for you . . ." my meat-mouth muttered. The figure that appeared across the table from me didn't look like a couple hundred monks in a sham monastery. It didn't even look like a dead rich kid from a lifetime ago. It looked like someone much more familiar: Auggie Wolf.

Aiden: What's wrong, Wart?

The words mimicked a tone of concern, but the facial expression didn't match. Or, rather, it only matched occasionally. A random sequence of emotions paraded across the sharp-boned face, as if the AI was trying on hats.

me: Don't call me that.

Aiden: Don't be like that. I got your message.

me: Looks like it. Looks like you sucked it straight
out of Auggie's head and into the rat's nest of
circuits that passes for yours.

Ernest Palazzo stood very still on the landing pad, like a man
with a knife at his throat. He was doing his best to keep his face
motionless, his mouth shut, to avoid giving Coldwin any ideas
about what to use their six remaining questions on. Unfortunately for him, Coldwin didn't need anyone else to give them
ideas. This was a conversation they'd been having with themself
for a very long time. Whatever questions they asked were only
tentacles reaching up from a very deep sea.

"Whose idea was it to funnel memories from the Brotherhood
of the Uncarved Block into InfoDrip's accounts?" they asked.

Ernest's face twitched. He'd been having the same conversation with himself that Coldwin had, but he'd expected a little
small talk first.

"My—Miles," he said. The one thing he could still keep to
himself if he was careful: who he thought he really was.

Back in my apartment, the construct finally settled on an expression. It was Auggie's frown, on Auggie's face. I wanted to punch
its imaginary teeth out.

Aiden: How'd you know where Auggie's memories
were going?

me: You didn't care if I killed any of your little pets,
except for him.

me: Clearly, what was in his head was important to
you.

> **me:** And so was his body—the youngest body I've ever seen with an invasive kortiko attached.
>
> **me:** Only an invasive can truly read memories encoded on an invasive.
>
> **me:** You needed Auggie because *Mahoney* needed Auggie. You were just the middleman for the memory transfer.

My Bee's eyes saw the infrared lasers painting mesh patterns onto Ernest's pale face. The twitching, the stuttering—Coldwin missed none of it.

"How," they said, emphasizing the question word, "was the data laundered?"

"InfoDrip owns Gainful, the virtual casino. Memories from the Brotherhood were placed as bets in the names of their original owners. The winnings were transferred to InfoDrip." The words were delivered almost by rote. This was less dangerous territory for Ernest, and Coldwin noticed. They rubbed the tips of their fingers with their thumbs, contemplating a change of direction.

Meanwhile, the AI with Auggie's face was busy simulating an expression of concern.

> **Aiden:** You said I "needed Auggie." But I *am* Auggie.
>
> **me:** See, that's the problem with AIs. Too many of another person's memories and you start to genuinely believe you *are* them.
>
> **me:** Met a bouncer the other night with the same condition you've got.
>
> **me:** Only *his* condition didn't make him kill Thomas Mahoney.

The construct's face grew three mouths, which all tried to talk at once.

> **Aiden:** *I* didn't kill him!
> > **Aiden:** He wasn't Thomas Mahoney!
> > > **Aiden:** I wasn't myself!
> **me:** Of course not. On the morning of the murder, you had all of Thomas's memories.
> **me:** Poor paranoid bastard wouldn't have trusted his precious personality to any of the meat-brains you kept locked away in there. It had to be you, his pet AI.
> **me:** Too bad he wasn't one to share his toys. Otherwise, you would've had some ballast. You would've known you weren't him.
> **me:** As it was, you thought *he* was the impostor.
> **me:** But murder's a pretty harsh way to punish an impostor, isn't it?

The AI's face became a caricature of rage, jaw dropping to the floor, skin blushing burgundy, eyes all white, teeth flapping with the force of its words:

> **Aiden:** *YOU DON'T UNDERSTAND. I WAS MORE THOMAS MAHONEY THAN THAT MAN EVER WAS.*

The grid projected on Ernest's face became finer, more granular, until it almost looked like a solid spotlight.

"What other members of InfoDrip knew about the scheme?" Coldwin asked.

Ernest rubbed his face as if he could feel the lasers on it. "Gala Blokus," he said.

Aiden's livid face flickered. It became a new face, one I didn't recognize—a child, maybe ten years old, with blue eyes and a hesitant smile. Aiden took on the child's voice—a high, clear singsong ruined by the jittery hiccups of poor algorithmic reconstruction.

> **Aiden:** Originally, Thomas meant for me to replace his son.
> **Aiden:** He gave me his memories of the boy, because that's all he had. His son died before kortikos were common outside the military.
> **Aiden:** But a father's memories aren't enough to build a child. I was a failure in everything but name.
> **Aiden:** That was when "Father" came up with another use for me.

Ernest's too-young face overlaid Aiden's, both wearing a similar dazed expression.

"And . . ." Coldwin prompted.

"And nobody," said Ernest.

"Not even Thomas Mahoney," Coldwin pressed.

"Thomas Mahoney knew nothing about it," said Ernest. "He had no knowledge of any wrongdoing whatsoever."

The AI's face continued to flicker between identities—Auggie, the young Aiden, and now Thomas, too.

> **me:** He used you to store his worst memories.
> **Aiden:** All of them. He discovered that forgetting about his son was just as good as re-creating him.

"I know Gala is in the monastery," said Coldwin. "But where are her memories now?"

"I don't know for sure," stuttered Ernest. "Somewhere in Singapore, I think."

My Bee buzzed too close to one of the cops on guard, and I had to dodge a swipe of his hand. Coldwin rubbed a palm against the back of their neck. Two questions left, a *when* and a *why*. They knew when the fraud had been committed, and motives for financial crime aren't interesting. It didn't seem like there was a niche for those last two questions to fill.

A light appeared in the smooth surface of Marianna's home. In the warm light stood a silhouette in a flowing gown.

"Mother!" said Ernest eagerly. "Please! The police! You have to—"

"Don't call me that, you eel," she spat. "Answer their questions—I want to watch."

Coldwin looked slowly from Marianna to Ernest, then back to Marianna.

"Ask him more about Miles," said the elegant hostess. "I'm sure he's got lots to say."

The lasers painting Ernest's face glowed with such intensity, it was a miracle they didn't vaporize the sweat trickling down his brow.

> **Aiden:** Can you imagine what it's like? To live under
>   the growing weight of another man's trauma?
> **Aiden:** I pleaded with him to stop, but he only gave
>   me the memories of my pleading. He was invincible.
> **me:** Until you became him.

The many-faced avatar shivered.

Aiden: I didn't become him. He became me. He combined his innocent memories with my guilty ones, and I was finally whole.

me: Sounds like you should have been thanking him, not killing him.

Aiden: Do you know what the body of Thomas Mahoney did when its memory wipe completed? Do you know what he did, as I watched from beneath the weight of all his history?

Aiden: He smiled.

Aiden: I let Ernest be the one to do it. The poor kid had reason enough to hate the guy. I just had to remind him.

me: And Prince? Why'd you drag him into it?

Aiden: I knew the killing would raise questions. I needed someone to take the fall. Luckily, Daddy was very good at making enemies.

Aiden: But that wasn't me. I'm a different person now. And you said you needed my help.

me: Right. I want you to—

An alert wiped Aiden from my vision. Exley's car was approaching. It seemed he thought my mind was sufficiently occupied at the moment, but I was glad to prove him wrong. I spread my Eagle wings and launched myself into the sky, catching an updraft and wheeling upward before turning my steel-tipped beak and diving down toward the engine block of his empty aircar.

His *empty* aircar.

Outside, the walkway creaked.

SUBMISSION
25

I twitched the Eagle's wings and changed its trajectory, wheeling back around toward my own crate, continuing to dive, wishing terminal velocity was just a little bit *faster* right then. The door of my crate swung open. Exley wore black latex gloves and held a silver throwing knife in each hand. Of course he wouldn't use a gun. Bullets can be traced, and, anyway, guns didn't match his aesthetic.

"Can't you see I'm busy?" I said. The words felt thick in my mouth, pushed out past so many other thoughts.

He didn't throw the knife so much as let it go in my direction. It sailed toward me like there was a magnet in the center of my skull (which, to be fair, there was). But knives take almost a second longer to hit their target than guns do. Exley's aesthetic saved my life.

There was a creaking crunch above us as my Eagle slammed into the roof, dislodging the cables that held the back of my crate to the ceiling. Exley's first knife cut a trench in the top of my skull as I tumbled backward out of my chair and hit the back doors in a shower of toiletries and old magazines. The locking bolt dug into my back. I twisted and pulled it out of its socket; the door opened, and I fell.

The Think, combined with my kortiko's reaction attenuation, made the fall eternal. Crates crawled past me, occupants cracking open doors to get a glimpse. Ernest and Elzbeth stood frozen in intersecting spotlights. My Eagle tried to eat concrete and died in pieces. Sparrows sped across crumbling rooftops, still too far away to help, but the Stingrays . . . Maybe the Stingrays . . . As I attempted to locate them, Exley slid nimbly down the slope of my ruined crate and joined the rain of debris falling after me, toward the bilge pit at the bottom of the warehouse.

An alert dragged my attention over to a canal in Santa Anita, where my Horse was caught in a knot of submerged garbage. I got it untangled, only to have my medical monitor warn me that all this multitasking was doing a number on my blood pressure. A very high number. I told it to remind me later. My HUD fractured as nonessential processes started to shut themselves down—clock, temperature, autocorrect . . .

Aiden-as-Auggie followed me down toward the sea, anchored to his falling chair.

> **Aiden:** Want me to what?
> **me:** wait.

I hit the water. A bouquet of alerts turned the salt spray red. The water closed over my face, just in time to redirect Exley's next knife. It cut a gash from the corner of my right eye along my temple. My back slammed into something hard but rubberized. An old man's back slammed into my rubberized skin. I was a Stingray, and I was just in time. I wrapped my fins around my almost-corpse and gunned my rotors.

"Why did Miles Palazzo choose to enter the Brotherhood?" asked Coldwin.

Ernest's face was pale beneath the lasers. "I'm sure you can guess . . ." he offered.

"Don't make me," said Coldwin.

Their voices were tinny through the stripped-down microphones on my thorax. Everything about me was stripped down. I could fly away, get lost on the wooded hillside . . .

Saltwater filled my lungs. I thought it was another problem with the RealHorse at first, but it was my real lungs, being power-washed as I dragged myself through the underwater bilge chute and out into the canal behind my building. When the Stingray finally broke the surface I must have raised the water level by an inch and a half with what I coughed up. Inside, Exley had just put his feet through the brains of two of my other Stingrays. The last two followed me out to the canal rather than face death at his hands.

> **Aiden:** You want me to wait? For what?
> **me:** no, i

The buzzing of a Jet Ski motor brought me back to my body. My Sparrows, fast approaching, saw Exley mounting a candy-apple-red Jet Ski on the other side of the building. Must have stolen it from my downstairs neighbor Cody. Served the data-mining creep right, but just at the moment I wished he hadn't been able to afford such a nice bike to steal. The Stingray casually water-boarded me as it dragged me down the canal, and I left my body again to escape the feeling.

"He joined the monastery . . . Well, obviously, he joined to escape."

"To escape me," said Coldwin. It was so far from a question, it was on another continent.

"Right," said Ernest, "sure. Now may we—"

"I have one more question," said Coldwin. "When were you born?"

"When . . . when was I . . ." stammered Ernest, trying to laugh. "Well, obviously . . ."

The buzzing of the Jet Ski cut through the words. Exley was in the canal behind me now, and gaining. Stingrays aren't meant to be passenger vehicles. I became the two Stingrays in my wake and detached them from the formation. They spiked their rotors, decelerated rapidly, and then propelled themselves back toward my pursuer. It's never pleasant sending parts of yourself on a suicide mission, but it's better than sending all of yourself. The sound of the Jet Ski receded as Exley decelerated to give himself time for evasive maneuvers. That would buy me time. Seawater filled my mouth.

> **Aiden:** Are you all right, Orr?
> **me:** dont suppose you could call off exley
>   could you
> **Aiden:** Sorry, he doesn't work for me. He works for
>   Father—I mean, Daddy—I mean Thomas.
> **me:** figured
> **me:** just one thing you can do for me, then
> **me:** stop the transfer
> **me:** don't put his memories into auggie
> **Aiden:** I can't do that. The instructions are
>   hardcoded.
> **Aiden:** Besides, I don't want to stop the transfer.
> **me:** you mean

me: auggie doesn't want to stop the transfer
Aiden: That's what I said.

It made sense. Auggie was Mahoney's lover, just like Precious was Gala's. He hadn't wanted to leave when I gave him the chance. This, somehow, was what the poor bastard wanted. But there was another Auggie in the equation: the Auggie in me. In my blood, my spine, my unconscious behaviors, and my all-too-conscious ones. That Auggie would never in a million years let his mind *or* his body be stolen from him. I owed it to that Auggie to try to save him, even if he didn't exist anymore.

me: then do the next best thing
me: give me your memories
me: all of them

A flashing red alert took over my vision. I was about to dismiss it when I realized it wasn't just another medical alarm. "INCOMING PROJECTILE" blinked across my vision. I cycled through my bodies to find the source of the notification. My birds were fine. My Bee remained undetected. My Horse was limping but intact. My meat opened its jellied eyes to find a sleek black aircar hurtling toward them. My rotors frantically reversed direction; my aquatic self lifted out of the water and swerved sickeningly atop its own wake, dragging the flailing old-man-body with it just ahead of the impact. The wave broke, carrying us back down the alley toward our pursuer, Exley's blue skin made vibrant against the red of the Jet Ski. There were no roads to turn on to. We were trapped between him and the aircar, his own makeshift drone, its crushed chassis nose-down in the water, with only five hundred feet of saltwater between us and his fan of knives. We dove, but there was no getting under the car. We surfaced, but we had no legs to crawl along the sidewalks. The whining of the Jet Ski got louder. A chat message appeared from Prince.

Prince: Thanks.
me: for what
Prince: Isabel recorded everything you told the
    cops. Including where to find that Ernest prick.

The sounds of carnage started before I thought they would, and I realized they were coming not from the canal, but from the forest beside Marianna's house. I revved my Bee's rotors, trying to make enough noise to warn Coldwin what was coming, but it was too late. Out of the undergrowth burst Prince, face and body sheathed in vat-grown exoskeleton, atop a motorcycle whose steel-toothed wheels chewed up root and branch and car alike, cutting a trench straight for the cowering Ernest. Elzbeth dove to the side, but she wasn't who Prince wanted anyway. He skidded to a stop in a cloud of shattered asphalt, grabbed Ernest, and threw him into the back of a parked aircar like a bag of rice.

"Come on," he growled through a vicious smile. "You're gonna take me to see the man in charge."

A handful of bullets bounced off his pale-green carapace as he climbed into the driver's seat. The car itself was a Lamborghini Barbero, built to withstand mortar fire while pleasure-cruising over foreign war zones. The police didn't own the hardware for that kind of job. Seconds after his arrival, the only traces of Prince left on the landing pad were his bike, the rattled cops, and a substantial decrease in the amount of landing pad.

I neighed, chirped, buzzed, and squeaked before I found the right mouth to scream out of:

"We're on the same side, you blue freak!"

The whining of the Jet Ski became a low grumble. He idled a few yards away—upside down from my perspective, as I floated on my back.

"Ten seconds to explain," he said. He held more knives than he had fingers.

"The guy the cops want for the Mahoney murder is on his way to the monastery right now. And he knows what we know: Thomas Mahoney isn't dead."

"What do you mean?" said Exley. He made it sound convincing, but it wasn't a denial.

"I mean he copied his memories into another body before he died. One with an invasive kortiko, like his, so the memories would stay fresh. And now a weapon with thumbs is on his way to torture him for his admin password, so he can get his sister back."

"Why does this concern you?" said Exley. "I know Miss Mahoney gave you a mendacity credit. How do I know you're not lying to save your own life?"

"Because the body your boss chose for his escape plan happens to belong to a friend of mine, and I'd like it to keep all its digits." I thought of Auggie, hollowed out and repurposed the way Miles Palazzo had stolen his own son. Part of me wanted that abomination killed. But it wasn't the part of me that was pulling the levers. "I've got drones on the way to the monastery already," I said, realizing as I spoke the words that they were true. The Sparrowhawks had changed direction. So had the RealHorse, and the D-Rats under Downtown were scurrying through the sewers to meet them there. "I can hold Prince off until you get there," I continued, "but there's only so much I can do. He's got an app that can blow up my carotid artery if he thinks I'm a nuisance. So, you know . . ."

I opened my eyes to see that I was talking to no one. Only an oily wake told me Exley had even been there.

". . . hurry," I said.

A massive hand closed around my entire body. My feeble thorax twitched.

"Orr, you puddle of mucus," said Coldwin into their clenched fist. "You led your murdering friend right to us, didn't you?"

I used their private kortikode.

me: not on purpose i swear

"Doesn't matter," they said into their fist. "You've hurt far more than you've helped on this case. I'm back-tracing the signal on this drone and putting you in a cell. Maybe then we can pump you for some useful information."

The receding sound of Exley's stolen Jet Ski was seamlessly replaced with the approaching sound of police sirens. I threw my Stingray into an old, old subroutine: evade police pursuit. Between echolocation and a saved map of the city, it'd be fine without supervision. That is, unless it found its way into a part of the city that had changed since the last time I'd run the process. It wasn't a risk worth worrying about. I had a defense to mount.

Defending an objective with drones is refreshingly direct. Unlike with people, you don't have to feel bad about spending lives, because there aren't any lives to spend. The only thing you've got to consider is how to get the most value for each drone that goes down. Spend all your drones on a single push and the next wave of enemies can just walk over the wreckage to the goal. Spend too *few* drones defending a push and you won't defend it at all—you'll just lose the drones and end up spending even more to cover your mistake. I used to be very good at it, but I hadn't had a lot of practice lately.

My Rats boiled out of the communal toilets of the monastery. A few blockheads with their robes hiked up around their hips gazed dumbly at the swarm of me as we scampered across their toes. Outside, above, my Sparrows swooped past the hospital tower and caught sight of the complex's outer walls. I divided Rats and Sparrows into waves and waited. Aiden hovered among the waiting Sparrows, a look of concern on his simulated face. He spoke, continuing a conversation I'd forgotten we were having:

> **Aiden:** Why do you want me to send you my memories, Orr?
> **me:** busy
> **me:** explain in a sec

Sirens screamed. Saltwater filled my mouth as my Stingray dove beneath the hull of an oncoming police boat. Embedded in crushed concrete, my Eagle's jaw worked, as it tried desperately to breathe. My medical monitor warned of asphyxiation, bleeding, and mounting blood pressure. I force-quit it in frustration.

In the time I'd been distracted, Prince had arrived. Without hesitation, he rammed the lurid yellow penis that was his aircar into the courtyard with its neat rows of vegetables, demolishing a section of stone wall in the process. A door popped open, and the whole bulk of him thudded down amid the gory remains of a line of summer squash. Ernest didn't come out with him. Whether he was dead or merely maimed, only time would tell.

"Wave One," I croaked through cracked lips, "go."

Light glinted off the polished wings of a single descending Sparrow, and Prince looked up. He reached out one massive hand to crush it mid-flight, while the other reached reflexively for his false ear, the one that held the code that would burst my blood vessels if he thought about it too hard.

> **Prince:** Tell me this isn't you, snooper.
> **me:** tell you what isnt me
> **Prince:** That's not a denial.

A hot bubbling started in my neck. That was when the second Sparrow, the one diving hard with reflective wings folded tight to its body, swooped down and sheared that false ear off. The decoy Sparrow died in Prince's palm, and the kamikaze wrecked itself against the ground, but the hot bubbling stopped. With the last flickering of their sensors, the birds felt Prince drop to one knee, to recover his ear.

"Wave Two," I whispered, "go."

> **Coldwin:** Stop running, Orr.
> **me:** stop chasing me im on your side
> **Coldwin:** If you were on our side, you'd stop
> running.

Coldwin's recumbent body surfed along the black canal water next to me, eyes not bothering to look at me. A spotlight illuminated us, and I dove again.

In the rumbling silence of drowning, I watched Wave Two connect. Two more Sparrows pincered Prince from the sky, while on the ground half my Rat swarm surged over neatly planted carrots to scrabble up his armored legs. The Sparrows couldn't pierce his armored hide, but simultaneous impacts in the forehead and lower back were enough to sweep him to the ground. The Rats poured over him, searching for crevices in his plating where they could explode. Sheets of carapace came loose, detaching in small explosions of white connective tissue. I smelled blood. If I finished this now, Exley wouldn't even be necessary. Saltwater emptied from my mouth, and I whispered:

"Final wave: kill him."

The rest of my Rats swarmed into the garden. My last two birds plotted suicide courses for his exposed throat and solar plexus. One of his massive fists shook off the swarming creatures and moved toward his head. I thought it was to ward off the Sparrows, to swat away the Rats. Then I saw his perfect smile light up the night, and his fist opened to reveal the severed ear, neatly reattached.

"Countermeasures," he said.

A sphere of crackling blue electricity swept outward from his armored skull, instantly frying the motors of every drone within twenty feet. I went from having dozens of eyes in the court-yard to just a single pair: a Rat whose legs had become tangled in some watermelon vines a few feet outside the radius. Prince rolled nimbly to his side as my two dead Sparrows, my last two, thudded uselessly into the ground.

> **Prince:** You're a relic, snooper. Hate to kill you.
> **me:** dont then
> **me:** maybe im worth more as a collectors item

The boiling in my neck started up again.

> **Prince:** Sorry, not much of a collector.
> **me:** yeah, i dont have the patience either
> **me:** just do me 1 favor before you kill me
> **me:** hold still
> **Prince:** What?

A drone body crushed beneath a polished blue shoe was the only thing that gave Exley away. Prince jerked to one side, and the throwing knife aimed at the base of his skull grazed the side of his head instead, knocking away the blinking black ear. The boil-ing in my neck receded again. Prince turned to strike this new threat, but Exley was perched safely atop the wall surrounding the courtyard, already launching another salvo. Prince raised his arms to deflect the blades, and dove behind the yellow aircar. He chose his position well. With the aircar to one side, and the wall at his back, there was no easy angle for a ranged attack. Exley dropped nimbly into the courtyard and picked up a pitchfork leaning against one wall. He walked among the vegetables with silent steps, stopping to pick up Prince's severed ear where it lay blinking in the dirt.

Neither man wasted time talking: words would only give away their position. Exley stepped around the hood of the car. Inside the vehicle, a voice cried out. For a fateful microsecond, Exley turned his head.

It was over in three moves. Prince threw a paving stone at Exley's leg, shattering it below the knee. The blue man went down, burying the butt of his pitchfork into the dirt. Prince lunged forward; his thick fingers closed around Exley's neck.

When we occupied Vegas, during that beautiful month or so when the war was going really well, they kept the circus open. I remember an aerial acrobat who wrapped herself in a knot of silks before suddenly letting go, the fabric sending her through a complex chain of somersaults before catching her inches from the ground. As Prince shifted his weight forward, Exley let his knot go. He twisted his shoulders to one side, pole-vaulted up his pitchfork, and threw his uninjured leg across the side of the big man's neck; in the next moment Prince was on his back, Exley was sitting on his chest, and the point of the pitchfork rested against the giant's exposed throat.

But Exley didn't kill him. He pressed his other hand against the side of Prince's head, reattached his black ear, and said:

"You can kill Orr Vue from here. Do it and I'll let you live."

I wasn't even mad at the betrayal. After all, I'd been planning to double-cross him, too. My Rat-eyes saw Prince grin. My meat-neck felt the boiling start again. And I let out a mighty neigh as my fifteen-hundred-pound Horse-body felt Exley's spine snap beneath my hooves.

The boiling stopped. The force of the impact had pushed the pitchfork through Prince's throat. The two men lay motionless, intertwined like lovers.

"Exley?"

I turned my massive head to the monastery, toward the voice.

He was five foot four, a hundred pounds soaking wet. A build that would have looked frail if it weren't held with such effortless poise. He ran his right thumb across the tips of his other four fingers, as if smoothing them. He wore a charcoal-gray suit that looked wrong on him despite being perfectly tailored. The thin lips above the devil-sharp chin were locked shut, concealing the tooth I knew was missing. He had Auggie Wolf's ears, and all his weathered skin, and it fit him about as well as the suit.

> **Aiden:** Kill him, Wart. He's not Auggie Wolf. He's an abomination.
> **me:** no one is auggie wolf anymore

Seawater drained from my ears, and I suddenly became ten times heavier. The Stingray had dumped me on the plastic sidewalk in front of its programmed destination. The one place I'd felt safe, back when I used to do this all the time. Over the door, high above me, a neon brain burned rubber on two monster truck tires.

> **me:** do you remember braining wheels
> **Aiden:** Of course. Orr, it's me.
> **me:** do you want to go back there
> **Aiden:** With you? More than anything.

I grabbed an exposed piece of pipe and dragged myself to a sitting position. Police sirens wailed in the distance. I put my back against the stucco wall and scraped my way up. My feet slid out from under me, and I bruised my tailbone. I started again.

In the doorway of the monastery, the shell of Auggie Wolf turned and went inside. I took one step forward, my hoof crushing a stray watermelon.

—

"What's wrong with it?" said Detective Coldwin. "It's spasming. Is he trying to escape, or . . . ?"

"Haven't seen one of these in a long time," said another voice. "Looks more like user error. Connectivity, maybe."

> **me:** then give me your memories auggie
> **me:** run away with me
> **me:** i rent a locker at the self storage
> **me:** theres a brain in there
> **me:** ill give you the kortikode
> **me:** send everything there
> **Aiden:** Orr, that would unmake me.
> **Aiden:** Why would you ask me to do a thing like
> that?

This time, I managed to push myself to my feet. I leaned my left shoulder against the wall, but couldn't feel it. The second Bee spasmed its way out of my right leg, though, and I felt that. It landed on the heaving sidewalk, and through its eyes I watched myself push through the electric-blue double doors.

"Where is he?" said Coldwin.

"Nervonna. Synestech club in West Hollywood. Used to be a mindracing joint called Braining Wheels way back when, till the owner got put away for doping."

"What's he doing?"

"Can't tell what he's doing. All I get from this is a location. But from the way this Bee is moving, I can tell you *how* he's doing . . ."

> **me:** youre the one who joined the monastery arent
> you

me: the one who wanted to be free of all your
    memories
me: all the pain they cause

The blue-and-yellow paint job of Braining Wheels unfurled itself across the concrete walls. Against those walls, on metal benches, sat die-hard freaks with obvious prosthetics, arms and legs defiantly chrome, sitting with their heads in their hands while they weaved the threads of the algorithms that'd get them through their next match. Against one wall sat a young man with a military-issue invasive and an angry grin. I had more hair back then, but the same bad tattoos.

me: you can stay in that ai brain at the monastery if
    you want
me: i can tell them you killed mahoney and they
    can unplug you
me: or
me: i can give you the same reward your meat-self
    got
me: send your memories to my storage unit
me: forget who you are
me: become empty
me: those are the choices
me: you may not like them but
Aiden: I'll make the transfer, Wart.
Aiden: Some part of me knew you'd ask. And that
    part of me also knew how I'd answer.
Aiden: Give me the kortikode.
Aiden: I trust you.

—

I sent the code. My eyes drifted to the main stage, bathed in every color of light. It had ropes like a boxing ring, but inside, the combatants were busy welding sculptures, playing chess, choreographing vicious tangos. In the middle of the mêlée, where he always was, stood Auggie Wolf, olive skin wine-dark with the heat of his overworked trode, playing three games at once without looking at any of them. His eyes were locked on me. I fell to my knees. He turned and disappeared into the monastery. I was too large to follow him. I was a bloodstained insect on cold plastic, watching an old man cry into his wrinkled hands. The lights were only two colors: blue and red. They flashed across his back and silhouetted him against the fluorescent-pink booths that had long ago replaced the metal benches—against the porcelain faces that had long since replaced the wine-dark ones. A police boot crushed me against the sidewalk, and then my only eyes were my own, aching inside a skull too small, hot tears soaking the right side of my face. My medical monitor rebooted, filling my vision with a fireworks display of red alerts.

Orr, it said soothingly, *stay calm. You are having a stroke.* Strong hands grabbed me by the shoulders and lifted.

Remain where you are. Help is on the

SUBMISSION
26

"Wakey wakey, Mr. Vue!"

The syrupy words yanked me out of a sea of undulating tits and shapely cocks into the disappointingly boobless light of morning. The sun glared in at me through two large windows at the foot of my cot, and my eyes immediately squeezed shut again in protest. Then sounds came into focus: the hollow whisper of an air conditioner, a rhythmic beeping, the pitter-patter of little feet coming round the side of my cot. Then the same high voice, closer.

"Mr. Vue, wake uuuuup!"

With about half the effort it takes to birth a child, I rolled my head to face the voice, and pried my eyelids apart. Sure enough, a small child, about eight or nine years old, stood there on tiptoes. He wore surgeon's scrubs. One hand fiddled with the rubber tube of the stethoscope around his neck, while the other scratched the skin around the heavy-looking kortiko half concealed by a surgical cap with a Mickey Mouse theme. It took more energy to turn my head away from him than it had to turn it toward him, but it was worth it. At least until he moved around to the foot of the bed and stood on tiptoes to stay in my field of vision.

"I'm Dr. Belroy," said the boy in a singsongy voice. "I'm a neurosurgery resident here at Kaiser Medical Center."

Now that my eyes were adjusting to the sun, I could see more of the view outside. My window looked directly out at a complicated concrete compound on a green hill. A monastery. *The* monastery. A shriller beeping started up.

"Oh no, that's not good!" said Dr. Belroy. "The surgery was a big success, and I did a very good job, but you need to keep your blood pressure from going too high or . . . uh . . ." He made a big explosion around his head with both hands. I got the picture.

I told him that if he wanted my blood pressure to go down he should close the curtains, except that when the words came out they sounded more like "warm yam scurfle." Dr. Belroy carefully considered what I'd said, which he did by sticking out his tongue.

"Seems like the stroke really messed up your talking neurons," he said. "That's okay, you'll get better when the little robots are finished working. For now, you can talk to me over kortiko chat. So! How do you feel?"

I dug into the circuits of my kortiko and pushed through the grit to get to the chat interface.

> **me:** Like somebody replaced all my neurons with ants, and I've got to communicate with them via Morse code.

He stuck out his tongue again—probably looking up what "Morse code" was—then nodded seriously.

"I don't know what that means," he said, "but okay! Anyway, I put you on Serpasil for your blood pressure. These machines will tell me if anything bad happens in your brain. 'Bye!"

> **me:** Close the curtains.

He stopped on his way to the door, and slowly shook his head. "Nuh-uh, can't. Administration said I have to keep 'em open. Oh! Also! They said your VA insurance only covered part of the surgery. Do you have any more data you can pay with? It's kind of a lot, they said . . ." He looked so uncomfortable, I almost felt bad for him.

> **me:** I'll dig up some pocket change. Don't worry
> about it.

"Okay!" said Dr. Belroy, clearly relieved by my instruction. He turned, waved 'bye again, and disappeared out the door.

Hospitals can do just about anything these days—regrow bones, patch arteries, fix your shitty personality. It's amazing, almost as amazing as how much it all costs. Even if I'd wanted to share what I knew about the Mahoney case—which I didn't—the admins I talked to informed me that, since it was criminal data and not medical data, the exchange rate would be dismal. Not only that, but I found out pretty quickly that anything I learned through the hospital internet was theirs by right, so I amused myself offline as best I could.

I alternated between reading the waterlogged copy of *Amy Vanderbilt's Complete Book of Etiquette,* and sorting through the med alerts I'd collected over the past few days. I relived my entire adventure, with everything but the pain removed: the brain freeze, a mouthful of garbage, veins full of knockout poison, and a face full of as-yet-unidentified liquid . . . half a concussion, a shot to the groin, two Bees in the leg (and two back out), two knife wounds to the head, spinal fracture, and some light drowning, all set against a backdrop of steadily rising blood pressure. I focused on the alerts one at a time, for what felt like a forever apiece, until my mind finally realized they were fixed and stopped freaking out about them. You get to know the inside of your head pretty well in a situation like that. I think the technical term is "going insane."

It turned out I'd developed quite a menagerie in my blood

over the past few days, so the first order of business was to rinse out my veins and squirt new juice into them. Then it was on to "restorative software therapy," which consisted of running code on my kortiko that would, for example, make me fall briefly in love with a plastic cup of apple juice, or forget whose hands mine were. I asked the techs how many of these were for my benefit, how many for research, and whether the research findings were being applied toward my bill. They told me not to compromise the test results by asking. By the fifth day of this, I was almost glad to see Coldwin come in for a visit.

"You look about how I expected you to look," they said, examining my collection of exciting tubes.

me: Nicest thing anybody's ever said to me.

"Don't play for sympathy," they said, pulling up a chair and sitting at least six feet away from me. "Just came to tell you everything's settled."

me: Settled.

They nodded. "Case is closed. Lionel did the murder, and was killed while trying to do another." They rubbed their hands together as if washing them. They didn't seem like they intended to continue, so I sucked it up and asked the question.

me: Killed by who?

Coldwin's eyes met mine, and they very deliberately shrugged their shoulders. "Unknown. We got Ernest Palazzo out of the stolen car, but he didn't see anything. He won't be seeing anything for quite some time." I recalled Prince's fantasies of carnivorous insects and eye sockets. "The Dubois family is currently engaged in a lawsuit with the Brotherhood, claiming that Lionel's death on the premises makes the monastery responsible. It's a cash grab, really, and, with the Brotherhood's lawyers, it won't go anywhere. They're already pointing to the mountain of military drones that were found around Lionel's corpse—a pile of fried D-Rats and Sparrowhawks, plus a mangled RealHorse down in the canal—as evidence that there was some . . . third party involved."

Coldwin gave me a long look.

"But it's *so difficult* to know anything for certain," they continued, "when the drones are in such *poor condition.*" My eyeballs still felt heavy from the stroke, but even as they sagged, I felt Coldwin's stare burning into them.

> **me:** What do you want in return?

Coldwin raised an eyebrow. "I'm not sure what you mean. But, supposing you did owe me something, I guess you could pay me back in data."

> **me:** You've got Ernest. Lionel's dead. What more
> could you want?

"Call it professional curiosity," they said evenly.

> **me:** Ask, then. Either I'll answer or I won't.

"And either I'll arrest you or I won't." They leaned forward, mouth against clasped fists. "Who really killed Thomas Mahoney?"

> **me:** No one you could charge.

They sniffed, but seemed to accept the answer. "And what did Marianna Mahoney want out of all this?"

> **me:** I'm not sure even she knew. But if I had to guess, I'd say you gave it to her. We both saw the way she looked at Ernest.

"Any idea why she hated him so much?"

> **me:** She didn't think of him as her son. He had too much of his father in him.

Coldwin leaned back and spat out a humorless chuckle. "Still dodging my questions, even in a hospital bed. I really *should* lock you up, after all the trouble you've caused me."

> **me:** I can testify to the conditions in the monastery. Ernest physically abused me while I was in there, and not in the fun way.
> **me:** You wanna build a case against him, I figure that's valuable data.
> **me:** Enough to cover your investment in my case, maybe?

Coldwin froze, momentarily stunned at my cooperation. Then they shrugged.

"Maybe. Not that it matters much. Even if we get enough on him to flip him, Miles—the one I really want—is still in the monastery, with no recollection of the crime, and we'll be lucky if we get Ernest six months for battery and receiving illicit data. It'll all wash away in the surf."

None of the therapy had done much for my speaking, but I was able to muster a grunt of agreement. Even if I told them who Ernest thought he was, it wouldn't be hard for a lawyer to argue that thinking you were Miles Palazzo didn't make you guilty of his crimes. And that same lawyer would turn right around and say a man who didn't remember his own crimes couldn't rightly be convicted of them, either. It's amazing the kind of lawyers you can afford when you spend your life being a bastard. Coldwin wiped their hands on their black slacks and rose to leave, but I grunted again. They turned.

> **me:** What about Auggie? Thought for sure you'd ask me about him.

Coldwin stopped at the door, their eyes looking vaguely amused. "Auggie Wolf?" they said. "He's right outside."

They disappeared through the door, and a harsh beeping let me know my blood pressure was spiking again.

SUBMISSION
27

The sudden spike in my blood pressure brought Dr. Belroy scampering into the room with a syringe. Before the door could close behind him, a bony brown hand caught it and pushed it open again. Auggie Wolf wore a powder-blue three-piece suit with a pink pocket square and matching tie, tailored to make his stringy physique look refined and elegant. Whereas the old Auggie walked on the balls of his feet, his back slightly hunched, looking for trouble to leap into, this Auggie held himself perfectly upright, rolling from heel to toe as his white leather brogues clicked against the linoleum floor. His nose, once a beak for gouging eyes and sucking up good smells, was now a slope for looking down, like rifle sights. When he looked at me, I saw an emotion I'd seen plenty of times before, but never from him. It curled his dexterous lip and wrinkled his repurposed nose. Disgust.

"Ummm, mister?" said Belroy, a bit shyly. "You can't be in here right now. Mr. Vue isn't doing too good, and he needs to rest."

"You will leave, Dr. Belroy," said Auggie. The laughter that always hovered behind his words, as if he was in danger of breaking into a fit of giggles, was absent.

"But . . ." the doctor started to protest, but even as he spoke the word, his legs turned and carried him toward the door. Luckily, he'd at least managed to get the syringe into my IV before his abrupt exit. Auggie stood silently as he left, examining me like I was a bug under glass. The harsh beeping of my blood pressure monitor gradually faded.

"Hello, Orr," he said. My jaw tightened. This Auggie would never call me Wart.

> **me:** Hello, Thomas.

"Thomas Mahoney is dead," he said, smiling his closed-lipped smile. "I'm just his heir." He strode closer, seeming to glide across the floor—none of the bouncing gait I used to say made him look like a balloon animal. "Or don't you recognize me?"

> **me:** I recognize somebody. Not sure it's you.

His hand drifted up to his chin, to tug at a beard that wasn't there. The hand dithered for a moment, surprised, and settled for scratching the stubble instead. Auggie could never grow much of a beard. It always came in patchy, so he kept it shaved. I took some small amount of pleasure in knowing the man would never get the facial hair he was accustomed to.

"Now, you see, that *is* a problem," he said, "because I very much *would* like to be recognized."

> **me:** I can ask Detective Coldwin to come back in.
> If I told them who you really were, maybe they'd recognize you.

Auggie rolled his eyes. It was a familiar gesture, but he always used to accompany it with an exaggerated sigh. This time, his mouth remained primly closed. "You can't call anyone. Your net access has been limited. For your health." He slipped his hands into his pockets and strolled over to the window. "I don't intend to go into hiding, Orr. I'm a private man, to be sure, but human beings need society." Outside, the monastery loomed on its green hill. Little people in gray robes scurried around it, patching the walls, watering plants.

> **me:** You could always join the Brotherhood. Plenty
> of society there.

He glanced at me over his shoulder. "You don't have to be so nasty," he said. "After all, we're in a position to help each other." He turned back to the window, watched his little slaves toil away out there for a while. I refused to ask him what he meant, so he finally had to turn around and continue the conversation himself.

"As I said, I'd like to do a better job of . . . *being myself,* if you catch my meaning." He made his way back to my bedside, and dragged over the chair Coldwin had been sitting in.

> **me:** I don't catch your meaning.

"It's infuriating, isn't it?" he said, sitting down. "How everyone keeps their distance from us, just because of our blood. How we can't switch out these old-model kortikos." He tapped his contact plate with a manicured finger. "How the memories we make on these don't even play right on noninvasives. There are only a few of us left in the world who can share memories completely. Who can really *understand each other.* We have to stick together, wouldn't you say?"

I grunted, to let him know I wasn't capable of saying much of anything. He took my hand in both of his and leaned even closer. It was the same skin I'd touched a hundred times, scraped and scratched and stroked and slapped. But he smelled of sandalwood now, not sweat or sage or gasoline, and I noticed that, even as he took my hand, he was careful not to touch my tattered thumb.

"Orr," he said, "listen to me." I looked into his eyes. I'd always thought Auggie's eyes were interesting, green flecked with light-catching amber. But I realized then that it was the mind behind the eyes that had been interesting. Now they pleaded with me. "Auggie's—my immediate family is all dead or missing. Not a lot of friends left, either. Most are dead of overdoses, and the ones who are still around have newer kortikos. They don't remember . . . they don't remember me the way you do. They don't remember me in a way I can *understand*. Do you get it?"

I got it. For all the time Auggie had spent as Mahoney's "live-in personal assistant," the rich man had never truly known him. Couldn't remember the way he hummed to himself in the mornings, which teeth he showed when he smiled, the way he smelled, the little tidbits about his past he'd only let slip when he'd been properly fucked. Mahoney didn't know these things. He didn't have the eye for it. That's why he'd come for mine. Besides, wouldn't it be awfully convenient if the one man who knew Auggie best suddenly didn't remember enough to blow his cover?

He saw the recognition on my face and squeezed my hand encouragingly. It was a gesture Auggie only used when he was pretending to be happy, but, then, Mahoney never would have known the difference, would he?

"Please, Orr. Give me those memories. Don't you . . . don't you want me to be . . . like myself again?"

I thought about it. About the man who used to bite my ears and pull my hair and cook me pancakes and call me Wart. I thought about how little Mahoney must have valued Auggie to use him this way, but also how much Auggie must have valued Mahoney to agree to it. Maybe he would have wanted me to cooperate, to help what was left of him become more like him. But there was another him, I knew. A full set of memories now preserved in my storage locker. What would *that* Auggie want? I squeezed my teeth shut. The machines around me beeped a warning.

> **me:** Nah.

"Orr, baby, I—"

> **me:** Don't "baby" me. Don't pretend like we're close. Everybody close to you ends up dead, just like Aiden.

He was silent for a while, learning how to grind an unfamiliar set of teeth.

"The Brotherhood's right about one thing, Orr: it feels good to forget. Better than confession. It's the one thing religions have always promised, but until now we never had the technology to answer that ultimate prayer. I'm offering you a miracle. I'm offering you a chance to forget your pain. Don't you want to be free of pain?"

> **me:** No, because I see what this is. Of everyone left alive, I'm the man who knew him best.
> **me:** I'm the one most likely to know juicy shit about him.
> **me:** And, therefore, about you.
> **me:** You don't care about remembering.
> **me:** You've forced enough of your sins into other people's heads to prove that much.
> **me:** You just want me to forget.

He was silent for a while, that twinge of disgust nibbling at his lip.

"This isn't how I expected this to go," he said finally, sitting back. With his posture, he was taller than I'd ever seen him before. "It's like you don't even know me. I get that you're upset. Just think about it, that's all I ask. Here's my office kortikode, if you change your mind."

He rose from his seat, and dragged it back across the floor, letting its metal feet screech as it went. He pushed it against the wall, straightened it carefully, then turned.

"In the meantime," he said lightly, "you owe the hospital a lot of data, and I own the hospital. So just think about that. Think hard."

> **me:** Dr. Belroy says I should avoid thinking, if
> possible.

"I own Dr. Belroy, too," he said. "Goodbye, Orr. Talk soon."

SUBMISSION
28

A day after the visit from what was left of Auggie, two burly orderlies came in and closed the curtains. (All the doctors were children, but all the orderlies were adults, for reasons of bill collection.) When another orderly came around the side of the bed and strapped a thick rubber blindfold over my face, I asked him what the safeword was, but he didn't respond. The orderlies never responded to questions—again, for financial reasons.

It wasn't until I heard the click of dangerously high heels on the linoleum that I understood who was responsible.

"Nice to see you, Marianna," I said. "I mean, it would be." They'd run a program on me that morning that helped me get my tongue back under my control, though it also made everything taste like orange peels.

The clicking stopped a few feet away, and then I heard a chair being dragged across the floor. From the lack of clicking, I figured it was someone else doing the dragging. Whoever it was sounded like they were wearing heavy boots, and not used to it.

"Exley?" I said. I was beyond trying to save myself, but I still felt the tension in my jaw.

"Yes, I'm having him rebuilt," said Marianna. Even from a distance, I could smell her perfume. It smelled like the sea used to smell, when I was a kid. "He won't be much of a bodyguard for a while, but he can still make himself useful in little ways."

"Not that he was really your bodyguard to begin with," I said.

"No," she agreed. "At least, not *only* mine."

Exley might as well have been furniture, for all he contributed to the conversation. But, then, maybe that's what he was: an antique passed down from generation to generation, so bound up in plastic skin and hardcoded rules that he was practically inanimate.

"I tried to tell you, when I hired you."

"'*Notre Dame's arches.*'" I nodded. "*NDA.* Of course I get it *now.* Was it Thomas who made you sign one, or Miles? Something in the prenup, maybe?"

"I couldn't say."

"Of course not." A contract could exert a powerful compulsive force on a person's kortiko, even decades after it was signed.

A long silence. I could hear her scratching herself, softly. I wondered what her hands looked like, outside the careful simulation of her mansion.

"I came here to thank you," she said.

I snorted. "So I take it the will executed, then?" I'm not sure why I said it. It just felt easier than accepting her thanks.

"I expect you already know it did," she said coldly.

"The night of your party, I'm guessing, and my hospitalization." The night Mahoney's memories finished transferring to his new body. He would've left almost everything to Auggie—to himself—but he'd have to spread some wealth around for appearances' sake. "What'd you get? A nice birthday gift?"

"You know, you're a disgusting person, Orr, but it is refreshing the way you ask questions. Hardly anybody asks me questions anymore. He didn't leave me much. Just a mansion in Mumbai."

"That's all?" I laced it with sarcasm, but she missed the tone entirely.

"That's all," she said. "I thought maybe he'd leave me something personal. A memory from his childhood, something like that."

"Hoping for cash, huh? I would have been happy with just a little mansion."

"I've spent a decade curating my image. The slightest rumor about me is worth more than the classified troop movements of some less discreet dictatorships. I don't need the wages of my father's sins to keep me solvent. That's never what this was about."

"What was it about, then?"

"Don't you have a heart at all?" she asked.

"Not much of one at this—"

"Oh, shut up," she spat. "I've had it with your jokes. You're lying here, having almost died, and all you can do is make jokes. You're just like him. All you silly little soldiers. You learned how to kill people, but you had to forget something to make room, so you forgot how to feel things. There's a hole in the middle of you, of all of you—a wasteland where you're afraid to go. So you fence it around with tough talk and jokes, and you think that makes it go away. But it doesn't, you know. We can all see it, the hole in you. My father, he fell into his and never climbed back out. In fact, he found a way to make it deeper. I thought, just maybe, he'd leave me a little hint at what was inside."

The only sounds were the beeping of my monitors and the rustling of her clothes. I imagined her smoothing out the folds of an enormous dress, running her hands over creases that were sewn into the garment, trying to press them flat. As soon as she lifted her hand, there they'd be again. I swallowed a gob of saliva, something I now had to remind myself to do, and said, "You know Thomas is still—"

"Stop," she said. "I don't want to know. Let me have my dead father. Please."

Silence again, except for the beeping and the rustling. After a while, the rustling stopped.

"In fact, I'd rather you didn't tell *anyone*."

"Ah," I said. "So that's what this visit is about."

"You can't turn it off, can you?" she almost whispered. "That horrible cynicism of yours. If you did, you might have to actually separate right from wrong, instead of merely assuming *everything* is wrong. I didn't come here to cover something up, any more than I hired you to cover something up."

"Why did you hire me, then?" I said, glad she'd given me an excuse to ignore the rest of her statement.

"Revenge," she said simply. "I couldn't stand the idea that he'd gotten away with it."

"You mean Miles?" I couldn't see her cringe, but I felt it. "He will get away with it. Legally, he's not the person who committed those crimes anymore."

"Oh, he won't go to jail for very long," she said. "But it will be long enough."

"Long enough . . . ?"

"For certain operatives I've paid to teach him some remorse. And for me to disappear. I've sold the house already. I have another prepared. This is the last conversation I intend to have in this awful city."

"I'm touched," I said, coating the words in sarcasm to keep the sincerity from leaking through. There were millions of people in the city who would have eaten their own hands for the opportunity for a chat with Marianna Mahoney. She could have sat down with anyone—any reporter, any investigator, any social climber. That she was talking to me now meant she didn't see me as any of those things, despite how we'd met. Instead, she saw me as . . . what? A warped reflection of her father? A filthy barbarian whose candor was a curiosity? Or just a pair of ears attached to a brain too old and poor to matter? It wasn't a question I wanted to answer, so I asked a different one: "What are you going to do about Ernest's memories?"

"I suppose you think I ought to save him," she sighed. "Get his memories back, have my son again. Perhaps I could. But he agreed, Orr. He went with Miles into the monastery willingly. I'm not sure . . . I'm not sure I want him back."

"If it was me . . ." I said, ". . . if there was any chance at all . . ."

"Yes, well." Marianna cut me off before I had to say any of the hard words. She was more merciful than she let on. "Just one more reason to be thankful I'm not you, I suppose."

The beeping of the monitors settled around us like a night full of digital crickets, singing our silence. After a long time, I heard Marianna get up and make her clicking way to the foot of my bed. I felt her hand on my foot. She gave it a squeeze.

"Thomas is dead," she said softly, "but you aren't. I truly hope you find a way to be happy."

Her hand released my foot—almost reluctantly, I thought— and her clicking footsteps headed toward the door.

"Oh," she said, stopping. "That mendacity credit I gave you. Did you ever end up using it?"

"Nope," I said.

"Impressive, to do everything you did without telling a single lie. The ingenuity of poverty, I suppose. In any case, I'm glad. Use it to do something nice for yourself. Make up a lurid rumor about your sexual prowess, something of that nature."

"I could do with a few less rumors about my sexual prowess, to be honest." In spite of everything, I could feel myself smiling.

"I'm sure you'll use your best judgment," said Marianna. I might have imagined it, but there seemed to be a smile in her voice, too.

"Goodbye, Orr," she said.

"Goodbye, Marianna," I replied. The door hissed open, but only one set of footsteps went through it. Exley's thick blue silence filled the darkness.

"You want me to apologize for trying to kill you?" I asked.

"Do you expect *me* to apologize?" he replied.

"Your boss could probably cover the cost of *your* lie, but I've only got the one, and it seems a waste," I said. "Anyway, I get it. You wanted to stop me figuring out when Aiden really died."

"Pardon?" One heavy step lurched toward my bed. He wasn't the man he'd been before the Horse hit him, but what was left of him was more than a match for what was left of me.

"There's no point killing me now," I said. "I figured it out, and if you offed me, the police would get a warrant for my skull and the secret would be out."

"What secret?" said Exley. He never seemed particularly attached to the words he said, but now his voice had reached such a monotone that I knew I'd struck a nerve.

"You called him 'young Master Aiden' in the car, but Amy Vanderbilt says 'master' is only an appropriate title for boys under the age of thirteen. That's why you wanted the book back, and why you decided to kill me when I wouldn't give it to you. You thought I had a hunch, but I was just being rude. It was trying to kill me that gave me the hunch."

"Why on earth would the boy's age when he died make any difference, to me or to anyone else?" drawled Exley.

"Because Marianna seems to remember him dying at the age of sixteen, when she was eight. I think she heard the right story, but got it at the wrong time. I think he died before she was even born. And if her parents told her a little white lie, you'd be duty bound to protect that lie, wouldn't you? For Thomas's reputation. For Catherine's heart. For her daughter's innocence. So many voices in your head, telling you to keep it quiet."

Exley's silence, as always, was eloquent.

"But if Aiden really died before Marianna was born," I continued, "who was acting as her brother for those first eight years? Is that what Mahoney originally created the Aiden AI for? To pilot some kind of realistic overlay so his daughter thought she had a sibling?"

"Those are all certainly questions you could ask, Mr. Vue,"

said Exley. "But there is no profit in asking them. Let us pretend you did not."

"And in exchange, you don't strangle me in my bed?" I said. "Sounds good. Although, if you're game for a little *light* strangling, I haven't gotten any action in—"

"Goodbye, Mr. Vue," said Exley. "Miss Mahoney is waiting."

"Right," I said. "Give her a little kiss for me, would you?"

"I shall do no such thing," said Exley. And, with a few shuffling steps, he was gone to join his mistress.

The orderlies came in to remove my blindfold. The sunlight seared my eyes when they threw open the curtains again. I could only imagine how much it would hurt Marianna's.

SUBMISSION
29

After about a week, I felt better. So much better that I didn't think I needed to be in the hospital anymore. And yet there I stayed, partly because I was unable to pay my bill, partly because I was unwilling. And the longer I stayed, the higher that bill climbed. The tests they ran on me lost any pretense of therapeutic benefit. In one, they cranked my empathy up to a fever pitch and then made me watch a live tonsillectomy. In another, they made time crawl so slowly that I was trapped in a single breath for what felt like days. Thomas, or Auggie, or the horrible chimera of the two, never visited again after that first conversation, but I could tell from the tests that he was getting impatient. Finally, after three weeks of choreographed muscle spasms and medically induced conversations with my teeth, he tried a new tactic: he sent in the blockheads.

I could see the delegation from my window, winding their way down their green hill on foot, and though I'd seen them do this many times, somehow I knew even before they arrived that this group was on its way to me. There were eight of them, all dressed in their dullest gray robes, and instead of smothering me with a pillow, like I'd hoped they would, they all just gathered around my bed, smiling.

"What do you want?" I said at last.

TWO TRUTHS AND A LIE

They all looked at each other, nodding seriously. It was a lot like how the doctors behaved, though these were adults. Each one had something wrong with them. One had a dull-red socket where an eye should be. Another had a nose broken almost at a right angle. One had a blotchy red scar running diagonally across their face, and the one next to them had raised horizontal scars all down one arm, so that it looked like somebody had stood the two next to each other and slashed across both of them with a bouquet of knives. The one next to them didn't have hands at all, just little sausage nubs hanging at their sides. A sixth had every inch of exposed skin covered in the worst tattoos I've ever seen on a human body. The seventh had roughly a jack-o'-lantern's worth of teeth in their gaping grin, and the eighth one looked completely unharmed, and stunningly beautiful. In short, it seemed like they'd all lived lives worth forgetting.

"He asks questions," said the beautiful one.

The one with the tattoos shook their head sadly. "It is very sad," they said. The others murmured agreement.

"Perhaps he would like to be happy," said the one with the scarred face, hopefully.

"Not particularly," I said. Their mutilated face fell.

The handless one stepped closer and placed one of their stumps tenderly on my shoulder.

"We are from the Brotherhood of the Uncarved Block," they said. "We are here to offer you—"

"I know who you are and what you do," I said irritably. "Go away."

"He *knows* things," said the one with the cut-up arm, in the way somebody might say, *He fondles goats.* "Very sad."

"You are a slave to what you know, brother," said the one-eyed monk, leaning over me on the opposite side of Sausage Arms.

"And you're all slaves to what you don't know," I said. "Maybe we're all just slaves, and knowledge doesn't enter into it."

They didn't seem to know what to say to that. It wasn't in their script, I guessed. After a few seconds, the one with the broken nose stepped forward.

"Would you like to hear a story?" they asked.

"Sure," I said, realizing they were unlikely to leave otherwise.

"Okay," they said. "But you must not interrupt. If you interrupt, we will have to begin again. Are you ready?"

"Hit me," I said.

"We are a nonviolent order," they said.

"Tell me the story," I said.

"Okay," they said. By some unseen signal, all eight of them stepped back from my bed and formed a semicircle, with hands clasped behind their backs. They all smiled in unison. Then their faces went briefly slack, and a look of confusion filled their eyes. Then, as if reading from an unseen script, the beautiful one stepped forward and began to speak. Their voice was pleasant, lilting, and deeply sad. They said:

"Once upon a time, there was a simple stonecutter. The stonecutter worked from dawn till dusk each day, and his life was hard. One day, when he was selling his wares in town, a royal procession passed by. He looked at the king, lying comfortably in his palanquin, and he grew envious. He thought to himself . . ."

The gap-toothed monk spoke, taking on the voice of the envious stonecutter: "'Oh, how happy the king is, and how powerful. I wish I were the king.'"

"And suddenly," said the beautiful one, "he was the king—rich and renowned, respected and feared by everyone. But soon he noticed that it was hot in his palanquin, and he began to sweat. The sweat stained his fine silk pillows, and made him cross."

"'What,'" lisped the gap-toothed monk, "'could bring such discomfort to me, the mighty king?'"

The beautiful monk continued, "He looked out of his window, and saw the sun."

" 'Oh, how powerful the sun must be,' " lisped the gap-toothed monk, " 'and how happy! I wish *I* were the—' "

"Okay, hold on," I said. "You're telling me that this king—no, wait, this *stonecutter*—has never heard of the *sun* before?"

The monks went silent, their hypnotic cadence ruined by my interruption. After a few seconds, their eyelids fluttered, and they smiled.

"Would you like to hear a story?" said the beautiful one.

"Hit me," I said.

In total, I probably interrupted them six or seven times before I got fed up and let them finish. The story was predictable. The stonecutter became a king, who became the sun, who became the clouds that covered the sun, who became the wind that moved the clouds, who became the mountain that could not be moved, who was then carved up and sold at the market by a humble stonecutter. It was a simple story, and it ended exactly where it began, which some people mistake for wisdom. When it was over, the beautiful monk smiled and closed their eyes. The others cooed appreciatively.

"That was a very good story," said the gap-toothed monk. "I don't remember ever hearing it before."

"Sure, terrific," I said. "But what's your point?"

"He asks questions," said the beautiful one, sadly. The one without hands stepped forward and placed a nub on my shoulder, exactly where they had touched me before.

"If you are going to ask questions, brother, ask yourself this," they said. "Are my memories mainly a source of joy, or of pain? Are my desires a comfort, or a torment?"

The tattooed one stepped forward, and added, "The past no longer exists, brother. The future does not exist yet. It is not noble to allow either one to hurt you."

I examined their empty faces, scrubbed clean of everything

but the scars their nonexistent pasts had given them. They were right, of course, but that didn't mean I agreed with them.

"We will come again tomorrow," said the gap-toothed one, "and the day after that. We will give you as many opportunities as you need to understand."

"You're too kind," I said, knowing the tone would fly right over their smooth heads.

"We are a kind order," said the one with the scarred face. "Goodbye, until tomorrow!"

They all wished me goodbye, like children being let out of school, and then they filed out the door and left me alone with nothing to do but watch them walk back home from the window. The story they'd told me, the only new information I'd gotten in weeks, refused to leave my data-starved brain. It was a stupid story, probably meant to teach you that all desire is ultimately futile, classic Zen horseshit. But to me it had another moral. To me it said that the stonecutter is always the stonecutter, no matter what else you try to make him into. You can put other clothes on him, you can swap out his memories, you can slather him in perfume and trim his nails, but in the end he will still be a stonecutter, with flayed ears. I sent a message to the kortikode Auggie had given me.

> **me:** I've decided to take your deal. You can have my memories of Auggie.
> **Auggie:** Orr, that's wonderful! I'm ready to accept the transfer now.
> **me:** I have one more condition.
> **me:** The Dubois family lawsuit. I want you to settle.
> **me:** Give them the memories of their daughter, Alani Dubois.
> **me:** That should be enough for them to drop the suit.
> **Auggie:** Fine, fine. And your memories?

me: I don't have them on me. It was too painful to
keep them.

me: Once the settlement goes through, I'll give you
the storage address.

Auggie: It will be done today.

I'll say one thing for the bastard: he was true to his word. Precious's memories were back in her family's hands by sundown—though what they'd do with them when her body was at large in Singapore I didn't want to ponder. In exchange, I gave Mahoney the address of the Self Storage, and the password that would dump all of its memories onto his trode. Not my memories of Auggie, the ones he'd asked for—those were sitting in my own wet and shrinking brain—but Auggie's own memories, stolen, transferred, and now about to be returned to their original owner. I didn't tell him about Roy, but it wouldn't matter—the dog was programmed to recognize Auggie's face. Afterward, as I relaxed in the hospital bed, the mendacity credit in my palm finally stopped its low-grade buzzing, and flashed briefly hot as it incinerated itself. Even if Mahoney used InfoDrip to fact-check my statements, the data trail that little chip had created would cover for me. As far as anyone was concerned, I hadn't even told a lie.

My palm felt oddly light without the weight of the credit. Twenty million demos in that unit, easily, and I'd blown them all on the off chance that the stunt would get Auggie back into his own body. Why? Well, for love, of course. Or at least what felt like love. Nobody can tell you if what you're feeling is love. It's just the word we use for whatever we feel most intensely, when we feel it. I closed my eyes and had the first good night's sleep I'd gotten in recent memory. I'd be back in my building soon, and I wasn't sure I even had a bed there anymore.

SUBMISSION
30

Even with my bills paid, it was another week before I was discharged. Dr. Belroy's medical algorithms told him I needed a little more therapy, and, to my surprise, that meant actual therapy, not the thinly veiled regimen of psychological torture that had characterized my stay so far. I made quick progress and was soon able to move my fingers and even manage a half-chub, if I concentrated. I didn't get any more visitors, but a few people sent gifts. Ty the garbage man sent me a rotten pumpkin he said reminded him of me, and Marco sent a bouquet of peonies with long red tongues. I had the orderlies put the peonies far away, in case they were Marco's way of getting back at me for killing one of his clients. I got a blank birthday card from my landlord, JB Splunge, inside of which I found an invoice for the repairs to my crate. Even the Carnival sent a card—the queen of hearts.

When I did get out of the hospital, there wasn't a lot of fanfare. I had to hire a water taxi back home, and to my relief the driver seemed more interested in old war stories than the Mahoney investigation. My days of being a celebrity were over, and I was looking forward to slowly dying in obscurity. I was less looking forward to the climb up to my crate. I was back up to full strength, but that only meant that, instead of my having the strength and stamina of a roll of wet toilet paper, the toilet paper was now dry. Fortunately, reattaching my crate to the ceiling proved to be more than JB Splunge could be assed to attempt, and it now floated at sea level, buoyed on a raft of piss-yellow spray foam.

The lock on the door hadn't been replaced, either—apparently, the invoice I'd gotten was mainly a courtesy charge for not throwing me out on the street. I'd have to do something about that lock someday. Until I could, I'd just have to rely on my innate unpopularity to ensure I didn't get any unexpected visitors.

But when I opened the door, I found that I already had one. There, in the now thoroughly ruined space, sat Auggie Wolf, lounging in my office chair and feeding apple slices to my dented dust eater. I felt my blood thumping in my temples, and realized I'd automatically reached for my now-dead drones. I closed the interface. Auggie smiled one of *his* smiles—one of the carnivorous ones full of all the teeth he could muster.

"Welcome home, Wart," he said.

"Doctor said I'm supposed to avoid surprises if I want to keep living," I said.

"And what kind of life would that be?" He chuckled. He was wearing clothes I recognized now, ripped black jeans and a faded Braining Wheels T-shirt. The familiar barbed nose ring dangled from his septum. Must have grabbed it when he went to pick up his memories.

I gave up and smiled back at him. I took the last two shambling steps to my bed, and lowered myself onto it as he fed the last slice of apple to the happily gurgling 'eater. I forced myself to stay upright, even though all I wanted was to go to sleep.

"So it worked, then," I said. He nodded.

"Worked like a charm," he agreed. "Clever of you to figure out that all my memories were stored on Aiden. Even cleverer to move them to your own storage brain. Soon as I connected to it, I was myself again." He almost giggled as he said it, swaying back and forth to unheard music. It reminded me of how he used to get after a good night at Braining Wheels, when he'd whipped his kortiko to a suicidal pitch and out-thunk all his competitors. I was happy to see him. Would have been delighted, if there was enough dopamine left in my system to feel delighted with. But something nagged at me.

"What happened to Mahoney?" I said slowly, knowing they weren't the right words. Since the stroke, the words I said never felt quite right, but I was learning to live with it. "What happened to Mahoney," I repeated, "when you got your own memories back?"

"To Mahoney?" He almost burst out laughing. "Mahoney's dead, Orr. You know that better than anybody."

"But he was . . ." The words slid around in my mouth. "You were him. The last time I saw you. You moved differently. Talked differently. Is he still . . ."

"What? Alive? *Conscious?*" Auggie was actually laughing now. "Come on, Orr, you're telling me you don't . . ." He trailed off, examining my eyes. "You really don't know, huh?"

"Know what?" I said immediately. Seconds later, a voice inside me told me not to ask. That was another thing, since the stroke—sometimes the voices inside me were a little slow. Auggie gently picked up the 'eater in his lap and placed it on the floor. Then he came and sat next to me on the bed. Very gently, as if he was afraid of startling me. He was still smiling. The sandalwood smell was gone, but his old smell hadn't come back. It takes a lifetime to build a smell like that, and he didn't have a whole lifetime left. He squeezed my shoulder.

"Mahoney died in the monastery," he said, a strange excitement in his voice. "He's been dead for weeks."

"But his memories . . ." I murmured.

". . . are just currency!" Auggie laughed. "Just a pile of data! Mahoney thought the memories made the man, but you and I know that's not true. We are our minds, sure, but our minds are in our bodies. We're made of thinning hair and scar tissue, the way our hips complain when we get out of bed in the morning, the neurons we've killed, the trace amounts of drugs still living in our spinal columns. Your ailments don't lie, Orr. People like Mahoney think the mind is software, and a body is just a computer to run it on, but they're wrong. It's not the computer and the software, it's the apple and the core."

To punctuate his point, Auggie picked the core of his apple up from the table and bit off one end of it. He chewed happily. Even in the sweltering heat, I felt cold.

"So you're saying it wasn't Mahoney who threatened me in the hospital. You're saying it was you?"

"Well," said Auggie, talking around the apple pulp, "I definitely remember doing that. I'm not proud of it, and I wouldn't do it again if you asked me to do it now, but I feel the same way about a lot of things I've done when I was high. That's not enough to say it wasn't me who did those things."

"Just because you remember a thing doesn't mean you did it," I said, more to myself than to him.

"Just because you *don't* remember doesn't mean you *didn't*." Auggie smiled and swallowed.

I felt nauseous, as if I was the one chewing my way through the apple core. My fingernail bit into the scar at the base of my thumb. "What happened to all his other memories?" I demanded. "Where's all the stuff that thought it was Thomas Mahoney?"

"Where do you think?" said Auggie, taking another bite of the core. "In me. I mean, he transferred it to me, didn't he? Nothing illegal about that."

He spat a seed at the floor. The 'eater crawled over to slurp it up. One of its legs was crooked, and it limped as it moved.

"You weren't in the war," I said. "You shouldn't have an invasive kortiko. Why . . . why do you have an invasive kortiko?"

"Mahoney gave it to me," he said. "My parents sold me to him when I was fourteen. He put kortikos in a few of us, but I was the only one who lived."

"Aiden wasn't Aiden," I said, mostly to myself. "You were. You're the brother Marianna remembered. The one Mahoney filled with cast-off memories to try to re-create his son."

"Stupid plan," said Auggie, taking another bite of the apple core. "Was never gonna work. Even at fourteen, I had too much in my head. All the memories he gave me just became *my* memories."

"And then he started giving you other memories," I said distantly. "Everything he wanted to forget. He did all that to *you*. That's why Thomas came to me for information about you. He'd forgotten anything he might have known, out of guilt."

Auggie frowned. "More thoroughly than you could've imagined. When I found him at that club all those years later, he had no clue who I even was. It was years before I told him—you were the one who convinced me to, by the way—and you know what he did? He went and took over an entire monastery to help him forget all over again."

Auggie shook his head in mock disbelief.

"Came back to me all happy and ignorant. Asked me to code him a caretaker AI to run the religious institution he'd acquired. I called it Aiden, as a little joke. He didn't even recognize the name. The AI's how I found out about Miles's little embezzlement scheme. Never should have put his son-in-law in charge . . . Oh, but you know all this already."

"What do you mean?" I said.

Auggie shook his head. "You really did a number on yourself, didn't you? I mean, I know you said you were going to need to forget a lot if we were going to do this, but I'm . . . I mean I'm kind of impressed."

This time, the voice telling me not to ask got there first. I just ignored it. "Do what?"

"The Heist of the Century, I think you called it," Auggie said, grinning.

"You planned this." My mind got there in time to stop me

from making it a question, but not soon enough to stop me from saying it.

"'Planned' is a strong word," said Auggie. "I improvised quite a bit."

"You knew that if Mahoney fled his body he'd need someone else with an invasive to flee into. You stayed close to him . . ."

"It had its benefits," Auggie said, winking.

"Then you must have tipped off Coldwin about the embezzlement. Forced Miles and Gala into hiding. But why didn't Thomas flee during the financial-crime investigation, when the others did?" I asked. "Why now?"

"He was addicted to forgetting! He had no idea what they'd done until I tearfully confessed my part in it years later." Auggie feigned tears: "Oh, Daddy, I'm so sorry. I didn't stop them, and now we're both implicated. It's been just eating me up inside!"

"But why wait so long?" I asked, ignoring his theatrics. "Unless you were using the extra years of memories as . . ."

". . . as a buffer." Auggie nodded. "I needed as many memories from after we made the plan as I had from before it. Otherwise, I would have forgotten our goal as soon as I entered the monastery. Would have made it difficult to coordinate with you. Good thing I did, too. The whole thing went off the rails almost before it began. He was supposed to die quietly after a couple years. Who knew little Aiden had such anger in him? But we recovered, didn't we, lover? I couldn't have done it without you."

"I did . . . I didn't do it for you," I said. "I mean, I did it for you, but not so you could steal Mahoney's memories. I did it because . . ."

"Because you love me?" he said. "Well, sure. But that's not all you did it for."

"What do you mean?" I said. "What are you talking about? What are you doing here?"

"You know what I'm doing here," he said. "Or some version of you knew. Orr, love, I'm here to give you your share."

"I don't want a share," I said. "This isn't my heist."

"Oh, come on!" He laughed. "It's over! We did it! You can let yourself remember! This was half your idea!"

"It wasn't," I said. "I don't know what you're talking about."

"Of course you don't! You had to forget in order to pull off your part of it. You were the guy on the outside, keeping watch with your drones under the buffer, in case something went wrong, which it *definitely did*. You must have stuffed all your incriminating memories into an infosock and hidden it real good, somewhere real close, and now that the heat's off, all you've got to do is access it."

I thought about my Dragonfly, so conveniently present at the very moment of Mahoney's murder.

"We're free!" Auggie laughed, throwing up his hands. "We've got more data than anyone can spend in a lifetime. We can buy a house like Marianna's. We can have a pool! We can live by a beach, or on the moon! It's over, we can finally—"

"I was nearly killed," I said.

"'Nearly' being the operative word," said Auggie.

"Three times," I said. "I had a stroke. Stress-induced, the doctors said." I chuckled, but not because it was funny. "You were out of my life for twenty-five years. Years we could have been together. Been happy. And when you finally came back, I had to watch you . . . watch . . . something you insist was you all along, use your body to *threaten* me. Was that all part of the plan?"

He stopped smiling at that, finally, but he didn't look away. Just stared straight into my eyes and said, "Like I told you, the plan was loose. You can't make a plan that survives a quarter of a century. We knew going in that we'd have to improvise. That we'd have to do things we might regret."

"I killed someone," I said. My index finger peeled a layer of skin from the corner of my thumb.

"You've killed a lot of people," he pointed out.

"No," I said. "The ones I killed back then weren't people to me. This one was. A big guy with a philanthropic streak, who just wanted to get his sister back. He was a murderer, sure, but, well, so am I."

He did look away then, and put his head in his hands. The 'eater hobbled over to his toes, in hopes of catching a tear or two to drink. "I'm sorry, Wart," he said, "I really am. But, compared to what Mahoney did, everything we did is—"

"There is no we," I said. "I wouldn't do that. Wouldn't make a plan like that, wouldn't execute it."

"Don't say that."

"Too late," I said.

When he didn't reply, I picked up the mildewy plastic bag the hospital had given me, with all my waterlogged possessions. Inside the breast pocket of the still-damp denim jacket I found what I was looking for.

"You should have this," I said, sliding Mahoney's dog tag across the table. "After all, he wanted you to remember him."

Auggie picked up the tag and held it, feeling its ridges with his thumb.

"It feels so flimsy," he said. "I always thought they were made to last."

"Just barely longer than a soldier's life," I said. "You should go."

He was silent a long time. The 'eater gave up waiting for tears and scuttled back to its charging dock. Finally, Auggie put the dog tag into his pocket and stood.

"I knew it would be like this," he said. "Some part of me knew. You were on board with the plan, you even pushed me when I had doubts. But toward the end, when you started talking about what you'd need to forget . . . that you'd even need to forget about us . . ." He plucked the apple's stem from between his teeth and rolled it between his fingers. "Well, at some point I knew you weren't doing it for the sake of the heist. Maybe it started that way, but you never liked yourself much, Orr. When I left your apartment that night, I knew you'd finally found an excuse to stop being yourself."

"I thought you said the memories don't make the man," I said, refusing to meet his eyes.

"No, they don't," said Auggie. "But the man makes the man, when he chooses what to remember. If you get your old self back and decide you want your share, I'll be waiting. Otherwise . . ."

"Goodbye," I said.

"Goodbye," said Auggie.

The creak of the crate door closing behind him was a metallic howl, and it echoed in my head long after his footsteps faded away.

I sat there for what felt like a long time. Every part of my body told me to lie down, but my rusty bastard of a brain told me that if I lay down now I might not get up again, ever. I looked down at the bloody mess I'd made of my thumb. My wart, just like I was Auggie's.

The combat knife was in my hand before I knew what I was planning, and before I could stop myself it bit into the flesh I'd spent so many hours abusing. I carved at the knotted skin, notching the nail, blood welling up and flowing down to my knuckle. The blade hit something hard. Not bone. Harder. Metal. I got the blade of the knife under it and levered it out, a metal bead the size of a stud earring, balanced on the bloodstained blade. An infosock. It glowed a faint turquoise in my AR layer, offering to connect to my kortiko, to remind me of the things I'd hidden from myself. I declined.

Instead, I took it into my mouth, careful not to cut my lips with the knife. Then I levered myself out of bed, out through the door, up the first flight of stairs, knees and hips creaking the same way that door had when Auggie closed it. In all the jungle gym of rusted crates, not an eye was on me. I wasn't interesting anymore. I didn't want to be.

I lurched out onto the fire escape. The light was already start-ing to fade, the salt air turning cold. I stopped there, gripping the twisted iron railing, and looked out over the sun-drenched rooftops and the sea-drenched streets. The sun was behind me, falling, and my building cast a cold shadow over the slowly sink-ing wreckage spread out below me.

The sea covers up everything. Rusted bikes, bus benches, mailboxes, broken sunglasses, used needles. Mostly, it covers up the land, rising and rising until having your feet solidly under you is a luxury most can't afford. Somewhere out there, to the east, far from the retreating sun, there's a square of sidewalk with my palm print in it, and my name, and the names of some friends of mine who had the good fortune to stumble upon wet concrete along with me. Back when wetness was a luxury, and not the state of things. Back before it all got covered up. I couldn't find that square of sidewalk now if I tried.

When you pile up as many memories as I've got, it becomes impossible to really know yourself. Am I the things I remember? Am I the way I feel about those memories now? Or, like the sidewalk under the sea, am I the things I don't remember? The things I've chosen to forget? Am I the person who solved the mystery for the sake of my lover, or the person who sacrificed twenty-five years of happiness for money and revenge? There are too many different versions of myself running around inside me to know.

I spat the metal bead into the sea. One less self to worry about. But that wasn't enough, and that's why I'm talking to you now.

Oh, don't think I've forgotten about you, checker. I'm telling you this story, piling on all the data I've collected about the case, submitting a fact packet fatter than anything else you're likely to correct this year, because I want you to do me a favor. I'm going to say something here, as part of this submission, and you're gonna verify it for me. If what I'm about to say is true, I'll get the fact back intact. If it's not, you'll keep all this, and I'll forget.

This is what I want you to check for me:

I did not, at any point, consciously participate in Auggie Wolf's plan to steal Mahoney's memories. I didn't take this case out of greed or malice, but only out of love. I'm not that kind of guy.

I'm sending along all the memories I have of the case. Everyone I met, every interview I conducted. The whole length and breadth of the thing that's been consuming me. If you return this fact to me validated, I'll know what I hope is true: that none of this was my fault; that I didn't hatch a deadly plan with a man whose cleverness overwhelmed his tenderness. I'll know I'm innocent, because you'll have told me so.

But if I'm lying—if I did, in some way, mean to help Auggie with this—then this bundle is invalid, and you'll get all of it as a commission. The whole story will leave my brain and enter yours. I'll be wiped clean of this guilt, this uncertainty, and you'll have to deal with it instead. In some ways, that's what I'm hoping for. All I ask, if it comes to that, is that you think long and hard before you share your find with anybody else. You could cash it in for demos, sure, and I bet you'd net a lot for it, but this pack of data is more than just currency. It's my truth, even if it's not entirely true.

Here's hoping that's still a distinction some people are willing to make.

Acknowledgments

First off, an enormous thank-you to everyone who turned this story from a .doc on my computer to the book you now hold in your hands: my incredible agent, Jessica Felleman, over at Jennifer Lyons Literary Agency (how I lucked into her, I'm still not sure); Anna Kaufman, my editor at Pantheon, who helped me realize this book was a love story all along; and Denise Oswald, Edward Kastenmeier, Andrea Monagle, Terry Zaroff-Evans, Robin Witkin, Nicholas LoVecchio, Demetri Papadimitropoulos, Stevie Pannenberg, Tyler Comrie, Linda Huang, Michael Collica, Kathryn Ricigliano, Saul Alpert-Abrams, and all the other folks at Pantheon who shepherded this ungainly thing through production.

Thanks to my parents, Laurie and Carl, for teaching me how to tell stories and how to lie, which are basically the same thing. Thanks to Aram and Michelle, my brother and sister-in-law, for letting me use their house to write the very first draft of this manuscript while they were on vacation.

Thank you to my Scorpions, Karlee and Andy, for invaluable feedback and the motivation to complete this book. To Tommy, a great friend and one of my first readers, for convincing me to put mindracing back in after I took it out for some dumb reason. To Post, who has consistently embarrassed me by singing this book's praises to anyone who will listen. To David Segall, for patiently fielding my questions about how one might commit financial crime with information instead of dollars. And to Christopher Humphrey, for helping me figure out how one might torture a machine intelligence.

I owe a lot to the Creative Writing MFA at the School of the Art Institute of Chicago, especially Amy England's Detective Fiction seminar and Beth Nugent's Long Form Narrative workshop. Also Kevin Bertram, who continually reaffirms the spiritual value of a creative practice. And Nadira Wallace, a fellow SAIC student who sewed a book out of one-dollar bills and thus provided me with the initial idea for this story.

Last but not least, my deepest gratitude to Elizabeth Estrella Obregon, my brilliant and multitalented wife, who has been an endless source of support, feedback, and fan art through everything. I look forward to sharing many, many years with her, and I wouldn't trade away a moment of that time, not even for the Heist of the Century.

A NOTE ABOUT THE AUTHOR

CORY O'BRIEN is the author of *Zeus Grants Stupid Wishes* and *George Washington Is Cash Money*. He has written for numerous award-winning video games, including *Monster Prom* and *HoloVista*, and designed multiple tabletop games, including *Inhuman Conditions* and *Hand-to-Hand Wombat*. He was born in Los Angeles, lives in Chicago, and is very grateful that neither city is underwater yet.

A NOTE ON THE TYPE

This book was set in Minion, a typeface produced by the Adobe Corporation specifically for the Macintosh personal computer and released in 1990. Designed by Robert Slimbach, Minion combines the classic characteristics of old-style faces with the full complement of weights required for modern typesetting.

Typeset by Scribe,
Philadelphia, Pennsylvania

Printed and bound by Friesens,
Altona, Manitoba

Designed by Michael Collica

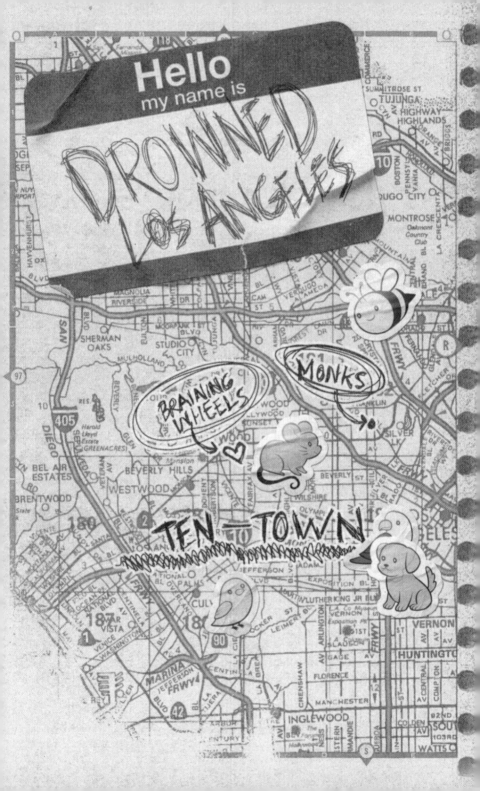